I0676955

# TALES FROM
# SCOTTISH BALLADS

# TALES FROM SCOTTISH BALLADS

## ELIZABETH W. GRIERSON

**WILDSIDE PRESS**

# TALES FROM SCOTTISH BALLADS

Published by Wildside Press LLC.

To
MY TWO FIRESIDE CRITICS
A. S. G. AND J. B. G.

# CONTENTS

# THE LOCHMABEN HARPER

*"Oh, heard ye of a silly harper,*
*Wha lang lived in Lochmaben town,*
*How he did gang to fair England,*
*To steal King Henry's wanton brown?"*

Once upon a time, there was an old man in Lochmaben, who made his livelihood by going round the country playing on his harp. He was very old, and very blind, and there was such a simple air about him, that people were inclined to think that he had not all his wits, and they always called him "The silly Lochmaben Harper."

Now Lochmaben is in Dumfriesshire, not very far from the English border, and the old man sometimes took his harp and made long journeys into England, playing at all the houses that he passed on the road.

Once when he returned from one of these journeys, he told everyone how he had seen the English King, King Henry, who happened to be living at that time at a castle in the north of England, and although he thought the King a very fine-looking man indeed, he thought far more of a frisky brown horse which his Majesty had been riding, and he had made up his mind that some day it should be his.

All the people laughed loudly when they heard this, and looked at one another and tapped their foreheads, and said, "Poor old man, his brain is a little touched; he grows sillier, and sillier;" but the Harper only smiled to himself, and went home to his cottage, where his wife was busy making porridge for his supper.

"Wife," he said, setting down his harp in the corner of the room, "I am going to steal the King of England's brown horse."

"Are you?" said his wife, and then she went on stirring the porridge. She knew her husband better than the neighbours did, and she knew that when he said a thing, he generally managed to do it.

The old man sat looking into the fire for a long time, and at last he said, "I will need a horse with a foal, to help me: if I can find that, I can do it."

"Tush!" said his wife, as she lifted the pan from the fire and poured the boiling porridge carefully into two bowls; "if that is all that thou needest, the brown horse is thine. Hast forgotten the old gray mare thou left at home in the stable? Whilst thou wert gone, she bore a fine gray foal."

"Ah!" said the old Harper, his eyes kindling. "Is she fond of her foal?"

"Fond of it, say you? I warrant bolts and bars would not keep her from it. Ride thou away on the old mare, and I will keep the foal at home; and I promise thee she will bring home the brown horse as straight as a die, without thy aid, if thou desire it."

"Thou art a clever woman, Janet: thou thinkest of everything," said her husband proudly, as she handed him his bowlful of porridge, and then sat down to sup her own at the other side of the fire, chuckling to herself, partly at her husband's words of praise, and partly at the simplicity of the neighbours, who called him a silly old harper.

Next morning the old man went into the stable, and, taking a halter from the wall, he hid it in his stocking; then he led out his old gray mare, who neighed and whinnied in distress at having to leave her little foal behind her. Indeed he had some difficulty in getting her to start, for when he had mounted her, and turned her head along the Carlisle road, she backed, and reared, and sidled, and made such a fuss, that quite a crowd collected round her, crying, "Come and see the silly Harper of Lochmaben start to bring home the King of England's brown horse."

At last the Harper got the mare to start, and he rode, and he rode, playing on his harp all the time, until he came to the castle where the King of England was. And, as luck would have it, who should come to the gate, just as he arrived, but King Henry himself. Now his Majesty loved music, and the old man really played very well, so he asked him to come into the great hall of the castle, and let all the company hear him play.

At this invitation the Harper jumped joyously down from his horse, as if to make haste to go in, and then he hesitated.

"Nay, but if it please your Majesty," he said humbly, "my old nag is footsore and weary: mayhap there is a stall in your Majesty's stable where she might rest the night."

Now the King loved all animals, and it pleased him that the old man should be so mindful of his beast; and seeing one of the stablemen in the distance, he turned his head and cried carelessly, "Here, sirrah! Take this old man's nag, and put it in a stall in the stable where my own brown horse stands, and see to it that it has a good supper of oats and a comfortable litter of hay."

Then he led the Harper into the hall where all his nobles were, and I need not tell you that the old man played his very best. He struck up such a merry tune that before long everybody began to dance, and the very servants came creeping to the door to listen. The cooks left their pans, and the chambermaids their dusters, the butlers their pantries; and, best of all, the stablemen came from the stables without remembering to lock the doors.

After a time, when they had all grown weary of dancing, the clever old man began to play such soft, soothing, quiet music, that everyone began to nod, and at last fell fast asleep.

He played on for a time, till he was certain that no one was left awake, then he laid down his harp, and slipped off his shoes, and stole silently down the broad staircase, smiling to himself as he did so.

With noiseless footsteps he crept to the stable door, which, as he expected, he found unlocked, and entered, and for one moment he stood looking about him in wonder, for it was the most splendid stable he had ever seen, with thirty horses standing side by side, in one long row. They were all beautiful horses, but the finest of all, was King Henry's favourite brown horse, which he always rode himself.

The old Harper knew it at once, and, quick as thought, he loosed it, and, drawing the halter which he had brought with him out of his stocking, he slipped it over its head.

Then he loosed his own old gray mare, and tied the end of the halter to her tail, so that, wherever she went, the brown horse was bound to follow. He chuckled to himself as he led the two animals out of the stable and across the courtyard, to the great wrought-iron gate, and when he had opened this, he let the gray mare go, giving her a good smack on the ribs as he did so. And the old gray mare, remembering her little foal shut up in the stable at home, took off at the gallop, straight across country, over hedges, and ditches, and walls, and fences, pull-ing the King's brown horse after her at such a rate that he had never even a chance to bite her tail, as he had thought of doing at first, when he was angry at being tied to it.

Although the mare was old, she was very fleet of foot, and before the day broke she was standing with her companion be-fore her master's cottage at Lochmaben. Her stable door was locked, so she began to neigh with all her might, and at last the noise awoke the Harper's wife.

Now the old couple had a little servant girl who slept in the attic, and the old woman called to her sharply, "Get up at once, thou lazy wench! dost thou not hear thy master and his mare at the door?"

The girl did as she was bid, and, dressing herself hastily, went to the door and looked through the keyhole to see if it were really her master. She saw no one there save the gray mare and a strange brown horse.

"Oh mistress, mistress, get up," she cried in astonishment, running into the kitchen. "What do you think has happened? The gray mare has gotten a brown foal."

"Hold thy clavers!" retorted the old woman; "methinks thou art blinded by the moonlight, if thou knowest not the difference between a full-grown horse and a two-months'-old foal. Go and look out again and bring me word if 'tis not a brown horse which the mare has brought with her."

The girl ran to the door, and presently came back to say that she had been mistaken, and that it was a brown horse, and that all the neighbours were peeping out of their windows to see what the noise was about.

The old woman laughed as she rose and dressed herself, and went out with the girl to help her to tie up the two horses.

"'Tis the silly old Harper of Lochmaben they call him," she said to herself, "but I wonder how many of them would have had the wit to gain a new horse so easily?"

Meanwhile at the English castle the Harper had stolen si-lently back to the hall after he had let the horses loose, and, tak-ing up his harp again, he harped softly until the morning broke, and the sleeping men round him began to awake.

The King and his nobles called loudly for breakfast, and the servants crept hastily away, afraid lest it might come to be known that they had left their work the evening before to listen to the stranger's music.

The cooks went back to their pans, and the chambermaids to their dusters, and the stablemen and grooms trooped out of doors to look after the horses; but presently they all came rushing back again, helter-skelter, with pale faces, for the stable door had been left open, and the King's favourite brown horse had been stolen, as well as the Harper's old gray mare. For a long time no one dare tell the King, but at last the head stableman ventured upstairs and broke the news to the Master-of-the-Horse, and the Master-of-the-Horse told the Lord Chamberlain, and the Lord Chamberlain told the King.

At first his Majesty was very angry, and threatened to dismiss all the grooms, but his attention was soon diverted by the cunning old Harper, who threw down his harp, and pretended to be in great distress.

"I am ruined, I am ruined!" he exclaimed, "for I lost the gray mare's foal just before I left Scotland, and I looked to the price of it for the rent, and now the old gray mare herself is gone, and how am I to travel about and earn my daily bread without her?"

Now the King was very kind-hearted, and he was sorry for the poor old man, for he believed every word of his story, so he clapped him on the back, and bade him play some more of his wonderful music, and promised to make up to him for his losses.

Then the wicked old Harper rejoiced, for he knew that his trick had succeeded, and he picked up his harp again, and played so beautifully that the King forgot all about the loss of his favourite horse.

All that day the Harper played to him, and on the morrow, when he would set out for home, in spite of all his entreaties that he would stay longer, he made his treasurer give him three times the value of his old gray mare, in solid gold, because he said that, if his servants had locked the stable door, the mare would not have been stolen, and, besides that, he gave him the price of the foal, which the wicked old man had said that he had lost. "For," said the King, "'tis a pity that such a marvellous harper should lack the money to pay his rent."

Then the cunning old Harper went home in triumph to Lochmaben, and the good King never knew till the end of his life how terribly he had been cheated.

# THE LAIRD O' LOGIE

*"I will sing if ye will hearken,*
*If ye will hearken unto me;*
*the king has ta'en a poor prisoner,*
*The wanton laird o' young Logie."*

It was Twelfth-night, and in the royal Palace of Holyrood a great masked ball was being held, for the King, James VI., and his young wife, Anne of Denmark, had been keeping Christmas there, and the old walls rang with gaiety such as had not been since the ill-fated days of Mary Stuart.

It was a merry scene; everyone was in fancy dress, and wore a mask, so that even their dearest friends could not know them, and great was the merriment caused by the efforts which some of the dancers made to guess the names of their partners.

One couple in the throng, however, appeared to know and recognise each other, for, as a tall slim maiden dressed as a nun, who had been dancing with a stout old monk, passed a young man in the splendid dress of a French noble, she dropped her handkerchief, and, as the young Frenchman picked it up and gave it to her, she managed to exchange a whisper with him, unnoticed by her elderly partner.

Ten minutes later she might have been seen, stealing cautiously down a dark, narrow flight of stairs, that led to a little postern, which she opened with a key which she drew from her girdle, and, closing it behind her, stepped out on the stretch of short green turf, which ran along one side of the quaint chapel. It was bright moonlight, but she stole behind one of the buttresses that cast heavy shadows on the grass, and waited.

Nearly a quarter of an hour passed before another figure issued from the same little postern and joined her. This time it was the young French noble, his finery hidden by a guard's long cloak.

"Pardon me, sweetheart," he said, throwing aside his disguise and putting his hand caressingly on her shoulder, "but 'tis not my fault that thou art here before me. I had to dance a minuet with her Majesty the Queen; she was anxious to show the court dames how 'tis done in Denmark, and, as thou knowest, I have learned the Danish steps passably well dancing it so often with thee. So I was called on, and Arthur Seaton, and a mention was made of thee, but Gertrud Van Hollbell volunteered to fill thy place."

"Gertrud is a good-natured wench, and I will tell her so; but did her Majesty not notice my absence?"

"Nay, verily, she was so busy talking with me, and I gave her no time to miss thee," said the young man, laughing, but his companion's face was troubled. They had taken off their masks, and a stranger looking at them would have taken them for what they seemed to be, a dark-haired, black-eyed Frenchman, and a fair English nun. But Hugh Weymes of Logie was a simple Scottish gentleman, in spite of his dress, and looks; and the maiden, Mistress Margaret Twynlace, was a Dane, who had come over, along with one or two others, as maid-in-waiting to the young Queen, who had insisted on having some of her own countrywomen about her.

Mistress Margaret's fair hair, and fairer skin, so different from that of the young Scotch ladies, had quite captivated young Weymes, and the two had been openly betrothed.

They had plenty of chances of speaking to each other in the palace, where Weymes was stationed in his capacity of gentleman of the King's household, and the young man was somewhat at a loss to understand why Margaret should have arranged a secret meeting which might bring them both into trouble were it known, for Queen Anne was very strict, and would have no lightsome maids about her, and were it to reach her ears that Margaret had met a man in the dark, even although it was the man she intended to marry, she would think nothing of packing her off to Denmark at a day's notice.

Now, as this was the very last thing that Hugh wanted to happen, his voice had a touch of reproach in it, as he began to point out the trouble that might ensue if any prying servant should chance to see them, or if Margaret's absence were noticed by the Queen.

But the girl hardly listened to him.

"What doth it matter whether I am sent home or not?" she said passionately. "Thou canst join me there and Denmark is as fair as Scotland; but it boots not to joke and laugh, for I have heavy news to tell thee. Thou must fly for thy life. 'Tis known that thou hast had dealings with my Lord of Bothwell, that traitor to the King, and thy life is in danger."

The young man looked at her in surprise. "Nay, sweet Meg," he said, "but methinks the Christmas junketing hath turned thy brain, for no man can bring a word against me, and I stand high in his Majesty's favour. Someone hath been filling thy ears with old wives' tales."

"But I know thou art in danger," she persisted, wringing her hands in despair when she saw how lightly he took the news. "I do not understand all the court quarrels, for this land is not my land, but I know that my Lord Bothwell hates the King, and that the King distrusts my Lord Bothwell, and, knowing this, can I not see that there is danger in thy having been seen talking to the Earl in a house in the Cowgate? and, moreover, it is said that he gave thee a packet which thou art supposed to have carried hither. Would that I could persuade thee to fly, to take ship at Leith, and cross over to Denmark; my parents would harbour thee till the storm blew past."

Margaret was in deadly earnest, but her lover only laughed again, and assured her that she had been listening to idle tales. To him it seemed incredible that he could get into any trouble because he had lately held some intercourse with his father's old friend, the Earl of Bothwell, and had, at his request, carried back a sealed packet to give to one of the officials at the palace, on his return from a trip to France. It was true that Lord Bothwell was in disfavour with the King, who suspected him of plotting against his person, but Hugh believed that his royal master was mistaken, and, as he had only been about the court a couple of months or so, he had not yet learned how dangerous it was to hold intercourse with men who were counted the King's enemies.

So he soothed Margaret's fears with playful words, promising to be more discreet in the future, and keep aloof from the Earl, and in a short time they were back in the ballroom, and he, at least, was dancing as merrily as if there was no such word as treason.

For two or three weeks after the Twelfth-night ball, life at Holyrood went on so quietly that Margaret Twynlace was inclined to think that her lover had been right, and that she had put more meaning into the rumours which she had heard than they were intended to convey, and, as she saw him going quietly about his duties, apparently in as high favour as before with the King, she shook off her load of anxiety, and tried to forget that she had ever heard the Earl of Bothwell's name.

But without warning the blow fell. One morning, as she was seated in the Queen's ante-chamber, busily engaged, along with the other maids, in sewing a piece of tapestry which was to be hung, when finished, in the Queen's bedroom, Lady Hamilton entered the room in haste, bearing dire tidings.

It had become known at the palace the evening before, that a plot had been discovered, planned by the Earl of Bothwell, to seize the King and keep him a prisoner, while the Earl was declared regent. As it was known that young Hugh Weymes, one of the King's gentlemen, had been seen in conversation with him some weeks before, he had been seized and his boxes searched, and in them had been found a sealed packet, containing letters to one of the King's councillors, who was now in France, asking his assistance, and signed by Bothwell himself.

The gentleman had not returned — probably word had been sent to him of his danger — but young Weymes had been promptly arrested, although he disclaimed all knowledge of the contents of the packet, and had been placed under the care of Sir John Carmichael, keeper of the King's guard, until he could be tried.

"And there will only be one sentence for him," said the old lady grimly; "it's beheaded he will be. 'Tis a pity, for he was a well-favoured youth; but what else could he expect, meddling with such matters?" and then she left the room, eager to find some fresh listeners to whom she could tell her tale.

As the door closed behind her a sudden stillness fell over the little room. No one spoke, although some of the girls glanced pityingly at Margaret, who sat, as if turned to stone, with a still, white face, and staring eyes. Gertrud Van Hollbell, her country-woman and bosom friend, rose at last, and went and put her arms round her.

"He is a favourite with the Queen, Margaret, and so art thou," she whispered, "and after all it was not he who wrote the letter. If I were in thy place, I would beg her Majesty, and she will beg the King, and he will be pardoned."

But Margaret shook her head with a wan smile. She knew

too well the terrible danger in which her lover stood, and she rightly guessed that the Queen would have no power to avert it.

At that moment the door opened, and the Queen herself entered, and all the maidens stood up to receive her. She looked grave and sad, and her eyes filled with tears as they fell on Margaret, who had been her playmate when they were both children in far-away Denmark, and who was her favourite maid-of-honour.

Seeing this, kind-hearted Gertrud gave her friend a little push. "See," she whispered, "she is sorry for thee; if thou go now and beg of her she will grant thy request."

Slowly, as if in a dream, the girl stepped forward, and knelt at her royal Mistress's feet, but the Queen laid her hand gently on her shoulder.

"'Tis useless asking me, Margaret," she said. "God knows I would have granted his pardon willingly. I do not believe that he meant treason to his Grace, only he should not have carried the packet; but I have besought the King already on his behalf and he will not hear me. Or his lords will not," she added in an undertone.

Then the girl found her voice. "Oh Madam, I will go to the King myself," she cried, "if you think there is any chance. Perhaps if I found him alone he might hear me. I shall tell him what I know is true, that Hugh never dreamt that there was treason in the packet which he carried."

"Thou canst try it, my child," said the Queen, "though I fear me 'twill be but little use. At the same time, the King is fond of thee, and thy betrothal to young Weymes pleased him well."

So, with a faint hope rising in her heart, Margaret withdrew to her little turret chamber, and there, with the help of the kind-hearted Gertrud, she dressed herself as carefully as she could.

She remembered how the King had praised a dull green dress which she had once worn, saying that in it she looked like a lily, so she put it on, and Gertrud curled her long yellow hair, and fastened it in two thick plaits behind, and sent her away on her errand with strong encouraging words; then she sat down and waited, wondering what the outcome of it all would be.

Alas! in little more than a quarter of an hour she heard steps coming heavily up the stairs, and when Margaret entered, it needed no look at her quivering face to know that she had failed.

"It is no use, Gertrud," she moaned, "no use, I tell thee. His Majesty might have let him off — I saw by his face that he was sorry — but who should come into the hall but my Lords Hamilton and Lennox, and then I knew all hope was gone. They are cruel, cruel men, and they would not hear of a pardon."

Gertrud did not speak; she knew that words of comfort would fall on deaf ears, even if she could find any words of comfort to say, so she only held out her arms, and gathered the poor heart-broken maiden into them, and in silence they sat, until the light faded, and the stars came out over Arthur's Seat. At last came a sound which made them both start. It was the grating noise of a key being turned in a lock, and the clang of bolts and bars, and then came the sound of marching feet, which passed right under their little window. Gertrud rose and looked out, but Margaret only shuddered. "They are taking him before the King," she said. "They will question him, and he will speak the truth, and he will lose his head for it."

She was right. The prisoner was being conducted to the presence of the King and the Lords of Council, to be questioned, and, as he openly acknowledged having spoken to the Earl of Bothwell, and did not deny having carried the packet, although he swore that he had no idea of its contents, his guilt was considered proved, and he was taken back to prison, there to await sentence, which everyone knew would be death.

From the little window Gertrud watched the soldiers of the King's guard lock and bar the great door, and give the key to Sir John Carmichael, their captain, who crossed the square swinging it on his finger.

"Would that I had that key for half an hour," she muttered to herself. "I would let the bird out of his cage, and old Karl Sevgen would do the rest."

Margaret started up from the floor where she had been crouching in her misery. "Old Karl Sevgen," she cried; "is he here?"

The old man was the captain of a little schooner which plied between Denmark and Leith, who often carried messages backwards and forwards between the Queen's maids and their friends.

"Ay," said Gertrud, glad to have succeeded in rousing her friend, and feeling somehow that there was hope in the sound of the old man's familiar name. "He sent up a message this evening — 'twas when thou wert with the King — and if we have anything to send with him it must be at Leith by the darkening to-morrow. I could get leave to go, if thou hadst any message," she added doubtfully, for she saw by Margaret's face that an idea had suddenly come to her, for she sat up and gazed into the twilight with bright eyes and flushed cheeks.

"Gertrud," she said at last, "I see a way, a dangerous one, 'tis true, but still it is a way. I dare not tell it thee. If it fails, the blame must fall on me, and me alone; but if thou canst get leave to go down to Leith and speak with old Karl alone, couldst thou tell him to look out for two passengers in the small hours of Wednesday morning? And say that when they are aboard the sooner he sails the better; and, Gertrud, tell him from me, for the love of Heaven, to be silent on the matter."

Gertrud nodded. "I'll do as thou sayest, dear heart," she said, "and pray God that whatever plan thou hast in thy wise little head may be successful; but now must thou go to the Queen. It is thy turn to-night to sleep in the ante-room."

"I know it," answered the girl, with a strange smile, and without saying any more she kissed her friend, and, bidding her good-night, left the room.

Outside the Queen's bed-chamber was a little ante-chamber, opening into a tiny passage, on the other side of which was a room occupied by the members of the King's bodyguard, who happened to be on duty for the week.

It was the Queen's custom to have one of her maids sleeping in the ante-room in case she needed her attendance through the night, and this week the duty fell to Margaret.

After her royal mistress had retired, the girl lay tossing on her narrow bed, thinking how best she could rescue the man she loved, and by the morning her plans were made.

"Gertrud," she said next day, when the two were bending over their needlework, somewhat apart from the other maids, "dost think that Karl could get thee a length of rope? It must be strong, but not too thick, so that I could conceal it about my person when I go to the Queen's closet to-night. Thou couldst carry it home in a parcel, and the serving man who goes with thee will think that it is something from Denmark."

"That can I," said Gertrud emphatically; "and if I have not a chance to see thee, I will leave it in the coffer in thy chamber."

"Leave what?" asked the inquisitive old dowager who was supposed to superintend the maids and their embroidery, who at that moment crossed the room for another bundle of tapestry thread, and overheard the last remark.

"A packet for Mistress Margaret, which she expects by the Danish boat," answered Gertrud promptly. "I have permission from her Majesty to go this evening on my palfrey to Leith, to deliver some mails to Captain Karl Sevgen, and to receive our packets in return."

"Ah," said the old dame kindly, "'tis a treat for thee doubtless to see one of thine own countrymen, even although he is but a common sailor," and she shuffled back placidly to her seat.

Margaret went on with her work in silence, blessing her friend in her heart for her ready wit, but she dare not look her thanks, in case some curious eye might note it.

Gertrud was as good as her word. When Margaret went up to her little room late in the evening, to get one or two things which she wanted before repairing to the Queen's private apartments, she found a packet, which would have disarmed all suspicions, lying on her coffer. For it looked exactly like the bundles which found their way every month or two to the Danish maids at Holyrood. It was sewn up in sailcloth, and was addressed to herself in rude Danish characters; but she knew what was in it, and in case the Queen might ask questions and laughingly desire to see her latest present from home, she slit off the sailcloth, which she hid in the coffer, and, unfolding the coil of rope, she wound it round and round her body, under her satin petticoat. Luckily she was tall, and very slender, and no one, unless they examined her very closely, would notice the difference in her figure. Then, taking up a great duffle cloak which she used when riding out in dirty weather, she made her way to her post.

It seemed long that night before Queen Anne dismissed her. The King lingered in the supper chamber, and the gentle Queen, full of sympathy for her favourite, sat in the little anteroom and talked to her of Denmark, and the happy days they had spent there. At last she departed, just as the clock on the tower of St Giles struck twelve, and Margaret was at liberty to unwind the coil of rope, and hide it among the bedclothes, and then, wrapping the warm cloak round her, she lay down and tried to wait quietly until it was safe to do what she intended to do.

There were voices for awhile in the next room — the King and Queen were talking — then they ceased entirely; but still she waited, until one o'clock rang out, and she heard the guards pass on their rounds.

Then she rose, and, taking off her shoes, crept gently across the tiny room and stealthily opened the door of the Queen's bedroom, and listened. All was quiet except for the regular breathing of the sleepers. A little coloured lamp which hung from the ceiling was burning softly, and by its light she could see the different objects in the room. Stealing to the dressing-table, she looked about for any trinkets that would answer her purpose. The King's comb lay there, carefully cut from black ivory, with gold stars let in along the rim; and there, among other dainty trifles, was the mother-of-pearl and silver knife, set with emeralds, which his Majesty had given the Queen as a keepsake, about the time of their marriage. Margaret picked up both of these, and then, retracing her steps, she closed the door behind her, and flung herself on her bed to listen in breathless silence in case anyone had heard her movements, and should come to ask what was wrong.

But all was quiet; not a soul had heard.

"The prisoner to be taken to the King now! Surely, fellow, thou art dreaming." Sir John Carmichael, captain of the King's guard, sat up in bed, and stared in astonishment at the soldier who had brought the order.

"Nay," said the man stolidly. "But 'twas one of the Queen's wenches who came to the guard-room, and told us, and as a token that it is true, and no joke, she brought these from his Majesty," and he held out the gilded comb and the little jewelled knife.

Sir John took them and turned them over in silence. He knew them well enough, and, moreover, it was no uncommon thing for the King, when he sent a messenger, as he often did, at an unaccustomed hour, to send also some trinket which lay beside him at the moment, as a token; therefore the honest gentleman suspected nothing, although he was loth to get out of bed.

There was no help for it, however; the message had come from the King, and King's messages must be obeyed, even though they seemed ill-timed and ridiculous.

"What in the world has ta'en his Majesty now?" he grumbled, as he got up reluctantly and began to hustle on his clothes. "Even though he wants to question the lad alone, could he not have waited till the morning? 'Tis the Queen's work, I warrant; she has a soft heart, and she will want his Majesty to hear the young man's defence when none of the Lords of the Council are by."

So saying, he took down the great key which hung on a nail at the head of his bed, and went off with the soldiers to arouse young Weymes, who seemed quite as surprised as Sir John at the sudden summons.

At the door of the Queen's ante-chamber they were met by the same maid-of-honour who had taken the tokens to the guard, and she, modestly shielding her face with a fold of her cloak, asked Sir John if he would remain in the guard-room with the soldiers until she called for him again, as the King wanted to question the prisoner alone in his chamber.

At the sound of her voice Hugh Logie started, although Sir John did not seem to recognise it, else his suspicions might have been aroused. He only waited until his prisoner followed the girl into the little room, then he locked the door behind them as a precaution, and withdrew with the soldiers into the guard-room, where he knew a bright fire and a tankard of ale were always to be found.

Once in the ante-room, the young man spoke. "What means this, Sweetheart?" he said. "What can the King want with me at this hour of night?"

"Hush!" answered the girl, laying a trembling finger on her lips, while her eyes danced in spite of the danger. "'Tis I who would speak with thee, but on board Karl Sevgen's boat at Leith, and not here. See," and she drew the rope from its hiding-place, "tie this round thy waist, and I will let thee down from the window; by God's mercy it looks out on a deserted part of the garden, where the guards but rarely come, and thou canst steal over the ditch, and down the garden, and round the Calton Hill, and so down to the sea at Leith. Karl's boat is there; he will be watching for thee. Thou wilt know her by her long black hull, and by a red light he will burn in the stern. Nay, Hugh," for he would have taken her in his arms. "The danger is not over yet, and we will have time to talk when we are at sea, for I am coming too; I dare not stay here to face the King alone. Only I can steal out by that little door in the tapestry" — luckily Sir John did not know that there was another way out — "and meet thee in the garden."

The window was not very high, and the night was dark, and no one chanced to pass that way as a figure slung itself down, and dropped lightly into the ditch; and, when a guard did come round, Hugh lay flat among the mud and nettles until he had passed, and by that time Margaret had stolen out by the little postern, and was waiting for him at the foot of the garden, and hand in hand they made their way over the rough uneven fields which lay between them and Leith.

Meanwhile, Sir John Carmichael drank ale, and talked with the guards, and waited; — and waited, and talked with the guards, and drank ale, until his patience was well-nigh gone. At last, just when the day was breaking, he went to the door of the ante-room to listen, and hearing nothing, he knocked, and receiving no answer, he unlocked the door and peeped in, not wishing to disturb the maid-of-honour, but merely to satisfy himself that all was right. The moment he saw the open window and the rope, he shouted to the guards, and rushed across the floor, and thundered at the door of the King's apartment, hoping against hope that the prisoner was still there.

But the King had been sleeping peacefully, and when he heard the story, he was very angry at first, and talked of arresting Sir John, and sent off horsemen, who rode furiously to Leith, in the hope of catching the Danish boat. But they came back with the news that she had sailed with the tide at three o'clock in the morning, after having taken two passengers on board; and, after all, he could say little to Carmichael, for had he not received the comb and the knife as tokens?

"Thou shouldst not have lingered so long at supper," said the Queen slyly, only too pleased at the turn events had taken. "Then hadst thou slept lighter, and would have awaked when the wench stole in to take the things."

King James burst into a great laugh. "By my troth, thou art right," he said, slapping his thigh. "The wench has been too clever for all of us, for the Lords of the Council, and Carmichael, and me, and she deserves her success. They must stay where they are for a time, for appearances' sake, but, heark 'ee, Anne, when thou art writing to Denmark, thou canst say that thou thinkest that my wrath will not last for ever."

Nor did it, and before many months had passed Hugh Weymes of Logie came home in triumph, bringing with him his young wife, who had dared so much and acted so boldly for his sake.

# KINMONT WILLIE

*"Oh, have ye na heard of the fause Sakelde?*
*Oh, have ye na heard of the keen Lord Scroope"*
*How they ha'e ta'en bauld Kinmont Willie,*
*On Haribee to hang him up?"*

I well remember the dull April morning, in the year 1596, when my father, William Armstrong of Kinmont, "Kinmont Willie," as he was called by all the countryside, set out with me for a ride into Cumberland.

As a rule, when he set his face that way, he rode armed, and with all his men behind him, for these were the old reiving days, when we folk who dwelt on the Scottish side of the Border thought we had a right to go and steal what we could, sheep, or oxen, or even hay, from the English loons, who, in their turn, would come slipping over from their side to take like liberties with us, and mayhap burn down a house or two in the by-going.

My father was aye in the thick and throng of these raids, for he was such a big powerful man that he was more than a match for three Englishmen, did he chance to meet them. Men called him an outlaw, but we thought little of that; most of the brave men on our side had been outlawed at one time or another, and it did them little ill: indeed, it was aye thought to be rather a feather in their cap.

Well, as I say, my father was not riding on business, as it were, this morning, for just then there was a truce for a day or two between the countries, the two Wardens of the Marches, Sir Walter Scott of Buccleuch, and My Lord Scroope, having sent their deputies to meet and settle some affairs at the Dayholme of Kershope, where a burn divides England from Scotland. My father and I had attended the Truce Muster, and were riding homeward with but a handful of men, when I took a sudden notion into my head, that I would like to cross the Border, and ride a few miles on English ground.

My birthday had fallen the week before (I was just eleven years old), and my father, aye kind to his motherless bairns, had given me a new pony, a little shaggy beast from Galloway, and, as I was keen to see how it would run beside a big man's horse, I had pled hard for permission to accompany him on it to the Muster.

As a rule I never rode with him. "I was too young for the work," he would say; but that day he gave his consent, only making the bargain that there should be no crying out or grumbling if I were tired or hungry long ere we got home again. I had laughed at the idea as I saddled my shaggy little nag, and, to make matters sure, I had gone to Janet, the kitchen wench, and begged her for a satchel of oatcakes and cheese, which I fastened to my saddle strap, little dreaming what need I would have of them before the day was out.

The Truce Muster had broken up sooner than he expected, so my father saw no reason why he should not grant my request, and let me have a canter on English soil, for on a day of truce we could cross the Border if we chose without the risk of being taken prisoners by Lord Scroope's men, and marched off to Carlisle Castle, while the English had a like privilege, and could ride down Liddesdale in open daylight, if they were so minded.

Scarce had we crossed the little burn, however, which runs between low-growing hazel bushes, and separates us from England, when two of the men rode right into a bog, and when, after some half-hour's work, we got the horses out again, we found that both of them wanted a shoe, and my father said at once that we must go straight home, in case they went lame.

At this I drew a long face. I had never been into England, and it was a sore disappointment to be turned back just when we had reached it.

"Well, well," said my father, laughing, ever soft-hearted where I was concerned, "I suppose I must e'en take thee a ride into Bewcastle, lad, since we have got this length. The men can go back with the horses; 'tis safe enough to go alone to-day."

So the men turned back, nothing loth, for Bewcastle Waste was no unknown land to them, and my father and I rode on for eight miles or so, over that most desolate country. Its bareness and loneliness disappointed me. Somehow I had expected that England would be quite different from Scotland, even although they were all one piece of land, with only a burn running between.

"Hast had enough?" said my father at last, noticing my

downcast face, and drawing rein. "Didst expect all the trees to be made of silver, and all the houses to be built of gold? Never mind, lad, every place looks much the same in the month of April, I trow, especially when it has been a backward season; but if summer were once and here, I'll let thee ride with the troop, and mayhap thou wilt get a glimpse of 'Merrie Carlisle,' as they call it. It lies over there, twelve miles or more from where we stand."

As he pointed out the direction with his whip, we both became aware of a large body of men, riding rapidly over the moor as if to meet us. My father eyed them keenly, his face growing grave as he did so.

"Who are they, father?" I asked with a sinking heart. I had lived long enough at Kinmont to know that men did not generally ride together in such numbers unless they were bent on mischief.

"It's Sakelde, the English Warden's deputy, and no friend o' mine," he answered with a frown, "and on any other day I would not have met him alone like this for a hundred merks; but the truce holds for three days yet, so we are quite safe; all the same, lad, we had better turn our horses round, and slip in behind that little hill; they may not have noticed us, and in that case 'tis no use rousing their curiosity."

Alas! we had no sooner set our horses to the trot, than it became apparent that not only were we observed, but that for some reason or other the leader of the band of horsemen was desirous of barring our way.

He gave an order, — we could see him pointing with his hand, — and at once his men spurred on their horses and began to spread out so as to surround us. Then my father swore a big oath, and plunged his spurs into his horse's sides. "Come on, Jock," he shouted, "sit tight and be a man; if we can only get over the hill edge at Kershope, they'll pay for this yet."

I will remember that race to my dying day. It appeared to last for hours, but it could not have lasted many minutes, ten at the most, during which time all the blood in my body seemed to be pounding and surging in my head, and the green grass and the sky to be flying past me, all mixed up together, and behind, and on all sides, came the pit-pat of horses' feet, and then someone seized my pony's rein, and brought him up with a jerk, and my father and I were sitting in the midst of two hundred armed riders, whose leader, a tall man, with a thin cunning face, regarded us with a triumphant smile.

"Neatly caught, thou thieving rogue," he said; "by my troth, neatly caught. Who would have thought that Kinmont Willie would have been such a fool as to venture so far from home without an escort? But I can supply the want, and thou shalt ride to Carlisle right well attended, and shall never now lack a guard till thou partest with thy life at Haribee."

As the last word fell on my ear, I had much ado to keep my seat, for I turned sick and faint, and all the crowd of men and horses seemed to whirl round and round. Haribee! Right well I knew that fateful name, for it was the place at Carlisle where they hanged prisoners. They could not hang my father — they dare not — for although he had been declared an outlaw, and might perhaps merit little love from the English, was not this a day of truce, when all men could ride where they would in safety?

" 'Tis a day of truce," I gasped with dry lips; but the men around me only laughed, and I could hear that my father's fierce remonstrance met with no better answer.

"Thou art well named, thou false Sakelde," I heard him say, and his voice shook with fury, "for no man of honour would break the King's truce in this way."

But Sakelde only gave orders to his men to bind their prisoner, saying, as he did so, "I warrant Lord Scroope will be too glad to see thee to think much about the truce, and if thou art so scrupulous, thou needest not be hanged for a couple of days; the walls of Carlisle Castle are thick enough to guard thee till then. Be quick, my lads," he went on, turning to his men; "we have a good fourteen miles to ride yet, and I have no mind to be benighted ere we reach firmer ground."

So they tied my father's feet together under his horse, and his hands behind his back, and fastened his bridle rein to that of a trooper, and the word was given for the men to form up, and they began to move forward as sharply as the boggy nature of the ground would allow.

I followed in the rear with a heavy heart. I could easily have escaped had I wanted to do so, for no one paid any attention to me; but I felt that, as long as I could, I must stay near my father, whose massive head and proud set face I could see towering above the surrounding soldiers, for he was many inches taller than any of them.

The spring evening was fast drawing to a close as we came to the banks of the Liddle, and splashed down a stony track to a place where there was a ford. As we paused for a moment or two to give the horses a drink, my father's voice rang out above the careless jesting of the troopers.

"Let me say good-bye to my eldest son, Sakelde, and send him home; or do the English war with bairns?"

I saw the blood rise to the English leader's thin sallow face at the taunt, but he answered quietly enough, "Let the boy speak to him and then go back," and a way was opened up for me to where my father sat, a bound and helpless prisoner, on his huge white horse.

One trooper, kinder than the rest, took my pony's rein as I slid off its back and ran to him. Many a time when I was little, had I had a ride on White Charlie, and I needed no help to scramble up to my old place on the big horse's neck.

My father could not move, but he looked down at me with all the anger and defiance gone out of his face, and a look on it which I had only seen there once before, and that was when he lifted me up on his knee after my mother died and told me that I must do my best to help him, and try to look after the little ones.

That look upset me altogether, and, forgetting the many eyes that watched us, and the fact that I was eleven years old, and almost a man, I threw my arms round his neck and kissed him again and again, sobbing and greeting as any bairn might have done, all the time.

"Ride home, laddie, and God be with ye. Remember if I fall that thou art the head of the house, and see that thou do honour to the name," he said aloud. Then he signed to me to go, and, just as I was clambering down, resting a toe in his stirrup, he made a tremendous effort and bent down over me. "If thou could'st but get word to the Lord of Buccleuch, laddie, 'tis my only chance. They dare not touch me for two days yet. Tell him I was ta'en by treachery at the time o' truce."

The whisper was so low I could hardly hear it, and yet in a moment I understood all it was meant to convey, and my heart beat until I thought that the whole of Sakelde's troopers must read my secret in my face as I passed through them to where my pony stood.

With a word of thanks I took the rein from the kindly man who had held it, and then stood watching the body of riders as they splashed through the ford, and disappeared in the twilight, leaving me alone.

But I felt there was work for me to do, and a ray of hope stole into my heart. True, it was more than twenty miles, as the crow flies, to Branksome Tower in Teviotdale, where my Lord of Buccleuch lived, and I did not know the road, which lay over some of the wildest hills of the Border country, but I knew that he was a great man, holding King James' commission as Warden of the Scottish Marches, and at his bidding the whole countryside would rise to a man. 'Twas well known that he bore no love to the English, and when he knew that my father had been taken in time of truce...! The fierce anger rose in my heart at the thought, and, burying my face in my pony's rough coat, I vowed a vow, boy as I was, to be at Branksome by the morning, or die in the attempt. I knew that it was no use going home to Kinmont for a man to ride with me, for it was out of my way, and would only be a waste of time.

It was almost dark now, but I knew that the moon would rise in three or four hours, and then there would be light enough for me to try to thread my way over the hills that lay between the valleys of the Teviot and Liddle. In the meantime, there was no special need to hurry, so I loosened my pony's rein, and let him nibble away at the short sweet grass which was just beginning to spring, while I unbuckled the bag of cakes which I had put up so gaily in the morning, and, taking one out, along with a bit of cheese, did my best to make a hearty meal. But I was not very successful, for when the heart is heavy, food goes down but slowly, and Janet's oatcake and the good ewe cheese, which at other times I found so toothsome, seemed fairly to stick in my throat, so at last I gave it up, and, taking the pony by the head, I began to lead him up the valley.

Although I had been down the Liddle as far as the ford once or twice before, it had always been in daylight, and my father had been with me; but I knew that as long as I kept close to the river I was all right for the first few miles, until the valley narrowed in, and then I must strike off among the high hills on my left.

It was slow work, for it was too dark to ride, and I dare not leave the water in case I lost my way, and by the time we had gone mayhap four or five miles, I had almost lost heart, for I was both tired and cold, and it seemed to me that half the night at least must be gone, and at this rate we would never reach Branksome at all.

At last, just when the tears were getting very near my eyes — for I was but a little chap to be set on such a desperate errand — I struck on a narrow road which led up a brae to my left, and going along it for a hundred yards or so, I saw a light which seemed to come from a cottage window. I stopped and looked at it, wondering if I dare go boldly up and knock.

In those lawless days one had to be cautious about going up to strange houses, for one never knew whether one would find a friend or an enemy within, so I determined to tie my pony to a tree, and steal noiselessly up to the building, and see what sort of place it was.

I did so, and found that the light came from a tiny thatched cottage standing by itself, sheltered by some fir trees. There appeared to be no dogs about, so I crept quite close to the little window, and peered in through a hole in the shutter. I could see the inside of the room quite plainly; it was poorly furnished, but beautifully clean. In a corner opposite the window stood a rough settle, while on a three-legged stool by the peat fire sat an old woman knitting busily, a collie dog at her feet.

There could be nothing to fear from her, so I knocked boldly at the door. The collie flew to the back of it barking furiously, but I heard the old woman calling him back, and presently she peeped out, asking who was there.

"'Tis I, Jock Armstrong of Kinmont," I said, "and I fain would be guided as to the quickest road to Branksome Tower."

The old woman peered over my head into the darkness, evidently expecting to see someone standing behind me.

"I ken Willie o' Kinmont; but he's a grown man," she said suspiciously, making as though she would shut the door.

"He's my father," I cried, vainly endeavouring to keep my voice steady, "and — and — I have a message to carry from him to the Lord of Buccleuch at Branksome." I would fain have told the whole story, but I knew it was better to be cautious. I was still no distance from the English Border, and it would take away the last chance of saving my father's life, were Sakelde to get to know that word of his doings were like to reach the Scottish Warden's ears.

"Loshsake, laddie!" exclaimed the old dame in astonishment, setting the door wide open so that the light might fall full on me, "'tis full twenty miles tae Branksome, an' it's a bad road ower the hills."

"But I have a pony," I said. "'Tis tied up down the roadway there, and the moon will rise."

"That it will in an hour or two, but all the same I misdoubt me that you'll lose your road. What's the matter wi' Kinmont Willie, that he has tae send a bairn like you his messages? Ye needna' be feared to speak out," she added as I hesitated; "Kinmont Willie is a friend of mine — at least, he did my goodman and me a good turn once — and I would like to pay it back again if I could."

I needed no second bidding; it was such a relief to have someone to share the burden, and I felt better as soon as I had told her, even although the telling brought the tears to my eyes.

The old woman listened attentively, and then shook her fist in the direction which the English had taken.

"He's a fause loon that Sakelde," she said, "and I'd walk to Carlisle any day to see him hanged. 'Twas he who stole our sheep, two years past at Martinmas, and 'twas your father brought them back again. But keep up your heart, my man; if you can get to the Bold Buccleuch he'll put things right, I'll warrant, and I'll do all I can for you. Go inbye, and sit down by the fire, and I'll go down the road and fetch the nag. You'll both be the better for a rest, and a bite o' something to eat, and when the moon is risen I'll take you up the hill, and show you the track. My goodman is away at Hawick market, or he would ha'e ridden a bit of the road wi' ye."

When I was a little fellow, before my mother died, she used to read me lessons out of her great Bible with the silver clasps, and of all the stories she read to me, I liked the lesson of the Good Samaritan best, and, looking back, now that I am a grown man, it seems to me that I met the Good Samaritan that night, only he was a woman.

After Allison Elliot, for that was her name, had brought my

pony into her cow-house, and seen that he was supplied with both hay and water, she returned to the cottage, and with her own hands took off my coarse woollen hose and heavy shoon, and spread them on the hearth to dry, then she made me lie down on the settle, and, covering me up with a plaid, she bade me go to sleep, promising to wake me the moment the moon rose.

It was nearly eleven o'clock when she shook me gently, bidding me get up and put on my shoon, as it was time to be going, and, sitting up, I found a supper of wheaten bread and hot milk on the table, which she told me to eat, while she wrapped herself in a plaid and went out for the nag.

What with the sleep, and the dry clothes, and the warm food, I promise you I felt twice the man I had done a few hours earlier, and I chattered quite gaily to her as she led my pony up a steep hillside behind the cottage, for the moon was only beginning to rise, and there was still but little light. After we had gone some two miles, we struck a bridle track, well trodden by horses' hoofs, which wound upwards between two high hills.

Here Allison paused and looked keenly at the ground.

"This is the path," she said; "you can hardly lose it, for there have been riders over it yesterday or the day before. Scott o' Haining and his men, most likely, going home from their meeting at the Kershope Burn. This will lead you over by Priesthaugh Swire, and down the Allan into Teviotdale. Beware of a bog which you will pass some two miles on this side of Priesthaugh. 'Tis the mire Queen Mary stuck in when she rode to visit her lover when he lay sick at Hermitage. May the Lord be good to you, laddie, and grant you a safe convoy, for ye carry a brave heart in that little body o' yours!"

I thanked her with all my might, promising to go back and see her if my errand were successful; then I turned my pony's head to the hills, and spurred him into a brisk canter. He was a willing little beast, and mightily refreshed by Allison Elliot's hay, and, as the moon was now shining clearly, we made steady progress; but it was a long lonely ride for a boy of my age, and once or twice my courage nearly failed me: once when my pony put his foot into a sheep drain, and stumbled, throwing me clean over his head, and again when I missed the track, and rode straight into the bog Allison had warned me about, and in which the little beast was near sticking altogether, and I lost a good hour getting him to firm land and finding the track again.

The bright morning sun was showing above the Eastern horizon before I left the weary hills behind me, but it was easy work to ride down the sloping banks of the Allan, and soon I came to the wooded valley of the Teviot.

Urging on my tired pony, I cantered down the level haughs which lay by the river side, and it was not long before Branksome came in sight, a high square house, with many rows of windows, flanked by a massive square tower at each corner.

I rode up to the great doorway through an avenue of beeches and knocked timidly on the wrought-iron knocker, for I had never been to such a big house in my life before, and I felt that I made but a sorry figure, splashed as I was with mud from head to foot.

The old seneschal who came to the door seemed to think so too, for he looked me up and down with a broad grin on his face before he asked who I was, and on what business I had come.

"To see my Lord of Buccleuch, and carry a message to him from William Armstrong of Kinmont," I replied, with as much dignity as I could muster, for the fellow's smile angered me, and I feared that he might not think it worth his while to tell the Warden of my arrival.

"Then thou shalt see Sir Walter at once, young sir, if thou wilt walk this way," said the man, mimicking my voice good-naturedly, and, hitching my pony's bridle to an iron ring in the door-post, he led me along a stone passage, straight into a great vaulted hall, in the centre of which stood a long wooden table, with a smaller one standing crossways on a dais at its head.

A crowd of squires and men-at-arms stood round the lower table, laughing and jesting as they helped themselves with their hunting knives to slices from the huge joints, or quaffed great tankards of ale, while up at the top sat my Lord of Buccleuch himself, surrounded by his knights, and waited on by smart pages in livery, boys about my own age.

As the old seneschal appeared in the doorway there was a sudden silence, while he announced in a loud voice that a messenger had arrived from William Armstrong of Kinmont; but when he stepped aside, and everyone saw that the messenger was only a little eleven-years-old lad, a loud laugh went round the hall, and the smart pages whispered together and pointed to my muddy clothes.

When the old seneschal saw this, he gave me a kindly nudge.

"Yonder is my Lord of Buccleuch at the top of the table," he whispered; "go right up to him, and speak out thy message boldly."

I did as I was bid, though I felt my cheeks burn as I walked up the great hall, among staring men and whispering pages, and when I reached the dais where the Warden sat, I knelt at his feet, cap in hand, as my father had taught me to do before my betters.

Sir Walter Scott, Lord of Buccleuch, of whom I had heard so much, was a young, stern-looking man, with curly brown hair and keen blue eyes. His word was law on the Borders, and people said that even the King, in far-off Edinburgh, stood in awe of him; but he leant forward and spoke kindly enough to me.

"So thou comest from Armstrong of Kinmont, boy; and had Kinmont Willie no better messenger at hand, that he had to fall back on a smatchet like thee?"

"There were plenty of men at Kinmont, an' it please your lordship," I answered, "had I had time to seek them; but a man called Sakelde hath ta'en my father prisoner, and carried him to Carlisle, and I have ridden all night to tell thee of it, for he is like to be hanged the day after to-morrow, if thou canst not save him."

Here my voice gave way, and I could only cling to the great man's knee, for my quivering lips refused to say any more.

Buccleuch put his arm round me, and spoke slowly, as one would speak to a bairn.

"And who is thy father, little man?"

"Kinmont Willie," I gasped, "and he was ta'en last night, in truce time."

I felt the arm that was round me stiffen, and there was silence for a moment, then my lord swore a great oath, and let his clenched fist fall so heavily on the table, that the red French wine which stood before him splashed right out of the beaker, a foot or two in the air.

"My Lord of Scroope shall answer for this," he cried. "Hath he forgotten that men name me the Bold Buccleuch, and that I am Keeper o' the Scottish Marches, to see that justice is done to high and low, gentle and simple?"

Then he gave some quick, sharp orders, and ten or twelve men left the room, and a minute later I saw them, through a casement, throw themselves astride their horses, and gallop out of the courtyard. At the sight my heart lightened, for I knew that whatever could be done for my father would be done, for these men had gone to "warn the waters," or, in other words, to carry the tidings far and wide, and bid all the men of the Western Border be ready to meet their chief at some given trysting-place, and ride with him to the rescue.

Meanwhile the Warden lifted me on his knee, and began asking me questions, while the pages gathered round, no longer jeering, but with wide-open eyes.

"Thou art a brave lad," he said at last, after I had told him the whole story, "and, with thy father's permission, I would fain have thee for one of my pages. We must tell him how well thou hast carried the message, and ask him if he can spare thee for a year or two."

At any other time my heart would have leapt at this un-heard-of good fortune, for to be a page in the Warden's household was the ambition of every well-born lad on the Border; but at that moment I felt as if Buccleuch hardly realised my father's danger.

"But he is lodged in Carlisle Castle, and men say the walls are thick," I said anxiously, "and it is garrisoned by my Lord Scroope's soldiers."

The Warden laughed.

"We will teach my Lord Scroope that there is no bird's nest that the Bold Buccleuch dare not harry," he said, and, seeing the look on his face, I was content.

Then, noticing how weary I was, he called one of the older pages, and bade him see that I had food and rest, and the boy, who had been one of the first to laugh before, but who now treated me with great respect, took me away to a little turret room which he shared with some of his fellows, and brought me a piece of venison pie, and then left me to go to sleep on his low pallet, promising to wake me when there were signs of the Warden and his men setting out.

I must have slept the whole day, for the little room was almost dark again, and the rain was beating wildly on the casement, when the boy came back. "My lord hath given orders for the horses to be saddled," he said, "and the trysting-place is Woodhouselee. I heard one squire tell another in the hall, for as a rule we pages know nothing, and are only expected to do as we are bid. I know not if my lord means thee to ride with him, but I was sent up to fetch thee."

It did not take me long to spring up and fasten my doublet, and follow my guide down to the great hall. Here all was bustle and confusion; men were standing about ready armed, making a hasty meal at the long table, which never seemed to be empty of its load of food, while outside in the courtyard some fifty or sixty horses were standing, ready saddled, with bags of fodder thrown over their necks.

Every few minutes a handful of men would ride up in the dusk, and, leaving their rough mountain ponies outside, would stride into the hall, and begin to eat as hard as they could, exchanging greetings between the mouthfuls. These were men from the neighbourhood, my friend informed me, mostly kinsmen of Buccleuch, and lairds in their own right, who had ridden to Branksome with their men to start with their chief.

There was Scott of Harden, and Scott of Goldilands, Scott of Commonside, and Scott of Allanhaugh, and many more whom I do not now remember, and they drank their ale, and laughed and joked, as if they were riding to a wedding, instead of on an errand which might cost them their lives.

Buccleuch himself was in the midst of them, booted and spurred, and presently his eye fell on me.

"Ha! my young cocksparrow," he cried. "Wilt ride with us to greet thy father, or are thy bones too weary? Small shame 'twould be to thee if they were."

"Oh, if it please thee, sire, let me ride," I said; "I am not too weary, if my pony is not," at which reply everyone laughed.

"I hear thy pony can scarce hirple on three legs," answered my lord, clapping me on my shoulder, "but I like a lad of spirit, and go thou shalt. Here, Red Rowan, take him up in front of thee, and see that a horse be led for Kinmont to ride home on."

I was about to protest that I was not a bairn to ride in front of any man, but Buccleuch turned away as if the matter were settled, and the big trooper who came up and took me in charge persuaded me to do as I was bid. "'Tis a dark night, laddie, and we ride fast," he said, "and my lord would be angered didst thou lose thy way, or fall behind," and although my pride was nettled at first, I was soon fain to confess that he was right, for the horses swung out into the wind and rain, and took to the hills at a steady trot, keeping together in the darkness in a way that astonished me. Red Rowan had a plaid on his shoulders which he twisted round me, and which sheltered me a little from the driving rain, and I think I must have dozed at intervals, for it seemed no time until we were over the hills, and down at Woodhouselee in Canonbie, where a great band of men were waiting for us, who had gathered from Liddesdale and Hermitage Water.

With scarcely a word they joined our ranks, and we rode silently and swiftly on, across the Esk, and the Graeme's country, until we reached the banks of the Eden.

Here we came to a standstill, for the river was so swollen with the recent rains that it seemed madness for any man to venture into the rushing torrent; but men who had ridden so far, and on such an errand, were not to be easily daunted.

"This way, lads, and keep your horses' heads to the stream," shouted a voice, and with a scramble we were down the bank, and the nags were swimming for dear life. I confess now, that at that moment I thought my last hour had come, for the swirling water was within an inch of my toes, and I clung to Red Rowan's coat with all the strength I had, and shut my eyes, and tried to think of my prayers. But it was soon over, and on the other side we waited a minute to see if any man were missing. Everyone was safe, however, and on we went till we were close on Carlisle, and could see the lights of the Castle rising up above the city wall.

Then Buccleuch called a halt, and everyone dismounted, and some forty men, throwing their bridle reins to their comrades, stepped to the front. Red Rowan was one of them, and I kept close to his side.

Everything must have been arranged beforehand, for not a word was spoken, but by the light of a single torch the little band arranged themselves in order, while I watched with wide-open eyes. They were not all armed, but they all had their hands full.

In the very front were ten men carrying hunting-horns and bugles; then came ten carrying three or four long ladders, which must have been brought with us on ponies' backs. Then came other ten, armed with great iron bars and forehammers; and only the last ten, among whom was the Warden himself and Red Rowan, were prepared as if for fighting.

At the word of command they set out, with long steady strides, and as no one noticed me, I went too, running all the time in order to keep up with them.

The Castle stood to the north side of the little city, close to the city wall, and the courtyard lay just below it. We stole up like cats in the darkness, fearful lest someone might hear us and give the alarm. Everyone seemed to be asleep, however, or else the roaring of the wind deadened the noise of our footsteps. In any case we reached the wall in safety, and as we stood at the bottom of it waiting till the men tied the ladders together, we could hear the sentries in the courtyard challenge as they went their rounds.

At last the ladders were ready, and Buccleuch gave his whispered orders before they were raised.

No man was to be killed, he said, if it could possibly be helped, as the two countries were at peace with each other, and he had no mind to stir up strife. All he wanted was the rescue of my father.

Then the ladders were raised, and bitter was the disappointment when it was found that they were too short. For a moment it seemed as if we had come all the weary way for nothing.

"It matters not, lads," said the Warden cheerily; "there be more ways of robbing a corbie's nest than one. Bide you here by the little postern, and Wat Scott and Red Rowan and I will prowl round, and see what we can see."

Along with these two stalwart men he vanished, while we crouched at the foot of the wall and waited; nor had we long to wait.

In ten minutes we could hear the bolts and bars being withdrawn, and the little door was opened by Buccleuch himself, who wore a triumphant smile. He had found a loophole at the back of the Castle left entirely unguarded, and without much difficulty he and his two companions had forced out a stone or two, until the hole was large enough for them to squeeze through, and had caught and bound the unsuspecting sentries as they came round, stuffing their mouths full of old clouts to hinder them from crying out and giving the alarm.

Once we were inside the courtyard he ordered the men with the iron bars and forehammers to be ready to beat open the doors, and then he gave the word to the men with the bugles and hunting horns.

Then began such a din as I had never heard before, and have never heard since. The bugles screeched, and the iron bars rang, and above all sounded the wild Border slogan, "Wha dare meddle wi' me?" which the men shouted with all their might. One would have thought that the whole men in Scotland were about the walls, instead of but forty.

And in good faith the people of the Castle, cowards that they were, and even my Lord Scroope himself, thought that they were beset by a whole army, and after one or two frightened peeps from out of windows, and behind doors, they shut themselves up as best they might in their own quarters, and left us to work our will, and beat down door after door until we came to the very innermost prison itself, where my father was chained hand and foot to the wall like any dog.

Just as the door was being burst open, my lord caught sight of me as I squeezed along the passage, anxious to see all that could be seen. He laid his hand on the men's shoulders and held them back.

"Let the bairn go first," he said; "it is his right, for he has saved him."

Then I darted across the cell, and stood at my father's side. What he said to me I never knew, only I saw that strange look once more on his face, and his eyes were very bright. Had he been a bairn or a woman I should have said he was like to weep. It was past in a moment, for there was little time to lose. At any instant the garrison might find out how few in numbers we were, and sally out to cut us off, so no time was wasted in trying to strike his chains off him.

With an iron bar Red Rowan wrenched the ring to which he was fastened, out of the wall, and, raising him on his back, carried him bodily down the narrow staircase, and out through the courtyard.

As we passed under my Lord Scroope's casement, my father, putting all his strength into his voice, called out a lusty "good night" to his lordship, which was echoed by the men with peals of laughter.

Then we hurried on to where the main body of troopers were waiting with the horses, and I warrant the shout that they raised when they saw us coming with my father in the midst of us, riding on Red Rowan's shoulder, might almost have been heard at Branksome itself.

When it died away we heard another sound which warned us that the laggards at the Castle had gathered their feeble courage, and were calling on the burghers of Carlisle to come to their aid, for every bell in the city was ringing, and we could see the flash of torches here and there.

Scarcely had the smiths struck the last fetter from my father's limbs than we heard the thunder of horses' hoofs behind us.

"To horse, lads," cried Buccleuch, and in another moment we were galloping towards the Eden, I in front of Red Rowan as before, and close to my father's side.

The English knew the lie of the land better than we did, for they were at the river before us, well-nigh a thousand of them, with Lord Scroope himself at their head. Apparently they never dreamed that we would attempt to swim the torrent, and thought we would have to show fight, for they were drawn up as if for a battle; but we dashed past them with a yell of defiance, and plunged into the flooded river, and once more we came safe to the other side. Once there we faced round, but the English made no attempt to follow; they sat on their horses, glowering at us in the dim light of the breaking day, but they said never a word.

Then my Lord of Buccleuch raised himself in his stirrups, and, plucking off his right glove, he flung it with all his might across the river, and, the wind catching it, it was blown right into their leader's face. "Take that, my Lord of Scroope," he cried; "mayhap 'twill cure thee of thy treachery, for if Sakelde took him, 'twas thou who harboured him, and if thou likest not my mode of visiting at thy Castle of Carlisle, thou canst call and lodge thy complaint at Branksome at thy leisure."

Then, with a laugh, he turned his horse's head and led us homewards, as the sun was rising and the world was waking up to another day.

# THE GUDE WALLACE

*"Would ye hear of William Wallace,*
*An' sek him as he goes, Into the lan' of Lanark,*
*Amang his mortal foes?*

*There were fyfteen English sojers,*
*Unto his ladye came,*
*Said, 'Gie us William Wallace,*
*That we may have him slain.'"*

I will tell you a tale of the Good Wallace, that brave and noble patriot who rose to deliver his country from the yoke of the English, and who spent his strength, and at last laid down his life, for that one end.

As all the world knows, the English King, Edward I., had defeated John Baliol at Dunbar, and he had laid claim to the kingdom of Scotland, and had poured his soldiers into that land.

Some of these soldiers, hearing of the strength, and wisdom, and prowess of the young champion who had arisen, like Gideon of old, for the succour of his people, determined to try to take him by stealth, before venturing to meet him in the open field.

'Twas known that Wallace was in the habit of visiting a lady, a friend of his, in the town of Lanark, so a band of these soldiers went to her house, and surrounded it, while the captain knocked at the door. When the lady opened it, and saw him, and saw also that her house was surrounded by his men, she was very much alarmed, which perhaps was not to be wondered at, for everyone was afraid of the English at that time.

The officer spoke to her in quite a friendly manner, however, and began to tell her about his own country, and how much richer and finer everything was there than in Scotland, and at last, when she was thoroughly interested, he hinted that it was in her power to marry an English lord if she cared to do so, and go and live in England altogether.

Now I am afraid that the lady was both silly and discontented, and it seemed to her that it would be a very fine thing indeed to be an English nobleman's wife, so she blushed and bridled, and looked up and down, and at last she asked how the thing could be managed.

"Well," said the officer cautiously, "there is only one condition, and that doth not seem to me to be a very hard one. It hath been told me that there is a rough and turbulent fellow who visits this house. His name is William Wallace, and because he is likely to stir up riots among the common people, it seems good to His Majesty, King Edward, that he should be taken prisoner. Would it be possible," and here his voice became very soft and persuasive, "for thee to let us know what night he intends to visit thee?"

At first the lady started back, and was very indignant with him for daring to suggest that she should do such a dishonourable thing.

"I am no traitor," she said proudly, "nor am I like Jael of old, who murdered the man who took shelter in her tent."

But the captain's voice was low and sweet, and the lady's nature was vain and fickle, and the prospect of marrying an English lord was very enticing, and so it came about that at last she yielded, and she told him how she was expecting young Wallace that very night at seven o'clock, and she promised to put a light in the window when he arrived.

Then the false woman went into her house and shut the door, and the soldiers set themselves to watch for the coming of their enemy.

How it happened I know not, but Wallace came, and walked boldly into the house without one of them seeing him, and he ran upstairs and knocked at the door of his friend's room.

When she opened it, he stood still, and stared at her in astonishment, for her face was pale and wild, and she looked at him with terror in her eyes. I warrant she had been wrestling with her conscience ever since she had spoken with the soldiers, and she had seen what an awful thing it is to be guilty of the blood of an innocent man.

"What ails thee?" cried Wallace, in his bluff, hearty way. "Thou lookest all distraught, as if thou hadst seen a ghost."

Then he held out his hand as if to greet her, but she stretched forth hers and pushed him away.

"Touch me not. I am like Judas, — Judas," she moaned,

"who betrayed the innocent blood, and whose fate is written in the Holy Book for a warning to all poor recreants like to me."

Sir William Wallace thought that she had gone mad. "Vex not thyself," he said kindly. "Methinks thou hast been reading, and thinking, till thou hast fevered thy poor brain. Thou art no Judas, but mine own true friend, in whose house I find safe shelter when I need to visit Lanark."

"Safe shelter!" she cried, with a bitter laugh, and she dragged him to the window, and pointed out in the dusk the figures of four soldiers who were leaning against the garden gate. "Safe shelter, say ye, when I have betrayed thee to the English; for this house is watched by fifteen soldiers; and I have but to put a lamp in the window, as a signal that thou art within, and they will come and slay thee."

"And what is thy reward for this deed of treachery?" asked Wallace, a look of contempt coming over his open face. "What pay did the English loons promise thee?"

"They promised me an English lord for a husband," sobbed the wretched woman, who now would have done anything in her power to undo the wrong that she had done. "But oh, sir, I fear me I have wrought sore dule to thee this day, and sore dule to Scotland. If thou canst get free from this house, which I fear me thou wilt never do, thou canst denounce me as a traitor. I care not if I die the death."

"Now Heaven forfend!" said Wallace, whose kindly heart was touched by her distress, although he despised her for her false deed; "it shall never be said that William Wallace avenged himself on a woman, no matter what her crime might be. I trusted thee, and thou hast proved false, and so from henceforth we must go our different ways; but if thou art truly sorry, thou mayest yet help me, and, as for me, if once I get clear away from these Southron knaves outside. I will think no more of the matter."

"But canst thou get clear away?" questioned the lady anxiously. "I fear me, now that it is past seven o'clock, they will keep stricter watch than they did when thou camest in. 'Twill be impossible for thee to pass out in safety, and if thou remainest here, they will search the house when they tire of waiting for my signal."

Wallace laughed.

"Impossible is not a word that I am well acquaint with, madam," he said, "and if, for the sake of the friendship that was between us in the days that are gone, thou wilt lend me some of thine attire, a gown and kirtle maybe, and a decent petticoat of homespun, and a cap such as wenches wear to shield their faces from the sun, I hope I may make good my escape under the very noses of these fellows."

Wondering to herself, the lady did as he asked her. She brought him a dark-coloured gown and kirtle, and a stout winsey petticoat, such as serving-maids wear, and after long search she found at the bottom of a drawer a milk-maid's cap.

Wallace proceeded to dress himself in these, and, when he had put them all on, and had clasped a leather belt round his waist, and wound an apron about his head, as lassies do to protect themselves from the rain or sun, and put the milk-maid's bonnet on top of all, I warrant even his own mother would not have known him.

"Now fetch me a milk-can," he said, "for I am no longer a soldier, but a modest maiden going to the well to draw water."

When she had brought it he bent low over her hand and gave it one kiss for the sake of old times; then he said farewell to her for ever, and opened the door, and walked boldly down the garden.

The four soldiers at the gate looked at one another in surprise when a tall damsel with a milk-can stood still at the foot of the garden path, and waited for them to open it. They had not known that the lady had a serving-maid.

"If it please thee, good sirs, to let me bye," broke in the maiden's voice in the gloom. "My mistress hath a sharp temper, and this water ought to have been fetched an hour ago."

She spoke with a lisp, and her accent was so outlandish that the men scarce understood what she said; but this they saw, that she wanted to go and draw water from the well, and they opened the gate to let her pass.

"If I dare leave my post, I would fain come and draw for thee," said one; "shame is it that such a pretty wench be left to go to the well alone."

The maiden paid no heed to the fellow's words, but tossed her head, and went quickly down the path to the well, taking such gigantic strides that the men gazed after her in wonder.

"Marry, but she covers the ground," said one.

"Certs, but I would rather walk one mile with her than two," said another.

"Methinks that we had better go after her and bring her back," cried a third. "I have heard say that this William Wallace, whom we are in search of, hath mighty long legs."

Horrified at the thought that they might have let the very man they were looking for escape, they hurried down the path after the serving-maid, and when they overtook her they found out in good sooth that she was William Wallace, for she drew a sword from under her kirtle, and killed all four of them, before they could lay hands on her.

When the four men lay dead before him, Wallace wasted no time over their burial, but drawing their bodies under a bush, where they were somewhat hidden from the passers-by, he hung the milk-can on a branch of a tree, and walked quietly away in the gathering darkness. No one who met a simple country girl walking out into the country ever dreamt of asking her who she was, or where she was going, and ere morning came, I promise you, her garments had been cast, and buried in a hole in the ground, and Wallace was making his way northward as fast as ever he could.

He had to be very careful which way he travelled, for there were soldiers quartered in many of the towns, who knew that there was a price set on his head, and who were only too anxious to catch him.

So he dare not venture into the towns, or into the districts where there were many houses, and it came to pass that, as he was nearing Perth, he was like to famish for want of food.

He had eaten almost nothing for three days, nor had he money wherewith to buy it.

Now, near to Perth there is a beautiful haugh or common, called the North Inch, which stretches along the river Tay, and as he was crossing that, he saw a pretty, rosy country girl washing clothes under a tree, and spreading them out to bleach in the sun. She looked so kind and so good-tempered that he thought he would speak to her, and mayhap, if he found that she lived near, he would ask her to give him something to eat.

So he went up to her, and greeted her pleasantly, and asked her what news there was in that part of the world.

"News," said she, looking up at him with a roguish smile, for it was not often that she had the opportunity of talking with such a gallant knight. "Nay, by my troth, I have no news, for I am but a poor working maiden, who toils hard for her living; but one thing I can tell thee, an' if thou be a true Scot at heart, thou wilt do all in thy power to shield him."

"To shield whom?" asked Wallace in surprise. "I know not of whom thou speakest."

"Why! Sir William Wallace," answered the girl, "that gallant man who will deliver this poor country of ours. 'Tis known that he is in these parts; he hath been traced from Lanark, and 'tis thought that he is making for the hills, where his followers are; and this very day a body of these cursed English have marched into the town, in order to search the country and take him. Look, seest thou that little hostelry yonder? There hath a band of them gone in there not half an hour ago. Certs, had I been a man, I would e'en have gone myself, and measured my strength against theirs. I tell thee this, because thou seemest a gallant fellow, and perchance thou canst do something to save the knight."

Wallace smiled. "Had I but a penny in my pocket," he said, "I would betake me to that little inn, just to see these English loons."

The maiden hesitated. She was poor, as she had said, and had to work hard for her living, but it chanced that that day she had half a crown in her pocket, which she had intended to spend in the town on her way home. But her kind heart was stirred with pity at the thought of such a goodly young man having no money in his pocket, and at last she took out the half-crown and gave it to him.

"Take this," she said, "and go and buy meat and drink with it, and if thou knowest where Wallace is, for the love of Heaven, betray him not to these English knaves."

"I will serve Wallace e'en as I serve myself," he said, "and more can no man promise," and, thanking her heartily for the piece of silver, he strode off in the direction of the little hostler-house, leaving her wondering what he meant by his strange answer.

Wallace had not gone very far on his way before he met a beggar man, coming limping along, clad in an old patched cloak.

This was the very thing the knight wanted.

"Hullo, old man," he said; "how goes the world with thee, and what news is there abroad in Perth?"

"News, master?" said the beggar. "No news that I know of, save that 'tis said that Sir William Wallace is somewhere hereabouts, and a party of English soldiers have come to hunt for him. As I craved a bite of bread at the door of that hostler-house down yonder, I saw fifteen of them within, eating and drinking."

"Say ye so, old man?" said Wallace. "That is right good news to me, for I have long had a desire to see an English soldier close at hand. See," and he drew the bright silver half-crown, which he had just received from the maiden, from his pocket, "here is a piece of white money for thee, if thou wilt sell me that old cloak of thine, and thy wallet. Faith, there be as many holes as patches in the cloak; it can scarce serve thee for a covering, and 'twill answer my purpose right well."

Joyfully the beggar agreed to the bargain, and Wallace was left with the cloak, which he threw over his shoulders, and which covered him from head to foot. Pulling his cap well over his eyes, and choosing a trusty thorn cudgel from a neighbouring thicket, he went limping up to the door of the little inn, and knocked.

The captain who was with the English soldiers opened it. He looked the lame beggar up and down.

"What dost thou want, thou cruikit carle?" he asked haughtily.

"An alms, master," answered the beggar humbly. "I am a poor lame man, and unable to work, and I travel the country from end to end, begging my daily bread."

"Ah," thought the captain to himself, "this man must hear all the country gossip. Likely enough he knows where Wallace is, or the direction in which 'tis thought he will travel."

He took a handful of gold from his pouch, and held it before the beggar's eyes.

"Did you ever hear of a man called William Wallace?" he asked slowly; "the country folk hereabouts talk a great deal of him. They call him 'hero,' and such-like names. But he is a traitor to our rightful King, King Edward, and I am here to take him, alive or dead. Hast ever heard of the fellow?"

"Ay," said the beggar, "I have both heard of him and seen

him. Moreover," and he looked at the gold, "I know where he is to be found."

An eager look came into the English knight's face. "I will pay thee fifty pounds down," he said, "fifty pounds of good red money, if thou wilt lead me to Sir William Wallace."

"Tell down the money on this bench," cried the beggar, "for it is in my power to grant thy request, and verily, I will never have a better offer, no, not if I wait till King Edward comes himself."

The English captain counted down the money on the old worm-eaten wooden bench that stood beside the door of the inn, and the beggar counted it after him, and picked it up, and put it carefully away in his wallet. Then he faced the Englishman with a strange gleam in his eyes.

"Thou wouldst fain see William Wallace," he said. "Then see him thou shalt, and feel the might of his arm too, which is more, belike, than thou bargainedst for," and, before the astonished captain could grasp his sword, he had let the beggar's cloak fall to the ground, and, lifting his stout cudgel, he had given him such a clout over the head, that his skull cracked like a nut, and he fell dead at his feet.

Without waiting to take breath, Wallace drew his sword, and, running lightly upstairs, he burst into the room where the soldiers were just finishing their meal, and before they could rise from the table and grasp their weapons, he had stabbed every one of them to the heart.

The innkeeper's wife, who had just come from the kitchen, and was serving the men rather unwillingly, for she had no love for the English, stood still and stared in amazement.

"God save us!" she said at last, as Wallace stopped and wiped his sword. "But are ye a man, or do you come from the Evil One himself?"

"I am William Wallace," said the stranger, "and I wish that all English soldiers who are in Scotland were even as these men are."

"Amen to that," said the old woman heartily, and then she dropped down on her knees before the embarrassed knight. "Hech, sirs," she said fervently, "to think that my eyes are looking on the Gude Wallace!"

"The Hungry Wallace, ye mean," said the knight with a

laugh. "If ye love me, woman, get up from thy knees, and set on meat and drink, for I have scarce tasted food these three days, and my strength is well-nigh gone."

"That will I, right speedily," she cried, and, jumping up, she ran to her husband and told him who the stranger was.

With great goodwill they began to prepare a meal, but hardly had it been dished up, and placed upon the table, before another band of soldiers marched up and surrounded the house. The beggar man had gone into Perth, and told people about the mysterious knight who had bought his old cloak in order that he might go and see the English soldiers, and when the rest of the soldiers in the town got to hear of it, they had suspected at once who he really was, and had come to the help of their companions.

Their suspicions proved true when they caught sight of Wallace through one of the windows.

"Come out, come out, thou false knight," they cried exultingly, "and think not that thou canst escape out of our hands. The tod[1] is taken in his hole this time, and right speedily shall he die."

With that they entered the house, and rushed upstairs, thinking that it would be an easy matter to capture the Scottish leader, for they knew that he had no follower with him. But the weak things of this world are able sometimes to confound the mighty, and they had not reckoned that the two old people to whom the inn belonged were prepared to shed the last drop of their blood, rather than that Wallace should come to harm in their house.

So the old man had taken down his broad claymore from the wall, and the old woman had seized a lance, and they stood one on each side of their guest, grasping their weapons with fevered zeal.

Then began a fierce and deadly onslaught in that little room, and many a time it seemed as if the three brave defenders must go down; but Wallace's arm had the strength of ten, and the old man laid on right bravely, and the old woman gave many a deadly thrust with her lance from behind, where she

1    Fox.

saw it was needed, and so it came to pass that at last every Englishman was slain, and Wallace and his bold helpers were left triumphant.

"Now, surely, I can eat in peace," said he, sitting down to his sorely needed meal, "and then must I begone. For, with thy help, I have done a work here this day that will raise all the English 'twixt Perth and Edinburgh. Mayhap, goodman, thou canst get help to throw these bodies into the river. 'Twill be better for thee that the English find them not in thy house, for I must up and away."

"That can I," said the old man, "for the good folk of Perth think much of thee, and very little of the English, therefore will they give me a hand."

So once more Wallace took the road to the North, and as he retraced his steps across the North Inch, he passed the rosy-cheeked maiden again, busy at her work. She was laying the clothes out to bleach now, and she gave him a friendly nod as he approached.

"I hope, fair sir, that thou hast seen the English," she said, "and that thou hast come by food at the same time?"

"That have I," said Wallace; "thanks to thy gentle charity, I have eaten and drunk to my heart's content. I have seen the English soldiers too, and, by my troth, the English soldiers have also seen me. The day that I visited that little hostler-house is not likely to be forgotten by the English army."

Then he put his hand in his pocket, and drew out twenty pounds in good red gold.

"Take that," he said to the astonished damsel, pressing the money into her hand as he spoke. "Thy half-crown brought me luck, and this is but thy rightful share of it."

So saying, he took his way quickly towards the hills, leaving the girl so bewildered, that, had it not been for the money in her hand, she would have been inclined to think that it was all a dream.

As it was, she never quite believed that it was a human being who had taken away her silver half-crown, and brought her back twenty gold pieces, but talked of ghosts, and visions; and some people, when they heard of the thirty English soldiers who lay dead in the little hostler-house, were inclined to be of her opinion.

# THE WARLOCK O' OAKWOOD

*"Ae gloamin' as the sinking sun*
*Gaed owre the wastlin' braes,*
*And shed on Oakwood's haunted towers*
*His bright but fading rays,*

*Auld Michael sat his leafu' lane*
*Down by the streamlet's side,*
*Beneath a spreading hazel bush,*
*And watched the passing tide."*

The bright rays of the setting sun were shining over the valley of Ettrick, and lighting up the stone turrets on the old tower of Oakwood.

For many a long year the old tower had stood empty, while its owner, Sir Michael Scott, one of the most learned men who ever lived, wandered in distant lands, far across the sea.

He had been a mere boy when he left it, to study at Durham and Oxford: then the love of learning had carried him first of all to Paris, where he had been famed for his skill in mathematics; then to Italy, and finally to Spain, where he had studied alchemy under the Moors, and had learned from them, so 'twas said, much of the magic of the East, so that he had power over spirits, and could command them to come and go at his bidding, and could read the stars, and cure the sick, and do many other wonderful things, which made all men regard him as a wizard.

And now that he had come back to his old home once more, the country folk avoided him, and gazed with awe at the great square tower where, they said, he spent most of his time, practising his magic art, and holding converse with the powers of darkness.

The King, on the other hand, thought much of this most learned knight, and would fain have seen more of him at his court in Edinburgh, but Sir Michael loved the country best, and spent most of his time there, writing, or reading, or making experiments.

This evening, however, he was not in his tower, but was sitting by the side of the Ettrick, studying with deepest interest all the sights and sounds of nature which were going on around him. For he loved nature, this studious, quiet, middle-aged man, and the sight of the little minnows darting about in the water, and the trouts hiding under the stones, and the partridges coming whirring across the cornfields, gave him as much pleasure as all the wonderful sights which he had seen in far-off lands.

Suddenly he raised his head and listened. Far away in the distance he seemed to hear the sound of trumpets, and the "thud," "thud" of horses' hoofs, as if a body of men were riding quickly towards him.

"Some strangers are approaching," he said to himself, "and if I am not mistaken they are soldiers. I will hasten home and learn their errand. Mayhap it is a message from his Majesty the King."

He rose to his feet slowly, for his limbs were somewhat cramped with sitting, and walked with stately dignity to the tower.

The riders had just arrived, and, as he expected, they bore a message from the King. As he approached, a knight clad in full armour rode forward, preceded by a man-at-arms, and, bending low over his horse's neck, presented to him a parchment packet, sealed with the Royal Seal.

"The King of Scotland, whom God preserve, sends greetings to his loyal cousin Sir Michael Scott," he said, "and whereas various French sailors have committed acts of piracy on the high seas, and have attacked and robbed divers Scottish vessels, he lays on him his Royal commands that he will betake himself to France with all speed, and deliver this packet into the hands of the French King. And, further, that he will demand that an answer to the writing contained therein be given him at once, and that he hasten back with all dispatch, and draw not rein, nor tarry, till he deliver the answer to the King in Edinburgh."

Sir Michael took the packet from the messenger's hand and bowed gravely. He was accustomed to receive such orders, and everyone wondered at the marvellously quick way in which he obeyed them.

"Carry my humblest greetings to his Majesty," he answered, "and assure him that I will lose no time, but will at once set about making my preparations. By dawn of day I will be gone, mounted on the swiftest steed that ever the eye of mortal man gazed upon."

"Is it swifter than the horse which his Majesty keeps for his own use at Dunfermline?" asked the soldier curiously. "For if it is, it must indeed be a noble animal, and 'twould fetch a good price among the barons of the court. Ever since his Majesty has turned his mind so much to horses, his courtiers have vied with each other to see which of them could become the possessor of the swiftest animal."

"My horse is not for sale," said Sir Michael shortly, "not though men offered me his weight in gold."

The young officer bowed again. There was something in Sir Michael's tone which forbade him asking to see the horse, much as he should have liked to do so; so, giving a signal to his men, he turned his horse's head in the direction of Edinburgh, and rode off, leaving Sir Michael standing on the doorstep gazing after them, a strange smile on his face.

"A good price," he repeated; "by my troth, 'twould need to be a very good price which would buy my good Diabolus from me. But I must go and summon him."

Muttering strangely to himself, he turned and entered the tower.

He went up the narrow, winding, stone stairs until he reached a little iron-studded door. This door was locked, but he opened it with a key which hung from his girdle, and, entering the low-roofed attic-room to which it led, he locked it again carefully behind him. The attic was at the top of the tower, and through the narrow windows which pierced three of its walls, a glorious view was to be had over the surrounding country.

But Sir Michael had not come up there to admire the view; he had other work to do — work which seemed to need mysterious preparations.

First of all, he proceeded to dress himself in a curiously shaped black cloak, and a hunting cap made of hair, which he took down from a nail in the wall. The cloak was very long, and completely enveloped his figure, and, when he had pulled the hairy cap well down over his eyes, no one would have taken him, I warrant, for the quiet, middle-aged, master of Oakwood.

When he was dressed he took down a leaden platter from a shelf by the door, and, opening a cupboard, he took out a little glass bottle full of a clear amber-coloured liquid, which glowed like melted fire. Setting down the platter on a little round table in the middle of the room, he dropped one or two drops of this liquid on it, and in an instant they broke into tongues of flame which curled up high above his head.

It was a strange and weird fire, enough to frighten any man, but the still, dark-robed figure standing beside it never moved, not even when a number of tiny little imps appeared, clad in scarlet, and green, and blue, and purple, and danced round and round it on the table, tossing their tiny arms, and twisting their queer little faces, as if they had gone mad.

He waited patiently until the little creatures had finished their dance and disappeared, then he seized the platter, and, going to one of the narrow windows, he flung it open, and, pushing the platter through it, he threw it, with its burning load, far out into the gathering twilight.

He watched the fire as it fell, in glowing fragments, among the oak trees which surrounded the tower, then he opened a small, black, leathern-bound book, which lay chained to a monk's desk which stood in a corner. Opening it he read a few words in an unknown tongue, then he turned to the window again and waved a little silver wand over his head three times.

"Come, Diabolus. Come, Diabolus," he muttered, and then he knelt on the floor and waited eagerly, his eyes fixed on the Western horizon.

The sun had sunk, but the sky was clear, and one or two stars had appeared, and were shining out peacefully, like little candles set in a golden haze.

Presently, however, big black clouds began to appear, and pile up, one against another, till the little stars were blotted out, and the whole sky became as black as night.

In a little time the dull muttering of thunder could be heard far away over the woods. It came nearer and nearer — crash upon crash, and roar upon roar — while the lightning flashed, and a perfect tempest of wind arose and lashed the branches of the tall trees into fury. Truly it was an awful storm.

The wizard felt the solid masonry of the tower rock beneath

him, but he was as calm as if only a little gust of wind had been passing on a summer's day.

Still he knelt on, peering eagerly into the darkness. At last his eyes grew bright and keen, for he saw a shadowy form come floating through the air, driven by the wind. He knew now that his charm had worked, and that this was his familiar spirit — the spirit over whom he had most control — who had come in the form of a great black horse, with flaming eyes, and flowing mane, to carry him over the sea to France.

With one bound he flew through the window, and alighted on its back.

"Now woe betide thee, Diabolus," he said, "if thou fliest not swiftly. For I must be in Paris by daylight to-morrow."

The huge black horse shook its mane, and snorted fiercely, as if it understood, and without more ado it flew on its way, its uncanny black-cloaked rider seated on its back.

As soon as they had disappeared, the storm died away, and the moon rose, and the little stars shone out over Oakwood Tower as clearly and quietly as if there had never been a cloud in the sky. Meanwhile Sir Michael Scott and his huge black charger were flying over hills, and valleys, and rivers, in the darkness. They even flew over the sea itself, and never halted until the day broke, and there, far below, lay the city of Paris, dimly seen in the gray morning light.

In the King's Palace the lackeys were hardly awake. They gazed at one another in astonishment when the heavy iron knocker on the great gate fell with a knock that echoed through the courtyard.

"Who dares to knock so loudly at this early hour?" asked the fat old porter in great indignation. "Whoever it be, I trow he may e'en wait outside till I have broken my fast."

But before he had done speaking the knocker fell once more, and there was something so commanding in the sound that the little man hurried off, grumbling to himself, to get the key.

"Beshrew me if it doth not sound like a messenger from some great king," said a man-at-arms who was standing by, and the porter's heart misgave him at the thought that perhaps by his tardiness he had got himself into trouble.

But when he opened the great door, instead of the company

of armed men whom he dreaded to see, there was only a solitary rider, muffled in a great black cloak, and wearing a hairy cap drawn down over his face, seated on an enormous black horse. The stranger's dress was so outlandish, and his horse so big, that the porter crossed himself.

"Surely 'tis the Evil One himself," he muttered; and when the lackeys heard his words, they crowded round the doorway. They, too, were puzzled at Sir Michael's appearance, and began to laugh and jeer at him.

"He is like a hooded crow," cried one.

"Nay, 'tis an old wife in her husband's clothes," shouted another.

"Surely the cloak belonged to Noah," cried a third.

But they started back in dismay when the muffled figure pushed up his cap, and demanded an audience of the King.

"I come from the King of Scotland," he said haughtily, "and his business brooks no delay."

A shout of laughter greeted his demand.

"Thou a messenger from the King of Scotland!" they cried. "A likely story, forsooth! The King of Scotland sends not beggars, in old rusty suits, as his ambassadors. No, no, my good fellow, thou askest us to believe too much. Whatever thou art, thou art not a king's messenger."

"What!" cried Sir Michael. "Ye refuse to do my bidding! and all because I am not decked out in crimson and gold, and ridest alone without a retinue. Well, ye shall see that it is not always wise to judge of a man by his outward appearance. Make way there." And without wasting any more words, he leaped from his horse, and, throwing its bridle over a pillar, he strode right through the middle of them, and made his way to the King's private apartment, without even waiting to be announced.

Now the King of France was accustomed to be treated with great ceremony, and when this dark-robed man strode into his bed-chamber, and held out the parchment packet to him, demanding an instant answer, he was very indignant, and refused to open it.

"Thou sayest that thou comest from the King of Scots," he said. "Well, I believe thee not. If thou wert Sir Michael Scott, as thou sayest thou art, thou wouldst have come with an armed escort, as befitted thy rank and station. Therefore begone, Sirrah, and count thyself happy that I have not had thee thrown into one of the palace dungeons, as a punishment for thy insolence."

"By my troth," cried Sir Michael angrily, "if this is the way thou wouldst answer my master's demands, I trow I can soon bring thee to a better frame of mind."

Without waiting for an answer, he flung down the parchment packet on the floor, and strode out of the room in the same way that he had entered, leaving the angry King gazing after him in astonishment.

"The fellow is mad," he cried to the nobles who stood round. "See to it that he is shut up until he comes to his senses."

But Sir Michael had already reached the courtyard, and passed through the great door to where his horse was waiting outside. He lowered his voice and spoke gently to the mighty beast.

"Stamp, my steed, and show the varlets that we are better than we seem to be," he said. And at his bidding the gigantic creature lifted one of its forefeet, and brought it down with all its might on the pavement.

In an instant it was as though an earthquake were passing over the city. The great towers of the Palace which frowned overhead rocked and swayed, and all the bells on a hundred church steeples chimed and jangled, until the air was thick with the sound of them.

The King and his courtiers were very much alarmed at these strange events, but they did not like to own that it was the mysterious stranger who was the cause of them. All the same, the King called a hurried council, and when the nobles were assembled, and seated in their places in the great hall, he opened the parchment packet, and took out the papers which it contained. When he had read them his face flushed with anger. The King of Scotland's demands were very urgent, and moreover they were stated in no uncertain language, and as he considered that he was a much more powerful monarch than King Alexander, he did not like to be dictated to.

"Ah," he said, "so my Lord of Scotland lays down his own terms with a high hand. Methinks he must learn that this is not the way to obtain favours from France."

"Ay, so in good sooth he must learn," repeated the nobles in one breath. "And in order that the lesson be made plain, we advise that his messenger be cast into prison, and that no notice be taken of his requests."

"Your advice pleases me well," said the King. "Command that the officers seize the fellow at once. Certs, he may think himself lucky that We permit his head to remain on his shoulders."

The command was given, but Sir Michael had been growing more and more impatient that no more notice seemed to be taken of his errand, and when the officers of the guard appeared, and, instead of handing him the French King's answer, as he had expected, laid their hands on him to drag him off to prison, his anger knew no bounds.

"What," he cried, "doth the King still refuse to listen? By my troth, he shall rue the delay," and once more he whispered in the black horse's ear, and once more the mighty creature lifted its great forefoot and brought it down with a crash on the pavement.

The effect was even more terrible than it had been before.

In an instant great thunder clouds rolled up from the horizon, and a fearful storm broke over the city. The thunder rolled and the lightning flashed, and strange and weird figures were seen floating in the air. The great bells which hung in the steeple of the great Cathedral of Notre Dame gave one awful crash, and then burst in two, while the towers and pinnacles of the splendid church came tumbling down in the darkness. The very foundations of the Palace were shaken, and rocked to and fro, till everyone within it was thrown to the ground. The King himself was hurled from his throne of state, and was so badly hurt that he cried aloud with pain and fear.

As for the courtiers, they lay about the floor in all directions, paralysed with terror, crossing themselves, and calling on the Saints to help them. They were so terrified that not one of them thought of going to their Royal Master's aid.

The King was the first to recover himself. "Alack! alack!" he groaned, rising to his feet. "Woe betide the day that brought this fellow to our land! Warlock or wizard, I know not which, but one of them he must be, for no mere mortal man could have had the power to work this harm to our city."

While he was speaking a loud trampling of feet was heard outside the great hall, and all the lackeys came tumbling in, pell-mell, without waiting to do their reverence, just as if the King had been any common man.

"O Sire," they cried, "grant the fellow anything and everything he asks, and let him be gone. He threatens that he will cause this awful beast to stamp yet once again, and, if he does, the whole land of France will be ruined. If your Majesty but knew what harm hath been wrought in the city already!"

"Yes, let him begone," wailed the courtiers, slowly beginning to pick themselves up from the floor, and feeling their bones to see if any of them were broken.

And, indeed, the King was nothing loth to grant their request, for he felt that if the mysterious stranger were allowed to stand at the door much longer his whole kingdom would be tumbling to pieces about his ears. Better far that the King of Scotland should be satisfied, even although it was sorely against his inclinations.

With trembling fingers he picked up the papers and once more read them. Then he wrote an answer promising to fulfil all the Scotch King's demands and he sealed up the packet, and flung it to the nearest lackey.

"Give it to him and bid him begone," he cried, and a sigh of relief went round the hall, as a minute later the man returned with the tidings that the great black horse and its outlandish rider had vanished.

"Heaven grant that when next my Cousin of Scotland sends an ambassador, he choose another man," said the King, and there was not a soul in all the palace who did not breathe a fervent "Amen."

Meanwhile, Sir Michael and his wonderful steed were speeding along on their homeward way. They had crossed the north of France, and were flying over the Straits of Dover, when the creature began to think that it might work a little mischief on its own account.

It had taken a sudden fancy to remain in France for a while, and it thought how nice it would be if it could pitch its master, whom it rather feared than loved, over its head into the water, and so be rid of him for ever.

It knew that as long as it was under his spell, it had to do his bidding, but it knew also that there were certain words which could break the spell even of a wizard, and it began to wonder if it would be possible to make Sir Michael pronounce one of these.

"Master," it said at last slyly, for when it wanted it had the power of speech, "I know little about Scottish ways, but I have oft-times been told that the old wives and children there mutter some words to themselves ere they go to bed. 'Tis some spell, I warrant, and I would fain know it. Canst tell me the words?"

Now the wily animal knew perfectly well what words the children of Scotland were taught to repeat as they knelt at night at their mother's knee, but it hoped that its master would answer without thinking.

But Sir Michael had not studied magic for long years for nothing, and he knew that if he answered that the women and children in Scotland bowed their knees and said their Pater Noster ere they went to bed, the holy words would break the spell, and he would be at the mercy of the fiend, who, when he needed him, was obliged to take the form of a horse, or serve him in any other way which he required.

So he shook the creature's bridle and answered sharply, "What is that to thee, Diabolus? Attend to the business thou hast in hand, and vex not thy soul with silly questions. If thou truly desirest to know what the bairns are taught to say at bed-time, then I would advise thee, when thou art in Scotland, and hast time to spare from thy wicked devices, to go and stand by a cottage window, and learn for thyself. Mayhap the knowledge will do thee good. In the meantime think no more of the matter, unless thou wouldst feel the weight of my wand on thy flanks."

Now, if there was one thing which the great horse feared, it was the wizard's magic wand, so he put his mind to his work, and flew with all the swiftness he possessed northwards over England, and across the Cheviots, until at last they came in sight of Edinburgh, and the Royal Palace of Holyrood.

Here Sir Michael slid from his back, and dismissed him with a little wave of his wand. "Avaunt, Diabolus," he said, and at the words the magic horse vanished into thin air, and, strange to say, the black cloak and hairy cap which the wizard had worn on the journey seemed to fall from him and vanish also, and he was left standing, a middle-aged, dignified gentle-man, clad in a suit of sober brown.

He hurried down to the Palace, and sought an instant audience of the King. The lackeys bowed low, and the doors flew open before him, as he was led into his Majesty's presence, for at the Court of Holyrood Sir Michael Scott was a very great person indeed.

But for once a frown gathered on King Alexander's face when he saw him. Kings expect to be obeyed, and he was not prepared to see the man appear whom he had ordered off to France with all speed the day before.

"What ho! Sir Michael," he said coldly. "Is this the way that thou carriest out our royal orders. In good sooth I wish I had chosen a more zealous messenger."

Sir Michael smiled gravely. "Wilt please my Sovereign Lord to receive this packet from the hand of the King of France?" he said with a stately bow. "Methinks that he will find that in it all his demands are granted, and that I have obeyed his behests to the best of my power."

The King was utterly taken aback. He wondered if Sir Michael were playing some trick on him, for it was absolutely impossible that he could have gone and come from France in twenty-four hours.

When he opened the packet, however, he saw that it was no trick. In utter amazement he called for his courtiers, and they crowded round him to examine the papers. They were all in order, and all the requests had been granted without more ado. Reparation was to be made for the damage that had been done to the Scottish ships, and in future all acts of piracy would be severely punished. It was evident that the papers had been taken to Paris, for there was the French King's own seal, and there was his name signed in his own handwriting, though how they had been carried thither so quickly, nobody ventured to say.

" 'Tis safer not to ask, your Majesty," whispered one old knight, making the sign of the Cross as he spoke, "for there are strange tales afloat, which say that the Lord of Oakwood keeps a familiar spirit in that ancient tower of his, who is ready to do his bidding at all times; and, by my soul, this goes far to prove it."

The King looked round uneasily, in case Sir Michael had heard this last sentence. He felt that if this were true, and he were a wizard, as men hinted, it was best not to incur his dis-

pleasure; but he need not have been afraid. The Lord of Oakwood loved not courts, and now that he had done his errand,
and the papers were safe in the King's hand, he had taken advantage of the astonishment of the courtiers to slip unobserved
through the crowd, and, having borrowed a horse from the royal
stables, he was now riding leisurely out of the city, on his way
home to his old tower on the banks of the Ettrick.

# MUCKLE-MOU'ED MEG

*"O wha hasna heard o' the bauld Juden Murray,*
*The Lord o' the Elibank Castle sae high?*
*An' wha hasna heard o' that notable foray,*
*Whan Willie o' Harden was catched wi' the kye?"*

Of all the towers and castles which belonged to the old Border reivers, there was none which was better suited to its purpose than the ancient house of Harden. It stood, as the house which succeeded it stands to this day, at the head of a deep and narrow glen, looking down on the Borthwick Water, not far from where it joins the Teviot.

It belonged to Walter Scott, "Wat o' Harden," as he was called, a near kinsman and faithful ally of the "Bold Buccleuch," who lived just over the hill, at Branksome.

Wat was a noted freebooter. Never was raid or foray but he was well to the front, and when, as generally happened, the raid or foray resulted in a drove of English cattle finding their way over the Liddesdale hills, and down into Teviotdale, the Master of Harden had no difficulty in guarding his share of the spoil. The entrance to his glen was so narrow, and its sides so steep and rocky, that he had only to drive the tired beasts into it, and set a strong guard at the lower end, and then he and his retainers could take things easily for a time, and live in plenty, till some fine day the beef would be done, and his wife, Dame Mary, whom folk named the "Flower of Yarrow" in her youth, would serve him up a pair of spurs underneath the great silver cover, as a hint that the larder was empty, and that it was full time that he should mount and ride for more.

'Twas little wonder that his five sons grew up to love this free roving life, to which they had always been accustomed, and that they took ill with the change when, in 1603, at the Union of the Crowns, Scotland and England became one country, and King James determined to put down raiding and reiving with a high hand.

It was difficult at first, but gradually a change came about. Courts of justice were established in the Border towns, where law-breakers were tried, and promptly punished, and the heads of the most powerful clans banded themselves together to put down bloodshed and robbery, and a time of quietness bade fair to settle down on the distressed district.

To the old folk, tired of incessant fighting, this change was welcome; but the younger men found their occupation gone, while as yet they had no thought of turning to some more peaceable pursuit. The young Scotts of Harden were no exceptions to this rule, and William, the eldest, found matters, after a time, quite unbearable. Moreover, his father's retainers were growing discontented with their quiet life, and scanty fare, for beef was not so plentiful at Harden now that Border law forbade its being stolen from England; so, without telling either his father or his brothers of his intention, he took a band of chosen men, and rode over, in the gray light of an early spring morning, to the house of William Hogg of Fauldshope, one of the chief retainers of the family.

William was a man of great bravery, and so fierce and strong that he had earned for himself the name of the "Wild Boar of Fauldshope."

He was still in bed when the party from Harden arrived, but rose hastily when they knocked. Great was his astonishment when he saw his young master with a band of armed men behind him.

"What cheer, Master?" he said, "and what doest thou out at this time of day? Faith, it minds me of the good old times, when some rider would come in haste to my door, to tell me that Auld Buccleuch had given orders to warn the water."[2]

"Heaven send that those times come back again," said young Harden piously, "else shall we soon be turned into a pack of old wives. The changes that have come to Harden be more than I can stand, Willie. Not so many years past we were aye as busy as a swarm of bees. When we had a mind, and had nought else to do, we leaped on our horses and headed towards Cumberland. There were ever some kine to be driven, or a house or two to be burned, or some poor widow to be avenged, or some prisoner to be released. So things went right merrily, and the

2    To call the countrymen to arms.

larder was always full. But now that this cursed peace hath come, and King Jamie reigns in London — plague on the man for leaving this bonnie land! — the place is as quiet as the grave, and the horses grow fat, and our men grow lean, and they quarrel and fight among themselves all day, an' all because they have nought else to do. Moreover, the pastures round Harden grow rough for want of eating. We need a drove of cattle to keep them down. So I have e'en come over to take counsel with thee, Will, for thou art a man after mine own heart, and I have brought a few of the knaves at my back. What think ye, man, is there no one we could rob? Fain would I ride over the Border to harry the men of Cumberland, but thou knowest how it is. My kinsman of Buccleuch is Warden of the Marches, and responsible for keeping the peace, and sore dule and woe would come to my father's house were I to stir up strife now that we are supposed to be all one land."

"Ay, by my troth," said Will of Fauldshope, "the fat would be in the fire if we were to ride into Cumberland nowadays; but, Master, the Warden hath no right to interfere with lawful quarrels. There is the Laird o' Elibank, for instance, old Sir Juden. Deil take me if anyone could blame us if we paid him a visit. For all the world knows how often some cows, or a calf or two, have vanished on a dark night from the hillsides at Harden, and though a Murray hath never yet been ta'en red-handed, it is easy to know where the larders o' Elibank get their plenishing. Turn about is fair play, say I, and now that the pastures at Harden are empty, 'tis time that we thought of taking our revenge. Sir Juden was a wily man in his youth, and sly as a polecat, but men say that nowadays he hath grown doited,[3] and does nought but sit with his wife and his three ugly daughters from morning till night. All the same, he hath managed to feather his nest right well. 'Twas told me at Candlemas that he hath no less than three hundred fat cattle grazing in the meadows that lie around Elibank."

Willie o' Harden slapped his thigh.

"That settles the matter," he cried, with a ring in his voice at the thought of the adventure that lay before him. "Three

---

3    In his dotage.

hundred kye are far too many for one old man to herd. Let him turn his mind to his three ill-faured[4] daughters, whom no man will wed because of their looks. This very night we will ride over into Ettrick, and lift a wheen[5] o' them. My father's Tower of Oakwood lies not far from Elibank, and when once we have driven the beasts into the Oakwood byres, 'twill take old Sir Juden all his time to prove that they ever belonged to him."

Late that afternoon Sir Juden Murray was having a daunder[6] in the low-lying haughs which lay along the banks of the Tweed, close to his old tower. His hands were clasped behind his back, under his coat tails, and his head was sunk low on his breast. He appeared to be deep in meditation, and so indeed he was. There was a matter which had been pressing heavily on his mind for some time, and it troubled him more every day.

The fact was, that it was a sore anxiety to him how he was going to provide for his three daughters, for Providence had endowed them with such very plain features that it seemed extremely unlikely that any gay wooer would ever stop before the door of Elibank. Meg, the eldest, was especially plain-looking. She was pale and thin, with colourless eyes, and a long pointed nose, and, to make matters worse, she had such a very wide mouth that she was known throughout the length and breadth of four counties as "Muckle-Mou'ed Meg o' Elibank."

No wonder her father sighed as he thought of her, for, in spite of his greed and his slyness, Sir Juden was an affectionate father, as fathers went in those days, and the lot of unmarried ladies of the upper class, at that time, was a hard one.

He was roused from his thoughts by someone shouting to him from the top of the neighbouring hill. It was one of his men-at-arms, and the old man stood for a moment with his hand at his ear, to listen to the fellow's words. They came faintly down the wind.

"I fear evil betakes us, Sir Juden, for far in the distance I hear bugles sounding at Oakwood Tower. I would have said

4    Plain-looking.
5    Few.
6    Gentle walk.

that the Scotts of Harden were riding, were it not for Buccleuch and his new laws."

Sir Juden shook his grizzled head. "Little cares Auld Wat o' Harden, or any o' his kind, either for Warden or laws, notwithstanding that the Warden is his own kith and kin. As like as not they have heard tell o' my bonnie drove of cattle, and would fain have some of them. Run, sirrah, and warn our friends; no one can find fault with us if we fight in self-defence."

No sooner had the first man disappeared to do his master's bidding, than another approached, running down the hillside as fast as he could. He was quite out of breath when he came up to the Laird, and no wonder, for he had run all the way from Philip-Cairn, one of the highest hills in the neighbourhood.

"Oh, Sir Juden," he gasped, "lose no time, but arm well, and warn well, if thou wouldst keep thine own. From the top of the hill I saw armed men in the distance, and it was not long ere I knew the knaves. 'Tis a band of reivers led by the young Knight of Harden, and, besides his own men, he hath with him the Wild Boar of Fauldshope, and all the Hoggs and the Brydons."

"By my troth, but thou bringest serious tidings," said Sir Juden, thoroughly alarmed, for he knew what deadly fighters Willie o' Harden and the Boar of Fauldshope were, and, without wasting words, he hurried away to his tower to make the best preparations he could for the coming fray.

He knew that even with all the friends who would muster round him, the men of Plora, and Traquair, and Ashiestiel, and Hollowlee, Harden's force would far outnumber his, and his only hope lay in outwitting the enemy, who were better known for their bravery than for their guile.

So when all his friends were assembled, instead of stationing them near the castle, he led them out to a steep hill-side, some miles away, where he knew the Scotts must pass with the cattle, on their way to Oakwood. As the night was dark, he bade each of them fasten a white feather in his cap, so that, when they were fighting, they would know who were their friends and who their foes, and he would not allow them to stand about on the hill-side, but made them lie down hidden in the heather until he gave them the signal to rise.

He knew well what he was doing, for he was as cunning as a fox, and neither the Knight of Harden nor the Wild Boar of

Fauldshope, brave though they were, were a match for him.

They, on their part, thought things were going splendidly, for when they rode up in the darkness of midnight to the Elibank haughs, all was quiet; not so much as a dog barked. It was not difficult to collect a goodly drove of fat cattle, and, as long as the animals were driven along a familiar path, all went well. But all the world knows the saying about "a cow in an unca loaning,"[7] and it held good in this case. The moment the animals' heads were turned to the hills that lay between Elibank and Oakwood the trouble began. They broke in confusion, and ran hither and thither in the darkness, lowing and crying in great bewilderment.

"Faith, but this will never do," exclaimed Will of Fauldshope; "if the beasts bellow at this rate, they will awaken old Sir Juden and his sons, and they will set on in pursuit. Not that that would matter much, but we may as well do the job with as little bloodshed as possible. See, I and my men will take a dozen or so, and push on over the hill. If once the way be trodden the rest will follow."

So Will of Fauldshope and his men went their way cheerily up the hill, and over its crest, and down the other side, on their way to Oakwood, with a handful of cattle before them, little recking that Sir Juden and his sons, whom they thought to be sleeping peacefully at Elibank, were crouching among the heather with their friends and retainers, or that they had ridden over a few of them on their way, and that, as soon as they were past, and out of earshot, and young Harden came on with the main body of the stolen cattle, the Murrays would rise and set on him with sudden fierceness, and after a sharp and bloody conflict would take him prisoner, and kill many a brave man.

Nor would Will have heard of the fight at all, until he had arrived at Oakwood, and his suspicions had been aroused by the fact that young Harden did not follow him, had it not been for a trusty fellow called Andrew o' Langhope, who was knocked down in the fight, and who thought that he could serve his master best by lying still. So he pretended to be dead, and lay

7    A cow in a strange lane or milking-place.

motionless until the fray was over, and poor young Scott bound hand and foot, and carried off in triumph by the Murrays; then he sprang to his feet, and ran off in pursuit of Will of Fauldshope as fast as his legs could carry him.

Now, if there was one man on earth whom the Wild Boar of Fauldshope and his men loved, it was the young Knight of Harden. He was so handsome, and brave, and debonair, a very leader among men, that I ween there was dire confusion among them when they heard Andrew o' Langhope's tale. A great oath fell from Will's lips as he threw off his jerkin and helmet, to ease his horse, and turned and galloped over the hill again, followed by all his company.

But in spite of their haste they were too late. The dawn was breaking as they reined up on the green in front of Elibank, and the gray morning light showed them that the stout oak door was closed, and the great iron gates made fast. By now young Harden was safe in the lowest dungeon, and right well they knew that only once again would he breathe the fresh air of heaven, and that would be when he was led out to die under the great dule-tree on the green.

Bitter tears of grief and rage filled the Boar of Fauldshope's eyes at the thought, but no more could be done, except to ride over to Harden, and tell old Sir Walter Scott of the fate that had befallen his eldest son.


"Juden, Juden." It was the Lady of Elibank's voice, and it woke her husband out of the only sound sleep he had had, for he had been terribly troubled with bad dreams all night: dreams not, as one would have imagined, of the fight which he had passed through, but of his eldest daughter Meg, and her sad lack of wooers.

"What is it?" he asked drowsily, as he looked across the room to where his worthy spouse, Dame Margaret Murray, already up and dressed, stood looking out of the narrow casement.

"I was just wondering," she said slowly, "what thou intendest to do with that poor young man?"

"Do," cried Sir Juden, wide awake now, and starting up in astonishment at the question, for his wife was not wont to be so pitiful towards any of his prisoners. "By'r Lady, but there is only one thing that I shall do. Hang the rogue, of course, and that right speedily."

"What," said the Lady of Elibank, and she turned and looked at her angry husband with an expression which seemed to say that at that moment he had taken leave of his senses; "hang the young Knight of Harden, when I have three ill-favoured daughters to marry off my hands! I wonder at ye, Juden! I aye thought ye had a modicum of common sense, and could look a long way in front of ye, but at this moment I am sorely inclined to doubt it. Mark my words, ye'll never again have such a chance as this. For, besides Harden, he is heir to some of the finest lands in Ettrick Forest.[8] There is Kirkhope, and Oakwood, and Bowhill. Think of our Meg; would ye not like to see the lassie mistress of these? And well I wot ye might, for the youth is a spritely young fellow, though given to adventure, as what brave young man is not? And I trow that he would put up with an ill-featured wife, rather than lose his life on our hanging-tree."

Sir Juden looked at his wife for full three minutes in silence, and then he broke into a loud laugh. "By my soul, thou art right, Margaret," he said. "Thou wert born with the wisdom of Solomon, though men would scarce think it to look at thee." And he began to dress himself, without more ado.

Less than two hours afterwards, the door of the dungeon where young Scott was confined was thrown open with a loud and grating noise, and three men-at-arms appeared, and requested the prisoner, all bound as he was, to follow them.

Willie obeyed without a word. He had dared, and had been defeated, and now he must pay the penalty that the times required, and like a brave man he would pay it uncomplainingly, but I warrant that, as he followed the men up the steep stone steps, his heart was heavy within him, and his thoughts were dwelling on the bonnie braes that lay around Harden, where he

---

8    These lands were sold to the Scotts of Buccleuch sometime afterwards, and the Duke of Buccleuch is the present owner.

had so often played when he was a bairn, with his mother, the gentle "Flower of Yarrow," watching over him, and which he knew he would never see again.

But, to his astonishment, instead of being led straight out to the "dule-tree," as he had expected, he was taken into the great hall, and stationed close to one of the narrow windows. A strange sight met his eyes.

The hall was full of armed men, who were looking about them with broad smiles of amusement, while, on a dais at the far end of the hall, were seated, in two large armchairs, his captor of the night before, Sir Juden Murray, and a severe-looking lady, in a wondrous head-dress, and a stiff silken gown, whom he took to be his wife.

Between them, blushing and hanging her head as if the ordeal was too much for her, was the plainest-looking maiden he had ever seen in his life. She was thin and ill-thriven-looking, very different from the buxom lassies he was accustomed to see: her eyes were colourless; her nose was long and pointed, and the size of her mouth would alone have proclaimed her to be the worthy couple's eldest daughter, Muckle-Mou'ed Meg.

Near the dais stood her two younger sisters. They were plain-looking girls also, but hardly so plain-looking as Meg, and they were laughing and whispering to one another, as if much amused by what was going on.

Sir Juden cleared his throat and crossed one thin leg slowly over the other, while he looked keenly at his prisoner from under his bushy eyebrows.

"Good morrow, young sir," he said at last; "so you and your friends thought that ye would like a score or two o' the Elibank kye. By whose warrant, may I ask, did ye ride, seeing that in those days peace is declared on the Border, and anyone who breaks it, breaks it at his own risk?"

"I rode at my own peril," answered the young man haughtily, for he did not like to be questioned in this manner, "and it is on mine own head that the blame must fall. Thou knowest that right well, Sir Juden, so it seems to me but waste of words to parley here."

"So thou knowest the fate that thy rash deed brings on thee," said Sir Juden hastily, his temper, never of the sweetest, rising rapidly at the young man's coolness. He would fain have hanged him without more ado, did prudence permit; and it was hard to sit still and bargain with him.

"So thou knowest that I have the right to hang thee, without further words," he continued; "and, by my faith, many a man would do it, too, without delay. But thou art young, William, and young blood must aye be roving, that I would fain remember, and so I offer thee another chance."

Here the Lord of Elibank paused and glanced at his wife, to see if he had said the right thing, for it was she who had arranged the scene beforehand, and had schooled her husband in the part he was to play.

Meanwhile young Harden, happening to meet Meg Murray's eyes, and puzzled by the look, half wistful, half imploring, which he saw there, glanced hastily out of the little casement beside which he was standing, and received a rude shock, in spite of all his courage, when he saw a strong rope, with a noose at the end of it, dangling from a stout branch of the dule-tree on the green, while a man-at-arms stood kicking the ground idly beside it, apparently waiting till he should be called on to act as executioner.

"So the old rascal is going to hang me after all," he said to himself; "then what, in Our Lady's name, means this strange mummery, and how comes that ill-favoured maiden to look at me as if her life depended on mine?"

At that moment, old Sir Juden, reassured by a nod from Dame Margaret, went on with his speech.

"I will therefore offer thee another chance, I say, and, moreover, I will throw a herd of the cattle which thou wert so anxious to steal into the bargain, if thou wilt promise, on thy part, to wed my daughter Meg within the space of four days."

Here the wily old man stopped, and the Lady of Elibank nodded her head again, while, as for young Harden, for the moment he was too astonished to speak.

So this was the meaning of it all. He was to be forced to marry the ugliest maiden in the south of Scotland in order to save his life. The vision of his mother's beauty rose before him, and the contrast between the Flower of Yarrow and Muckle-Mou'ed Meg o' Elibank struck him so sharply that he cried out in anger, "By my troth, but this thing shall never be. So do thy worst, Sir Juden."

"Think well before ye choose," said that knight, more disappointed than he would have cared to own at his prisoner's words, "for there are better things in this world than beauty, young man. Many a beautiful woman hath been but a thorn in her husband's side, and forbye[9] that, hast thou not learned in the Good Book — if ever ye find time to read it, which I fear me will be but seldom — that a prudent wife is more to be sought after than a bonnie one? And though my Meg here is mayhap no' sae well-favoured as the lassies over in Borthwick Water, or Teviotdale, I warrant there is not one of them who hath proved such a good daughter, or whose nature is so kind and generous."

Still young Harden hesitated, and glanced from the lady, who, poor thing, had hidden her face in her hands, to the gallows, and from the gallows back again to the lady.

Was ever mortal man in such a plight? Here he was, young, handsome, rich, and little more than four-and-twenty, and he must either lose his life on the green yonder, or marry a damsel whom everyone mocked at for her looks.

"If only I could be alone with her for five minutes," he thought to himself, "to see what she looks like, when there is no one to peep and peer at her. The maiden hath not a chance in the midst of this mannerless crowd, and methought her eyes were open and honest, as they looked into mine a little while ago."

At that moment Meg Murray lifted her head once more, and gazed round her like a stag at bay. Poor lassie, it had been bad enough to be jeered at by her father, and flouted and scolded by her mother, because of the unfortunately large mouth with which Providence had endowed her, without being put up for sale, as it were, in the presence of all her father's retainers, and find that the young man to whom she had been offered chose to suffer death rather than have her for a bride.

It was the bitterest moment of all her life, and, had she known it, it was the moment that fixed her destiny.

For young Willie of Harden saw that look, and something in it stirred his pity. Besides, he noticed that her pale face was

9    Besides.

sweet and innerly,[10]] and her gray eyes clear and true.

"Hold," he cried, just as Sir Juden, whose patience was quite exhausted, gave a signal to his men-at-arms to seize the prisoner, and hurry him off to the gallows, "I have changed my mind, and I accept the conditions. But I call all men to witness that I accept not the hand of this noble maiden of necessity, or against my will. I am a Scott, and, had I been minded to, I could have faced death. But I crave the honour of her hand from her father with all humility, and here I vow, before ye all, to do my best to be to her a loyal and a true man."

Loud cheers, and much jesting, followed this speech, and men would have crowded round the young Knight and made much of him, but he pushed his way in grim silence up the hall to where Meg o' Elibank stood trembling by her delighted parents.

She greeted him with a look which set him thinking of a bird which sees its cage flung open, and I wot that, though he did not know it, at that moment he began to love her.

Be that as it may, his words to Sir Juden were short and gruff. "Sir," he asked, "hast thou a priest in thy company? For, if so, let him come hither and finish what we have begun. I would fain spend this night in my own Tower of Oakwood."

Sir Juden and his lady were not a little taken aback at this sudden demand, for, now that the matter was settled to their satisfaction, they would have liked to have married their eldest daughter with more state and ceremony.

"There's no need of such haste," began Dame Margaret, with a look at her lord, "if your word is given, and the Laird satisfied. The morn, or even the next day might do. The lassie's providing[11] must be gathered together, for I would not like it said that a bride went out of Elibank with nothing but the clothes she stood in."

But young Harden interrupted her with small courtesy. "Let her be married now, or not at all," he said, and as the heir of Harden as a prospective son-in-law was very different from

10    Confiding.
11    Trousseau.

the heir of Harden as a prisoner, she feared to say him nay, lest he went back on his word.

So a priest was sent for, and in great haste William Scott of Harden was wedded to Margaret Murray of Elibank, and then they two set off alone, over the hills to the old Tower of Oakwood — he, with high thoughts of anger and revenge in his heart for the trick that had been played him; — she, poor thing, wondering wistfully what the future held in store for her.

The day was cold and wet, and halfway over the Hanging-shaw Height he heard a stifled sob behind him, and, looking over his shoulder, he saw his little woebegone bride trying in vain with her numbed fingers to guide her palfrey, which was floundering in a moss-hole, to firmer footing.

The sight would have touched a harder heart than Willie of Harden's, for he was a true son of his mother, and the Flower of Yarrow was aye kind-hearted; and suddenly all his anger vanished.

"God save us, lassie, but there's nothing to greet[12] about," he said, turning his horse and taking her reins from her poor stiff fingers, and, though the words were rough, his voice was strangely gentle. " 'Tis not thy fault that things have fallen out thus, and if I be a trifle angered, in good faith it is not with thee. Come," and, as he spoke, he stooped down and lifted her bodily from her saddle, and swung her up in front of him on his great black horse. "Leave that stupid beast of thine alone; 'twill find its way back to Elibank soon enough, I warrant. We will go over the hill quicker in this fashion, and thou wilt have more shelter from the rain. There is many a good nag on the hills at Harden, and, when she hears of our wedding, I doubt not but that my mother will have one trained for thee."

Poor Meg caught her breath. She did not feel so much afraid of her husband now that she was close to him, and his arm was round her; besides, the shelter from the rain was very pleasant; but still her heart misgave her.

"Thy Lady Mother, she is very beautiful," she faltered, "and doubtless she looked for beauty in her sons' wives."

Then, for ever and a day, all resentment went out of Willie

12   Cry.

of Harden's heart, and pure love and pity entered into it.

"If her sons' wives are but good women, my mother will be well content," he said, and with that he kissed her.

And I trow that that kiss marked the beginning of Meg Scott's happiness.

For happy she always was. She was aye plain-looking — nothing on earth could alter her features — but with great happiness comes a look of marvellous contentment, which can beautify the most homely face, and she was such a clever housekeeper (no one could salt beef as she could), and so modest and gentle, that her handsome husband grew to love her more and more, and I wot that her face became to him the bonniest and the sweetest face in the whole world.

Sons and daughters were born to them, strapping lads and fair-faced lassies, and, in after years, when old Wat o' Harden died, and Sir William reigned in his stead, in the old house at the head of the glen, he was wont to declare that for prudence, and virtue, and honour, there was no woman on earth to be compared with his own good wife Meg.

# DICK O' THE COW

*"Now Liddesdale has layen lang in,*
*There is na ryding there at a';*
*The horses are a' grown sae lither fat,*
*They downa stir out o' the sta'.*

*Fair Johnie Armstrong to Wilie did say —*
*'Billy, a riding we will gae;*
*England and us have lang been at feid;*
*Ablins we'll light on some bootie.'"*

It was somewhere about the year 1592, and Thomas, Lord
Scroope, sat at ease in his own apartment in Carlisle Castle. He
had finished supper, and was now resting in a great oak chair
before a roaring fire. A tankard of ale stood on a stool by his side
(for my Lord of Scroope loved good cheer above all things), and
his favourite hound lay stretched on the floor at his feet.

To judge by the look on his face, he was thinking pleasant
thoughts just then. He held the office of Warden of the English
Marches, as well as that of Governor of Carlisle Castle, and in
those lawless days the post was not an easy one. There was generally some raid or foray which had to be investigated, some
turbulent Scot pursued, or mayhap some noted freebooter
hung; but just at present the country-side was at peace, and the
Scotts, and Elliots, and Armstrongs, seemed to be content to
stay quietly at home on their own side of the Border.

So that very day he had sent off a good report to his royal
mistress, Queen Elizabeth, then holding her court in far-off
London, and now he was dreaming of paying a long deferred
visit to his Castle of Bolton in Lancashire.

A sharp knock at the door came as a sudden interruption to
these dreams. "Enter," he cried hastily, wondering to himself
what message could have arrived at the castle at that hour of
night.

It was his own poor fool who entered, for in Carlisle Castle
high state was kept, and Lord Scroope had his jester, like any
king.

The man was known to everyone as "Dick o' the Cow," the

reason probably being that his wife helped to eke out his scanty wages by keeping three cows, and selling their milk to the honest burghers of Carlisle. He was a harmless, light-hearted fellow, whom some men called half-witted, but who was much cleverer than he appeared at first sight to be.

As a rule he was always laughing and making jokes, but tonight his face was long and doleful.

"What ails thee, man?" cried Lord Scroope impatiently. "Methinks thou hast forgot thine office, else why comest thou here with a face that would make a merry man sad?"

"Alack, Master," answered the fool, "up till now I have been an honest man, but at last I must turn my hand to thieving, and for that reason I would crave thy leave to go over the Border into Liddesdale."

"Tush!" said the Warden impatiently, "I love not such jesting. I hear enough about thieving and reiving, and such-like business, without my very fool dinning it into my ears. Leave such matters for my Lord of Buccleuch and me to settle, Sirrah, and bethink thee of thy duty. 'Tis easier to crack jokes and sing songs in the safe shelter of Carlisle Castle than to ride out armed against these Scottish knaves."

But Dick knelt at his master's feet.

"This is no jest, my lord," he said. "For once in his life this poor fool is in earnest. For I am like to be ruined if I cannot have revenge. Thou knowest how my wife and I live in a little cottage just outside the city walls, and how, with my small earnings, I bought three milch cows. My wife is a steady woman and industrious, and she sells the milk which these three cows give, to the people in the city, and so she earns an honest penny."

"In good sooth, a very honest penny," repeated Lord Scroope, laughing, for 'twas well known in Carlisle that the milk which was sold by Dick o' the Cow's wife was thinner and dearer than any other milk sold in the town.

"Last night," went on the fool, "these Scottish thieves, the Armstrongs of Liddesdale, rode past the house, and, of course, they must needs drive these cows off, and, not content with that, they broke open the door, and stole the very coverlets off my bed. My wife bought these coverlets at the Michaelmas fair, and, I trow, what with the loss of them, and the loss of the cows, she is like to lose her reason. So, to comfort her, I have promised to bring them back. Therefore, my lord, I crave leave of thee to go over into Liddesdale, and see what I can lay my hands on there."

The blood rose to the Warden's face. "By my troth, but thou art not frightened to speak, Sirrah," he cried. "Am I not set here to preserve law and order, and thou wouldst have me give thee permission to steal?"

"Nay, not to steal," said the fool slyly; "I only crave leave to get back my own, or, at least, the money's worth for what was my own."

Lord Scroope pondered the request for a minute or two.

"After all," he thought to himself, "what can this one poor man do against such a powerful clan as the Armstrongs? He will be killed, most likely, and that will be the end of it. So there can be no great harm in letting him go."

"If I give thee leave, wilt thou swear that thou wilt steal from no one but those who stole from thee?" he asked at last.

"That I will," said Dick readily. "I give thee my troth, and there is my right hand upon it. Thou canst hang me for a thief myself, if I take as much as a bannock of bread from the house of any man who hath done me no harm."

So my Lord of Scroope let him go.

A blithe man was Dick o' the Cow as he went down the streets of Carlisle next morning, for he had money in his pocket, and a big scheme floating in his brain. It mattered little to him that men smiled to each other as they passed him, and whispered, "There goes my Lord of Scroope's poor jester."

"He laughs the longest who laughs the last," he thought to himself, "and mayhap all men will envy me before long."

First of all, he went and bought a pair of spurs, and a new bridle, which he carefully hid in his breeches pocket, then he turned his back on Carlisle and set out to walk over Bewcastle Waste into Liddesdale. It was a long walk, but he footed it bravely, and at last he arrived at Pudding-burn House, a strongly fortified place, held by John Armstrong, "The Laird's Jock," as he was called, son of the Laird of Mangerton, and a man of importance in the clan. He was known to be both just and generous, and the poor fool thought that he would go to him, and tell him his story, in the hope that he would force the rest of the Armstrongs to give him back his three cows. But when he came near the Pudding-burn House, he found to his dismay that the two Armstrongs who had stolen his cows, Johnie and Willie, had stopped there, on their way home, with all their men-at-arms, and, from the sounds of feasting and mirth which he heard as he approached, he suspected that one, at least, of his three cows had been killed to provide the supper.

"Ah well," thought he to himself, "I am but a poor fool, and there are three-and-thirty armed men against me. To fight is impossible, so I must e'en set my wits to work against their strength of arms."

So he walked boldly up to the house, and demanded to see the Laird's Jock. There was much laughter among the men-at-arms as he was led into the great hall, for everyone had heard of my Lord of Scroope's jester, and, when they knew that it was he, they all crowded round to see what he was like.

He knew his manners, and bowed right low before the master of the house. "God save thee, my good Laird's Jock," he said, "although I fear me I cannot wish so well to all thy company. For I come here to bring a complaint against two of these men — against Johnie and Willie Armstrong, who, with their followers, broke into my house near Carlisle these two nights past, and drove away my three good milk cows, forbye stealing three coverlets from my bed. And I crave that I get my own again, and that justice may be meted out to the dishonest varlets."

These words were greeted by a shout of laughter, for these were rough and lawless times, when might was right, and the strong tyrannised over the weak, and it seemed ridiculous to see this poor fool standing in the middle of all these armed moss-troopers, and expecting to be heard.

"He deserves to be hanged for his insolence," said Johnie Armstrong, who had been the leader of the company.

"Run him through with a sword," said Willie, laughing; "'tis less trouble, and 'twill serve the same end."

"No," cried another. "'Tis not worth while to kill him. He is but a fool at the best. Let us give him a good beating, and then let him go."

But the Laird's Jock heard them, and his voice rang out high above the rest. "Why harm the poor man?" he said. "After all, he hath but come to seek his own, and he must be both hungry and footsore." Then, turning to the fool, he added kindly, "Sit thyself down, my man, and rest thee a little. I am sorry that we cannot exactly give thee thy cattle back again, but at least we can give thee a slice from the leg of one of them. Beshrew me if I have tasted finer beef for many a long day."

Amid roars of laughter a slice of beef was cut from the enormous leg which lay roasted on the great table, and placed before Dick. But he could not eat it, he could only think what a fine cow it had been when it was alive. At last he slipped away unobserved out of the house, and, looking about for somewhere to sleep, he found an old tumble-down house filled with peats.

He crept into it, and lay there, wondering and scheming how he could avenge himself.

Now it had always been the custom at Mangerton Hall, where the Laird's Jock had been brought up, that whoever was not in time for one meal had to wait till the next, and he made the same rule hold good at Pudding-burn House.

As the poor fool lay among the peats, he could see what was going on through a crack in the door, and he noticed that, as the Armstrongs' men were both tired and hungry, they did not take time to put the key away safely after attending to their horses and locking the stable door, but flung it hastily up on the roof, where it could easily be found if it were wanted, and hurried off in case they were late for their supper.

"Here is my chance," he thought to himself, and, as soon as they were all gone into the house, he crept out, and took down the key, and entered the stable. Then he did a very cruel thing. He cut every horse, except three, on one of its hind legs, "tied it with St Mary's knot," as it was called; so that he made them all lame. Then he hastily drew the spurs and the new bridle out of his breeches pocket. He buckled on the spurs, and began to examine the three horses which he had not lamed. He knew to whom they belonged. Two of them, which were standing together, belonged to Johnie and Willie Armstrong, and were the very horses they had ridden when they stole the cows. The third, a splendid animal, which had a stall to itself, plainly belonged to the Laird's Jock.

"I will leave the Laird's Jock's," thought Dick to himself, "for I cannot take three, and he is a kind man; but Johnie's and Willie's must go. 'Twill perhaps teach them what comes of dishonest ways."

So saying, he slipped the bridle over the head of one horse, and tied a rope round the neck of the other, and, opening the stable door, he led them out quietly, and then, mounting one of them, he galloped away as fast as he could.

The next morning, when the men went to the stable to see after their horses, there were shouts of anger and consternation. And no wonder. For it was easy to be seen that thirty of the horses would never put foot to the ground again; other two were stolen; and there was only one, the beautiful bay mare which belonged to the Laird's Jock, which was of any use at all.

"Now who hath done this cruel thing?" cried the master of the house in great anger. "Let me know his name, and by my soul, he shall be punished."

"'Twas the varlet whom we all took to be such a fool," cried Johnie; "the rascal who came here last night whining for his precious cows. A thousand pities but we had done as I said, and hanged him on the nearest tree."

"Hold thy tongue and take blame to thyself," said the Laird's Jock sharply. "Did I not tell thee, ere thou rode to Carlisle, thou and Willie and thy thieving band, that the two countries were at peace, and if thou began this work once more, 'twas hard to say where it would end? Truly the tables are indeed turned. For this poor fool, as thou callest him, hath befooled us all, for the men's horses are maimed and useless, thine own and thy brother's are stolen, and there but remains this good bay mare of mine. Beshrew me, but it seems as if the fellow had some gratitude left that he did not touch her, for I love her as I never loved a horse before."

"Give her to me," cried Johnie Armstrong quickly, stung by this well-earned reproof, "and I will bring the two horses back, and the cunning fool with them, either alive or dead. 'Tis a far cry from here to Carlisle, and I trow he could ride but slowly in the darkness."

"A likely story," said the Laird's Jock. "The fool, as thou callest him, hath already stolen two good horses, and to send another after him would but be sending good siller after bad."

"An' dost thou think that he could take the horse from me?" asked Johnie indignantly, and he pleaded so hard to be allowed to pursue Dick, that at last the Laird's Jock gave him leave.

He wasted no time in seeking his armour, but, snatching up hastily his kinsman's doublet, sword, and helmet, he leaped on the bay mare and galloped away.

He rode so furiously that by midday he overtook Dick on Canonbie Lee, not far from Longtown.

The poor fool had had to ride slowly, for he was not very much accustomed to horses, and it was not easy for him to manage two. He looked round in alarm when he heard the thunder of hoofs behind him, but his face cleared when he saw that Johnie Armstrong was alone.

"I have outwitted a whole household," he thought to himself; "beshrew me if I cannot tackle one man, even although it be Johnie Armstrong."

All the same he put his horses to the gallop, and went on as fast as he could.

"Now hold, thou traitor thief, and stand for thy life," shouted Johnie in a passion.

Dick glanced hastily over his shoulder, and then he pulled his horses round suddenly. He could fight better than most men thought, when he was put to it.

"Art thou alone, Johnie?" he said tauntingly. "Then must I tell thee a little story. I am an unlettered man, being but a poor fool, as thou knowest, but I try to do my duty, and every Sunday I go to church in Carlisle city with my betters. And at our church we have a right good preacher, though his sermons run through my poor brain as if it were a sieve; but there are three words which I aye remember. The first two of these are 'faith' and 'conscience,' and it seems to me that ye lacked both of them when ye came stealing in the dark to my humble cottage, knowing full well that I could not defend myself, and stole my cows, and took my wife's coverlets. What the third word is, I cannot at this moment remember, but it means that when a man lacks faith and conscience he deserves to be punished, and therefore have I punished thee."

Johnie Armstrong felt that he was being laughed at, and, blind with fury, he took his lance and flung it at the fool, thinking to kill him. But he missed his aim, and it only glanced against Dick's doublet, and fell harmless to the ground.

Dick saw his advantage, and rode his horse straight at his enemy, and, taking his cudgel by the wrong end, he struck

Johnie such a blow on the head that he fell senseless to the ground.

Then was the fool a proud man. "Lord Scroope shall hear of this, Johnie," he said to himself, with a chuckle of delight, as he dismounted, and stripped the unconscious man of his coat-of-mail, his steel helmet, and his two-handed sword. He knew that if he went home empty-handed, and told his master that he had fought with Johnie Armstrong and defeated him, Lord Scroope would laugh him to scorn, for Johnie was known to be one of the best fighters on the Borders; but these would serve as proofs that his story was true.

Then, taking the bay mare by the bridle, he mounted his horse once more, and rode on to Carlisle in triumph.

When Johnie Armstrong came to his senses, he cursed the English and all belonging to them with right goodwill. "Now verily," he said to himself, as he turned his face ruefully towards Liddesdale, " 'twill be a hundred years and more ere anyone finds me fighting with a man who is called a fool again."

When Dick o' the Cow rode into the courtyard of Carlisle Castle with his three horses, the first man he met was My Lord of Scroope. Now the Warden knew the Laird's Jock's bay mare at once, and at the sight of her he flew into a violent passion. For he knew well enough that if Dick had stolen three horses from the Armstrongs, that powerful clan would soon ride over into Cumberland to avenge themselves, and had he not written to Queen Elizabeth, not three days before, of the peace which prevailed on the Borders?

"By my troth, fellow," he said in deep vexation, "I'll have thee hanged for this."

Poor Dick was much taken aback at this unlooked-for welcome. He had expected to be greeted as a hero, instead of being threatened with death.

" 'Twas thyself gave me leave to go, my Lord," he said sullenly.

"Ay, I gave thee leave to go and steal from those who stole from thee, an thou couldst," said Lord Scroope in reply; "but beshrew me if I ever gave thee leave to steal from the good Laird's Jock. He is a peaceful man, and a true, and meddles not the Border folk. 'Twas not he who stole thy cows."

Then Dick held up the coat-of-mail, and the helmet, and the

two-handed sword. "On my honour, I won them all in fair and open fight," he cried. "Johnie Armstrong stole my cows, and 'twas he who followed me on the Laird's Jock's mare, and clad in the Laird's Jock's armour. He would fain have slain me with his lance, but by God's grace it glanced from my doublet, and I felled him to the ground with my cudgel."

"Well done!" cried the Warden, slapping his thigh in his delight. "By my soul, but it was well done. My poor fool is more of a man than I thought he was. If the horse be the fair spoil of war, then will I buy her of thee. See, I will give thee fifteen pounds for her, and throw a milk cow into the bargain. 'Twill please thy wife to have milk again."

But Dick was not satisfied with this offer. "May the mother of all the witches fly away with me," he said, "if the horse is not worth more than fifteen pounds. No, no, my Lord, twenty pounds is her price, an if thou wilt not pay that for her, she goes with me to-morrow to be sold at Morton Fair."

Now Lord Scroope happened to know the worth of the mare, so he paid the money down without more ado, and he kept his word about the milk cow.

As Dick pocketed the money and took possession of the cow, he thought what a very clever fellow he was, and he held his head high as he rode out of the courtyard, and down the streets of Carlisle, still leading one horse, and driving the cow in front of him.

He had not gone very far before he met Lord Scroope's brother.

"Well met, fool," he cried, laying his hand on Dick's bridle rein. "Where in all the world didst get Johnie Armstrong's horse? I know 'tis his by the white feet and white forelock. Has my brother been having a fray with Scotland?"

"No," said the fool proudly, "but I have. The horse is mine by right of arms."

"Wilt sell him me?" asked the Warden's brother, who loved a good horse if only he could get him cheaply. "I will give thee ten pounds for him, and a milk cow into the bargain."

"Say twenty pounds," said Dick contemptuously, "and keep thy word about the milk cow, else the horse goes with me to Morton Fair."

Now the Warden's brother needed the horse, and, besides,

it was not dear even at twenty pounds, so he paid down the money, and told the fool where to go for the milk cow.

An hour later Dick appeared at his own cottage door, and shouted for his wife. She rubbed her eyes and blinked with astonishment when she saw her husband mounted on a good black horse, and driving two fat milk cows before him.

Like everyone else, she had always counted him a fool, and had never looked for much help from him. So the loss of the three cows had been a serious matter to her, for the money which their milk brought had done much towards keeping up the house, and clothing the children.

"Here, woman," he cried joyously, leaping from his horse, and emptying the gold out of his pockets into her apron. "Thou madest a great to-do over thy coverlets, but I trow that forty pounds of good red money will pay for them fully, and the three cows which we lost were but thin, starved creatures, compared with these two that I have brought back, and here is a good horse into the bargain."

It all seemed too good to be true, and Dick's wife rubbed her eyes once more. "Take care that they be not taken from thee," she said. "Methinks the Armstrongs will demand vengeance."

"They will not get it from My Lord of Scroope," answered Dick, "for 'twas he who gave me leave to go and steal from them. But mayhap we live too near the Borders for our own comfort, now that we are so rich. When a man hath made his fortune by his wits, as I have, he deserves a little peace in his old age. What wouldst thou think of going further South into Westmoreland, and taking up house near thy mother's kinsfolk?"

"I would think 'twas the wisest plan that ever entered that silly pate of thine," answered his wife, who had never liked to live in such an unsettled region.

So they packed up their belongings, and, getting leave from Lord Scroope, they went to live at Burghunder-Stanmuir, where they passed for quite rich and clever people.

# THE HEIR OF LINNE

*"Lithe and listen, gentlemen,*
*To sing a song I will beginne;*
*It is of a lord of faire Scotland,*
*Which was the unthrifty heire of Linne."*

There was trouble in the ancient Castle of Linne. Upstairs in his low-roofed, oak-panelled chamber the old lord lay dying, and the servants whispered to one another, that, when all was over, and he was gone, there would be many changes at the old place. For he had been a good master, kind and thoughtful to his servants, and generous to the poor. But his only son was a different kind of man, who thought only of his own enjoyment; and John o' the Scales, the steward on the estate, was a hard task-master, and was sure to oppress the poor and helpless when the old lord was no longer there to keep an eye on him.

By the sick man's bedside sat an old nurse, the tears running down her wrinkled face. She had come to the castle long years before, with the fair young mistress who had died when her boy was born. She had taken the child from his dying mother's arms, and had brought him up as if he had been her own, and many a time since he became a man she had mourned, along with his father, over his reckless and sinful ways.

Now she saw nothing before him but ruin, and she shook her head sadly, and muttered to herself as she sat in the darkened room.

"Janet," said the old lord suddenly, "go and tell the lad to speak to me. He loves not to be chided, and of late years I have said but little to him. It did no good, and only angered him. But there are things which must be said, and something warns me that I must make haste to say them."

Noiselessly the old woman left the room, and went to do his bidding, and presently slow, unwilling footsteps sounded on the staircase, and the Lord of Linne's only son entered.

His father's eye rested on him with a fondness which nothing could conceal. For, as is the way with fathers, he loved him still, in spite of all the trouble and sorrow and heartache which he had caused him.

He was a fine-looking young fellow, tall and strong, and debonair, but his face was already beginning to show traces of the wild and reckless life which he was leading.

"I am dying, my son," said his father, "and I have sent for thee to ask thee to make me one promise."

A shadow came over the young man's careless face. He feared that his father might ask him to give up some of his boon companions, or never to touch cards or wine again, and he knew that his will was so weak, that, even if he made the promise, he would break it within a month.

But his father knew this as well as he did, and it was none of these things that he was about to ask, for he knew that to ask them would be useless.

"'Tis but a little promise, lad," he went on, "and one that thou wilt find easy to keep. I am leaving thee a large estate, and plenty of gold, but I know too well that in the days to come thou wilt spend the gold and sell the land. Thou canst not do otherwise, if thou continuest to lead the life thou art leading now. But think not that I sent for thee to chide thee, lad; the day is past for that. Promise only, that when the time I speak of hath come, and thou must needs sell the land, that thou wilt refuse to part with one corner of it. 'Tis the little lodge which stands in the narrow glen far up on the moor. 'Tis a tumble-down old place, and no man would think it worth his while to pay thee a price for it. It would go for an old song wert thou to sell it. Therefore I pray thee to give me thy solemn promise that when thou partest with all the rest, thou wilt still remain master of that. For remember this, lad," and in his eagerness the old man raised himself in his bed, "when all else is lost, and the friends whom thou hast trusted turn their backs and frown on thee, then go to that old lodge, for in it, though thou mayest not think so now, there will always be a trusty friend waiting for thee. Say, wilt thou promise?"

"Of course I will, father," said the young man, much moved; "but I never mean to sell any of the land. I am not so bad as all that. But if it makes thee happier, I swear now in thy presence that I will never part with the old lodge."

With a sigh of satisfaction the old lord fell back on his pillow, and before his son could call for help he was dead.

For the first few weeks after his father's death, the Heir of

Linne seemed sobered, and as if he intended to lead a better life; but after a little while he forgot all about it, and began to riot and drink and gamble as hard as ever. He filled the old house with his friends, and wild revelry went on in it from morning till night.

He had always been wild and reckless; he was worse than ever now.

His father's friends shook their heads when they heard of his wild doings. "It cannot go on," they said. "He is doing no work, and he is throwing away his money right and left. Had he all the gold of the Indies, it would soon come to an end at this rate."

And they were right. It could not go on.

One day the young man found that not one penny remained of all the money which his father had left him, and there seemed nothing for it but to sell some of his land. Money must be got somehow, for he was deeply in debt. Besides, he had to live, and he had never been taught to work, and, even if he had, he was too lazy and idle to do it.

So away he went, and told his dilemma to his father's steward, John o' the Scales, who, as I have said, was a hard man, and a rogue into the bargain. He knew far more about money matters than his master's son, and when he heard the story which he had to tell him, his wicked heart gave a throb of joy.

Here, at last, was the very opportunity which he had been looking for: for, while the heir had been wasting his time, and spending his money, instead of looking after his estates, the dishonest steward had been filling his own pockets; and now he would fain turn a country gentleman.

So, with many fair words, and a great show of sympathy, he offered to buy the land for himself.

"Young men would be young men," he said, "and 'twas no wonder that a dashing young fellow, like the Heir of Linne, should wish to see the world, rather than stay quietly at home and look after his land. That was only fit for old men when they were past their prime. So, if he desired to part with the land, he would give him a fair price for it, and then there would be no need for him to trouble any more about money matters."

The foolish young man was quite ready to agree to this. All that he cared about was how to get money to pay his debts, and to enable him to go on gambling and drinking with his companions.

So when John o' the Scales named a price for the land, and drew up an agreement, he signed it readily, never dreaming that the cunning steward was cheating him, and that the land was worth at least three times as much as he was paying for it. There was only one corner of the estate which he refused to sell, and that was the narrow glen, far out on the hillside, where the old tumble-down lodge stood.

For the Heir of Linne was not wholly bad, and he had enough manliness left in him to remember the promise which he had made to his dying father.

So John o' the Scales became Lord of Linne, and a mighty big man he thought himself. He went to live, with his wife Joan, in the old castle, and he turned his back on his former friends, and tried to make everyone forget that up till now he had only been a steward.

Meanwhile the Heir of Linne, as people still called him — though, like Esau, he had sold his birthright — went away quite happily now that his pockets were once more filled with gold, and went on in his old ways, drinking, and gambling, and rioting, with his boon companions, as if he thought that this money would last for ever.

But of course it did not, and one fine day, nearly a year after he had sold his land, he found that his purse was quite empty again, except for a few small coins.

He had no more land to sell, and for the first time in his life he grew thoughtful, and began to wonder what he should do. But he never took the trouble to worry about anything, and he trusted that in the end it would all come right.

"I have no lack of friends," he thought to himself, "and in the past I have entertained them right royally; surely now it is their turn to entertain me, and by and by I shall look for work."

So with a light heart he travelled to Edinburgh, where most of his fine friends lived, never thinking but that they would be ready to receive him with open arms. Alas! he had yet to learn that the people who are most eager to share our prosperity are not always those who are readiest to share our adversity. With all his faults he had ever been open-handed and generous, and had lent his money freely, and he went boldly to their doors, intending to ask them to lend him money in return, now that he was in need of it.

But, to his surprise, instead of being glad to see him, one and all gave him the cold shoulder.

At the first house the servant came to the door with the message that his master was not at home, though the heir could have sworn that a moment before he had seen him peeping through the window.

The master of the next house was at home, but he began to make excuses, and to say how sorry he was, but he had just paid all his bills, and he had no more money by him; while at the third house his friend spoke to him quite sharply, just as if he had been a stranger, and told him that he ought to be ashamed of the way he had wasted his father's money, and sold his land, and that certainly he could not think of lending gold to him, as he would never expect to see it back again.

The poor young man went out into the street, feeling quite dazed with surprise.

"Ah, lack-a-day!" he said to himself bitterly. "So these are the men who called themselves my friends. As long as I was Heir of Linne, and master of my father's lands, they seemed to love me right well. Many a meal have they eaten at my table, and many a pound of mine hath gone into their pockets; and this is how they repay me."

After this things went from bad to worse. He tried to get work, but no one would hire him, and it was not very long before the Heir of Linne, who had been so proud and reckless in his brighter days, was going about in ragged clothes, begging his bread from door to door. No one who saw him now would have known him to be the bright-faced, handsome lad of whom the old lord had been so proud a few years before.

At last, one day when his courage was almost gone, the words which his father had spoken on his death-bed, and which he had forgotten up till now, flashed into his mind.

"He said that I would find a faithful friend in the little lodge up in the glen, when all my other friends had forsaken me," he said to himself. "I cannot think what he meant, but surely now is the time to test his words, for surely no man could be more forsaken than I am."

So he turned his face from the city, and wended his way

over hill and dale, moor and river, till he came to the little lodge, standing in the lonely glen, high up on the moors near the Castle of Linne.

He had hardly seen the tumble-down old place since he was a boy, and somehow, from his father's words, he expected to find someone living in it — his good old nurse, perhaps. He was so worn out and miserable that the tears came into his eyes at the mere thought of seeing her kindly face. But the old building was quite deserted, and, when he forced open the rusty lock, and entered, he found nothing but a low, dark, comfortless room. The walls were bare and damp, and the little window was so overgrown with ivy that scarcely any light could get in. There was not even a chair or a table in it, nothing but a long rope with a noose at the end of it, which hung dangling down from the ceiling.

As his eyes grew accustomed to the darkness, he noticed that on the rafter above the rope there was written in large letters —

*"Ah, graceless wretch, I knew that thou wouldst soon spoil all, and bring thyself to poverty. So, to hide thy shame, and bring thy sorrows to an end, I left this rope, which will prove thy best friend."*

"So my father knew the straits which my foolishness would bring me to, and he thought of this way of ending my life," said the poor young man to himself, and he felt so heart-broken, and so hopeless, that he put his head in the noose and tried to hang himself.

But this was not the end of which his father had been thinking when he wrote the words; he had only meant to give his son a lesson, which he hoped would be a warning to him. So, when he put his head in the noose, and took hold of the rope, the beam that it was fastened to gave way, and the whole ceiling came tumbling down on top of him.

For a long time he lay stunned on the floor, and when at last he came to himself, he could hardly remember what had happened. At last his eye fell on a packet, which had fallen down with the wood and the mortar, and was lying quite close to him.

He picked it up and opened it.

Inside there was a golden key, and a letter, which told him, that, if he would climb up through the hole in the ceiling, he would find a hidden room under the roof, and there, built into the wall, he would see three great chests standing together.

Wondering greatly to himself, he climbed up among the broken rafters, and he found that what the letter said was true. Sure enough there was a little dark room hidden under the roof, which no one had known of before, and there, standing side by side in the wall, were three iron-bound chests.

There was something written above them, as there had been something written above the rope, but this time the words filled him with hope. They ran thus: —

> *"Once more, my son, I set thee free;*
> *Amend thy Life and follies past:*
> *For if thou dost not amend thy life,*
> *This rope will be thy end at last."*

With trembling hands the Heir of Linne fitted the golden key into the lock of one of the chests. It opened it easily, and when he raised the lid, what was his joy to find that the chest was full of bags of good red gold. There was enough of it to buy back his father's land, and when he saw it he hid his face in his hands, and sobbed for very thankfulness.

The key opened the other two chests as well, and he found that one of them was also full of gold, while the other was full of silver.

It was plain that his father had known how recklessly he would spend his money, and had stored up these chests for him here in this hidden place, where no one was likely to find them, so that when he was penniless, and had learned how wicked and stupid he had been, he might get another chance if he liked to take it.

He had indeed learned a lesson.

With outstretched hands he vowed a vow that he would follow his father's advice and mend his ways, and that from henceforth he would try to be a better man, and lead a worthier life, and use this money in a better way.

Then he lifted out three bags of gold, and hid them in his ragged cloak, and locked up the chests again, and took his way down the hill to his father's castle.

When he arrived, he peeped in at one of the windows, and there he saw John o' the Scales, fat and prosperous-looking, sitting with his wife Joan at the head of the table, and beside them three gentlemen who lived in the neighbourhood. They were laughing, and feasting, and pledging each other in glasses of wine, and, as he looked at them, he wondered how he had ever allowed the sleek, cunning-looking steward to become Lord of Linne in his father's place.

With something of his old pride he knocked at the door, and demanded haughtily to speak with the master of the castle. He was taken straight to the dining-hall, and when John o' the Scales saw him standing in his rags he broke into a rude laugh.

"Well, Spendthrift," he cried, "and what may thine errand be?"

The heir wondered if this man, who, in the old days had flattered and fawned upon him, had any pity left, and he determined to try him.

"Good John o' the Scales," he said, "I have come hither to crave thy help. I pray thee to lend me forty pence."

It was not a large sum. John o' the Scales had often had twice as much from him, but the churlish fellow started up in a rage.

"Begone, thou thriftless loon," he cried; "thou needst not come hither to beg. I swear that not one penny wilt thou get from me. I know too well how thou squandered thy father's gold."

Then the heir turned to John o' the Scales' wife Joan. She was a woman; perhaps she would be more merciful.

"Sweet madam," he said, "for the sake of blessed charity, bestow some alms on a poor wayfarer."

But Joan o' the Scales was a hard woman, and she had never loved her master's son, so she answered rudely, "Nay, by my troth, but thou shalt get no alms from me. Thou art little better than a vagabond; if we had a law to punish such, right gladly would I see thee get thy deserts."

Now one of the guests who sat at the board with this rich and prosperous couple was a knight called Sir Ned Agnew. He was not rich, but he was a gentleman, and he had been a friend of the old lord, and had known the Heir when he was a boy, and now, when he saw him standing, ragged and hungry, in the hall that had once been his own, he could not bear that he should be driven away with hard and cruel words. Besides, he felt very indignant with John o' the Scales, for he knew that he had bought the land far too cheaply. He had not much money to lend, but he could always spare a little.

"Come back, come back," he cried hastily, as he saw the Heir turn as if to leave the house. "Whatever thou art now, thou wert once a right good fellow, and thou wert always ready to part with thy money to anyone who needed it. I am a poor man myself, but I can lend thee forty pence at least; in fact I think that I could lend thee eighty, if thou art in sore want." Then, turning to his host, he added, "The Heir of Linne is a friend of mine, and I will count it a favour if thou wilt let him have a seat at thy table. I think it is as little as thou canst do, seeing that thou hadst the best of the bargain about his land."

John o' the Scales was very angry, but he dare not say much, for he knew in his heart that what the knight said was true, and, moreover, he did not want to quarrel with him, for he liked to be able to go to market, where people were apt to think of him still as the castle steward, and boast about "my friend, Sir Ned."

"Nay, thou knowest 'tis false," he blustered, "and I'll take my vow that, far from making a good bargain, I lost money over that matter, and, to prove what I say, I am willing to offer this young man, in the presence of you all, his lands back again, for a hundred merks less than I gave for them."

"'Tis done," cried the Heir of Linne, and before the astonished John o' the Scales could speak, he had thrown down a piece of money on the table before him.

"'Tis a God's-penny," cried the guests in amazement, for when anyone threw down a piece of money in that way, it meant that they had accepted the bargain, and that the other man could not draw back.

Then the Heir pulled out the three bags of gold from under his cloak, and threw them down on the table before John o' the Scales, who began to look very grave. He had never dreamt, when he offered to let the young man buy back the land, that he would ever be able to do it. He had meant it as a joke, and the joke was very much like turning into a reality. His face grew longer and longer as the Heir emptied out the good red gold in a heap.

"Count it," he cried triumphantly. "It is all there, and honest money. It is thine, and the land is mine, and once more I am the Lord of Linne."

Both John o' the Scales and his wife were very much taken aback; but there was nothing to be done but to count the money and to gather it up. John would fain have asked to be taken back as steward again, but the young lord knew now how dishonest he had been, and would not hear of such a thing.

"No, no," he said, "it is honest men whom I want now, and men who will be my friends when I am poor, as well as when I am rich. I think I have found such a man here," and he turned to Sir Ned Agnew. "If thou wilt accept the post, I shall be glad to have thee for my steward, and for the keeper of my forests, and my deer, as well. And for everyone of the pence which thou wert willing to lend me, I will pay thee a full pound."

So once more the rightful lord reigned in the Castle of Linne, and to everyone's surprise he settled down, and grew so like his father, that strangers who came to the neighbourhood would not believe the stories which people told them of the wild things which he had done in his youth.

# BLACK AGNACE OF DUNBAR

*"Some sing o' lords, and some o' knichts,*
*An' some o' michty men o' war,*
*But I sing o' a leddy bricht,*
*The Black Agnace o' Dunnebar."*

It was in the year 1338, when Bruce's son was but a bairn, and Scotland was guided by a Regent, that we were left, a household of women, as it were, to guard my lord's strong Castle of Dunbar.

My lord himself, Cospatrick, Earl of Dunbar and March, had ridden off to join the Regent, Sir Andrew Moray, and help him to drive the English out of the land. For the English King, Edward III., thought it no shame to war with bairns, and since he had been joined by that false loon, Edward Baliol, he had succeeded in taking many of our Scottish fortresses, including Edinburgh Castle, and in planting an English army in our midst.

Now the Castle of Dunbar, as all folk know, is a strong Castle, standing as it doth well out to sea, on a mass of solid rock, and connected with the mainland only by one narrow strip of land, which is defended by a drawbridge and portcullis, and walls of solid masonry. Its other sides need no defence, for the wild waters of the Northern Sea beat about them with such fury that it is only at certain times of the tide that even peaceful boatmen can find a safe landing. Indeed, 'tis one of the strongest fortresses in the country, and because of its position, lying not so far from the East Border, and being guard as it were to the Lothians, and Edinburgh, it is often called "The Key of Scotland."

My lord deemed it impregnable, as long as it was well supplied with food, so he had little scruple in leaving his young wife and her two little daughters alone there, with a handful of men-at-arms, too old, most of them, to be of any further service in the field, to guard them.

She, on her part, was very well content to stay, for was she not a daughter of the famous Randolph, and did she not claim kinship with Bruce himself? So fear to her was a thing unknown.

I, who was a woman of fifty then, and am well-nigh ninety now, can truly say that in all the course of a long life, I never saw courage like to hers.

I remember, as though it were yesterday, that cold January morning when my lord set off to the Burgh Muir, where he was to meet with the Regent. When all was ready, and his men were mounted and drawn up, waiting for their master, my lady stepped forth joyously, in the sight of them all, and buckled on her husband's armour.

"Ride forth and do battle for thy country and thine infant King, poor babe," she said, "and vex not thy heart for us who are left behind. We deserve not the name we bear, if we cannot hold the Castle till thy return, even though it were against King Edward himself. Thinkest thou not so, Marian?" and she turned round to where I was standing, a few paces back, with little Mistress Marjory clinging to my skirts, and little Mistress Jean in my arms.

For though I was but her bower-woman, I was of the same clan as my lady, and had served in her family all my life. I had carried her in my arms as I now carried her little daughter, and, at her marriage, I had come with her to her husband's home.

"Indeed, Madam, I trow we can, God and the Saints helping us," I answered, and at her brave words the soldiers raised a great cheer, and my lord, who was usually a stern man, and slow to show his feelings, put his arm round her and kissed her on the lips.

"Spoken like my own true wife," he said. "But in good troth, Sweetheart, methinks there is nothing to fear. For very shame neither King Edward nor his Captains will war against a woman, and, e'en if they do, if thou but keep the gates locked, and the portcullis down, I defy any one of them to gain admittance. And, look ye, the well in the courtyard will never run dry — 'tis sunk in the solid rock — and besides the beeves that were salted down at Martinmas, and the meal that was laid in at the end of harvest, there are bags of grain hidden down in the dungeons, enough to feed a score of men for three months at least."

So saying, he leaped into his saddle, and rode out of the gateway, a gallant figure at the head of his troop of armed men, while we climbed to the top of the tower, and stood beside old Andrew, the watchman, and gazed after them until the last glint of their armour disappeared behind a rising hill.

After their departure all went well for a time. Indeed, it was as though the years had flown back, and my lady was once more a girl, so light-hearted and joyous was she, pleased with the novelty of being left governor of that great Castle. It seemed but a bit of play when, after ordering the house and setting the maidens to their tasks, she went round the walls with Walter Brand, a lame archer, who was gently born, and whom she had put in charge of our little fighting force, to see that all the men were at their posts.

And mere play it seemed to her still, when, some two weeks after my lord's departure, as she was sitting sewing in her little chamber, whose windows looked straight out over the sea, and I was rocking Mistress Jean's cradle, and humming a lullaby, little Mistress Marjory, who was five years old, and stirring for her age, came running down from the watch-tower, where she had been with old Andrew, and cried out that a great host of men on horseback were coming, and that old Andrew said that it was the English.

We were laughing at the bairn's story, and wondering who the strangers could be, when old Andrew himself appeared, a look of concern on his usually jocund face.

"Oh, my lady," he cried, "there be a body of armed men moving towards the Castle, led by a knight in splendid armour. A squire rides in front of him, carrying his banner; but the device is unknown to me, and I fear me it was never wrought by Scottish hands."

"Ah ha," laughed the Countess, rising and throwing away her tapestry. "Thou scentest an Englishman, dost thou, Andrew? Mayhap thy thoughts have run on them so much of late, that the habit hath dimmed thine eyes."

"Nay, nay, my lady," stammered old Andrew, half hurt by her gentle raillery, "mine een are keen enough as yet, although my limbs be old."

"'Tis but my sport, Andrew," she answered kindly. "I have always loved a jest, and I have no wish to grow old and grave before my time, even if I have the care of a whole Castle on my shoulders. But hark, there be the stranger's trumpets sounding before the gate. See to it that Walter Brand listens to his message, and answers it as befits the dignity of our house: and thou, do thou mount to thy watch-tower, and keep a good lookout on all that passes."

We waited in silence for some little space; we could hear the sound of voices, but no distinct words reached us.

At last Walter Brand came halting to the door and knocked. Like old Andrew, he wore an anxious look. He was devoted to the Countess, and was aye wont to be timorous where she was concerned.

" 'Tis the English Earl of Salisbury," he said, "who desires to speak with your Grace. I asked him to entrust his message to me, and I would deliver it, but he gave answer haughtily, that he would speak with no one but the Countess."

"Then speak with me he shall," said my lady, with a flash of her eye, "but he must e'en bring himself to catch my words as they drop like pearls from the top of the tower. Summon the archers, Walter, and let them stand behind me for a bodyguard: no man need know how old and frail they be, if they are high enough up, and keep somewhat in the background. And thou, Marian, attend me, for 'tis not fitting that the Countess of Dunbar and March should speak with a strange knight in her husband's absence, without a bower-woman standing by."

Casting her wimple round her, she ascended the steep stone stairs, and, as we followed, Walter Brand put his head close to mine. "I like it not," he said in his sober way, "for this Earl of Salisbury is a bold, brazen-faced fellow, and to my ears his voice rings not true. I fear me, he wishes no good to our lady. They say, moreover, that he is one of the best Captains that the King of England hath, and he hath at least two hundred men with him."

"Trust my lady to look after her own, and her husband's honour," I said sharply, for, good man though he was, Walter Brand aye angered me; he seemed ever over-anxious, a character I love not in a man.

All the same my heart sank, as we stepped out on the flat roof of the tower, and glanced down over the battlements.

I saw at once that Walter had spoken truly. Montague, Earl

of Salisbury, had a bold, bad face, and his words, though honeyed and low, had a false ring in them.

"My humblest greetings, fair lady," he cried; "my life is at thy service, for I heard but yesterday that thy lord, caitiff that he be, hath left thee alone among rough men, in this lonely wind-swept Castle. Methinks thou art accustomed to kinder treatment and therefore am I come to beg thee to open thy gates, and allow me to enter. By my soul, if thou wilt, I shall be thy servant to the death. Such beauty as thine was never meant to be wasted in the desert. Let me enter, and be thy friend, and I will deck thee with such jewels, — with gold and with pearls, that thou shalt be envied of all the ladies in Christendom."

My lady drew herself up proudly; but even yet she thought it was some sport, albeit not the sport that should have been offered to a noble dame in her husband's absence.

"Little care I for gold, or yet for pearls, my Lord of Salisbury," she said in grave displeasure. "I have jewels enough and to spare, and need not that a stranger should give them to me. As for the gates, I am a loyal wife, and I open them to no one until my good lord return."

Now, had my Lord of Salisbury been a true knight, or even a plain, honest, leal soldier, this answer of my lady's would have sufficed, and he would have parleyed no more, but would have departed, taking his men with him. But, villain that he was, his honeyed words rose up once more in answer.

"Oh, lady bright, oh, lady fair," he cried, "I pray thee have mercy on thy humble servant, and open thy gates and speak with him. Thou art far too beautiful to live in these cold Northern climes, among rough and brutal men. Come with me, and I will dress thee in cloth-of-gold, and take thee along with me to London. King Edward will welcome thee, for thy beauty will add lustre to his court, and we shall be married with all speed. I warrant the Countess of Salisbury will be a person of importance at the English court, and thou shalt have a retinue such as in this barren country ye little dream of. Thou shalt have both lords and knights to ride in thy train, and twenty little page boys to serve thee on bended knee; and hawks, and hounds, and horses galore, so thou wouldst join in the chase. Think of it, lady, and consider not thy rough and unkind lord. If he had loved thee in the least, would he have left thee in my power?"

Now the English lord's words were sweet, and he spoke in the soft Southern tongue, such as might wile a bird from the lift,[13] if the bird chanced to have little sense, and when he ceased I glanced at my lady in alarm, lest for a moment she were tempted.

Heaven forgive me for the thought.

She had drawn herself up to her full height, and her face of righteous anger might have frightened the Evil One himself; and, by my Faith, I am not so very sure that it was not the Evil One who spoke by the mouth of my Lord of Salisbury.

The Countess was very stately, and of wondrous beauty. "Black Agnace," the common folk were wont to call her, because of her raven hair and jet black eyes. Verily at that moment these eyes of hers burned like stars of fire.

"Now shame upon thee, Montague, Earl of Salisbury," she cried, and because of her indignation her voice rang out clear as a trumpet. "Open my gates to *thee*, forsooth! go to London with *thee*, and be married to *thee* there, and bear thy name, and ride in the chase with thy horses and hounds, as if I were thy lawful Countess. Shame on thee, I say. I trow thou callest thyself a belted Earl, and a Christian Knight, and thou comest to me, the wife of a belted Earl — who, thank God, is also a Christian Knight, and a good man and true, moreover, which is more than thou art — with words like these. Yea," and she drew a dainty little glove from her girdle, and threw it down at the Earl's feet, "I cry thrice shame on thee, and here I fling defiance in thy face. Keep thy cloth-of-gold for thine own knights' backs; and as for thy squires and pages, if thou hast so many of them, give them each a sword, and set them on a horse, and bring them here to swell thy company. Bring them here, I say, and let them try to batter down these walls, for in no other way wilt thou ever set foot in Dunbar Castle."

A subdued murmur, as if of applause, ran through the ranks of the armed men, who stood drawn up in a body behind the English Earl. For men love bravery wherever they chance

13   Sky.

to meet it, and I trow we must have seemed to them but a feeble company to take upon us the defence of the Castle, and to throw defiance in the teeth of their lord.

But the bravery of the Countess did not seem to strike their leader; possibly he was not accustomed to receive such answers from the lips of women. His face flushed an angry red as his squire picked up my lady's little white glove and handed it to him.

"Now, by my soul, Madam," he cried, "thou shalt find that it is no light matter to jeer at armed men. I have come to thee with all courtesy, asking thee to open thy Castle gates, and thou hast flouted me to my face. Well, so be it. When next I come, 'twill be with other words, and other weapons. Mayhap thou wilt be more eager to treat with me then."

"Bring what thou wilt, and come when thou wilt," answered my lady passionately, "thou shalt ever find the same answer waiting thee. These gates of mine open to no one save my own true lord."

With a low mocking bow the Earl turned his horse's head to the South, and galloped away, followed by his men.

We stood on the top of the tower and watched them, I, with a heart full of anxious thoughts for the time that was coming, my lady with her head held high, and her eyes flaming, while the men stood apart and whispered among themselves. For we all knew that, although the English had taken themselves off, it was only for a time, and that they would return without fail.

When the last horseman had disappeared among the belt of trees which lay between us and the Lammermuirs, my lady turned round, her bonnie face all soft and quivering.

"Will ye stand by me, my men?" she asked.

"That will we, till the death, my lady," answered they, and one after another they knelt at her feet and kissed her hand, while, as for me, I could but take her in my arms, as I had done oft-times when she was a little child, and pray God to strengthen her noble heart.

Her emotion passed as quickly as it had come, however, and in a moment she was herself again, laughing and merry as if it had all been a game of play.

"Come down, Walter; come down, my men," she cried; "we must e'en hold a council of war, and lay our plans; while old Andrew will keep watch for us, and tell us when the black-faced knave is like to return."

And when we went downstairs into the great hall, and found that the silly wenches had heard all that had passed, and were bemoaning themselves for lost, and frightening little Mistress Marjory and Mistress Jean well-nigh out of their senses, I warrant she did not spare them, but called them a pack of chicken-hearted, thin-blooded baggages, and threatened that if they did not hold their tongues, and turn to their duties at once, she would send them packing, and then they would be at the mercy of the English in good earnest.

After that we set to work and made such preparations as we could. We set the wenches to draw water from the well, and to bake a good store of bannocks to be ready in time of need, for the men must not be hungry when they fought. Walter Brand and two of the strongest men-at-arms set to work to strengthen the gates, by laying ponderous billets of wood against them, and clasping these in their places by strong iron bars; while the rest, led by old Andrew, went round the Castle, looking to the loopholes, and the battlements, and examining the cross-bows and other weapons.

Upstairs and downstairs went my lady, overlooking everything, thinking of everything, as became a daughter of the great Randolph, while I sat and kept the bairns, who, poor little lassies, were puzzled to know what all the stir and din was about.

And indeed it was none too soon to look to all these things, for although the country seemed quiet enough through the hours of that short afternoon, when night fell, and I was putting the bairns to bed, my lady helping me — for, when one bears a troubled heart (and her heart must have been troubled, in spite of her cheerful face), it aye seems lighter when the hands are full — a little page came running in to tell us that there were lights flickering to Southward among the trees.

"Now hold thy silly tongue, laddie," said I, for I was anxious that we should at least get one good night's rest before the storm and stress of war came upon us.

My lady looked up with a smile from where she was kneeling beside Mistress Jean's cradle. "Let him be, Marian," she said; "the lad meant it well, and 'tis good to know how the danger threatens. Come, we will go up and watch with old Andrew."

So, as soon as the bairns were asleep, we threw plaids over our heads, and crept up the narrow stairs to where old Andrew was watching in his own little tower, which stood out from the great tower like a corbie's[14] nest, and, crouching down behind the battlements to gain some shelter from the cruel wind, we watched the flickering lights coming nearer and nearer from the Southward, and listened to the shouting of men, and the tramp of horses' hoofs, which we could hear at times coming faintly through the storm.

For two long hours we waited, and then, as we could only guess what was taking place, it being far too dark to see, we crept down the narrow stairs again, stiff and chilled, and threw ourselves, all dressed as we were, on our beds.

The gray winter dawn of next morning showed us that the English Earl meant to do his best to reduce our fortress in good earnest, for a small army of men had been brought up in the night, from Berwick most likely, and they were encamped on a strip of greensward facing the Castle. They must have spent a busy night, for already the tents had been pitched, and fires lit, and the men were now engaged in cooking their breakfast, and attending to their horses. At the sight my heart grew heavier and heavier; but my lady's spirits seemed to rise.

"'Tis a brave sight, is it not, Marian?" she said. "In good troth, my Lord of Salisbury does us too much honour, in setting a camp down at our gates, to amuse us in our loneliness. Me-thinks that is his own tent, there on the right, with the pennon floating in front of it; and there are the mangonells behind," and she pointed to a row of strange-looking machines, which were drawn up on a hill a little way to the rear. "Well, 'tis a stony coast; his lordship will have no trouble in finding stones to load them with."

"What be they, madam?" I asked, for in all my life I had never seen such things before.

My lady laughed as she turned her head to greet Walter Brand, who came up the stairs at that moment.

"Welcome, Walter," she said merrily. "We are just taking the measure of our foes, and here is Marian, who has never seen

14   Crow's.

mangonells before, wondering what they are. They are engines for shooting stones with, Marian; for well the knaves know that arrows are but poor weapons with which to batter stone walls. But see, the fray begins, for yonder are the archers approaching, and yonder go the men down to the sea-shore to gather stones for the mangonells. Thou and I must e'en go down and leave the men to brave the storm. See to it, Walter, that they do not expose themselves unduly; we could ill afford to lose one of them."

Then began the weary onslaught which lasted for so many weeks. In good faith it seems to me that, had we known, when that first rush of arrows sounded through the air, how long it would be ere we were quiet again, we scarce would have had the courage to go on. And when those infernal engines were set off, and their volleys of stones and jagged pieces of iron sounded round our ears, the poor silly wenches lost their heads, and screamed aloud, while the bairns clung to my skirts, and hid their chubby faces in the folds.

But even then my lady was not daunted. Snatching up a napkin, she ran lightly up the stairs, and before anyone could stop her, she stepped forward to the battlements, and there, all unheeding of the danger in which she stood from the arrows of the enemy, she wiped the fragments of stone, and bits of loose mortar daintily from the walls, as if to show my Lord of Salisbury how little our Castle could be harmed by all the stones he liked to hurl against it.

It was bravely done, and again a murmur of admiration went through the English ranks; and — for I was peeping through a loophole — I trow that even the haughty Earl's face softened at the sight of her.

The story of that first day is but the story of many more days that followed. Showers of arrows flew from the cross-bows, volleys of stones fell from the mangonells, until we got so used to the sound of them, that by the third week the veriest coward among the maidens would go boldly up and wipe the dust away where a stone had been chipped, or another displaced, as calmly as our lady herself had done on that first terrible morning.

Their archers did little harm, for our men were so few, and our places of shelter so many, that they ran small risk of being hurt, and although one or two poor fellows were killed, and half a dozen more had wounds, it was nothing to be compared with the loss which the English suffered, for our archers had the whole army to take aim at, and I wot their shafts flew sure.

In vain they brought battering-rams and tried to batter down the doors. Our portcullis had resisted many an onslaught, and the gates behind it were made of oak a foot thick, and studded all over with iron nails, and they might as well have thought to batter down the Bass Rock itself.

So, in spite of all, as the weeks went by, we began to feel fairly safe and comfortable, although my lady never relaxed her vigilance, and went her round of the walls, early and late. At Walter's request she began to wear a morion on her head, and a breast-plate of fine steel, to protect her against any stray arrow, and in them, to my mind, she looked bonnier than ever. In good sooth, I think the very English soldiers loved her, not to speak of our own men; for whenever she appeared they would raise their caps as if in homage, and hum a couplet which ran in some wise thus —

"Come I early, come I late,
I find Annot at the gate,"

as if they would praise her for her tireless watchfulness. One day, Earl Montague himself, moved to admiration by the manner in which Walter Brand had sent his shaft through the heart of an English knight, cried out in the hearing of all his army, "There comes one of my lady's tire-pins; Agnace's love-shafts go straight to the heart." At which words all our men broke into a mighty shout, and cheered, and cheered again, till the walls rang, and the echoes floated back from far out over the sea.

In spite of their admiration at our lady's bravery, however, the English were determined to conquer the Castle, and after a time, when they saw that their battering-rams and mangonells availed little, they bethought them of a more dangerous weapon of warfare.

It was somewhere towards the end of February, when one fine day a mighty sound of hammering arose from the midst of their camp.

"What are they doing now, think ye, Walter?" asked my lady lightly. "Is it possible that they look for so long a siege that they are beginning to build houses for themselves? Truly they are wise, for if my Lord of Salisbury means to stay there until I open my gates to him, he will grow weary of braving these harsh East winds in no better shelter than a tent."

But for once Walter Brand had no answering smile to give her.

"I fear me 'tis a sow that they are making," he said, "and if that be so we had need to look to our arms."

"A sow," repeated the Countess in graver tones. "I have oft heard of such machines, but I never saw one. Thy words hint of danger, Walter. Is a sow then so deadly that our walls cannot resist its onslaught?"

"It is deadly because it brings the enemy nearer us, my lady," answered Walter. "Hitherto our walls have been our shelter; without them we could not stand a moment, for we are outnumbered by the English a score of times over. These sows, as men name them, are great wooden buildings, which can hold at least forty men inside, and with a platform above where other thirty can stand. They be mounted on two great wheels, and can be run close up to the walls, and as they are oft as high as a house, 'twill be an easy matter for the men who stand on the platform to set up ladders and scale our walls, and after that what chance will there be for our poor handful of men? 'Tis not for myself I fear," he went on, "nor yet for the men. We are soldiers and we can face death; but if thou wouldst not fall into the hands of this English Earl, my lady, I would advise that thou, and Marian, and little Mistress Marjory and Mistress Jean, should set out in the boat the first dark night, when it is calm. 'Tis but ten miles to the Bass, and thou couldst aye find shelter there."

Thus spake honest Walter, who was, as I have said, ever timorous where my lady was concerned; but at his words she shook her head.

"And leave the Castle, Walter?" she said. "That will I never do till I open its doors to my own true lord. As for this English Earl and his sows — tush! I care not for them. If they have wood we have rock, my lad, and I warrant 'twill be a right strong sow that will stand upright after a lump of Dunbar rock comes crashing down on its back; so keep up thy courage, and get out the picks and crowbars. If they build sows by day, we can quarry stones by night."

So saying, my lady shook her little white fist, by way of defiance, in the direction of the tents which studded the greensward opposite, while Walter went off to do her bidding, muttering to himself that the famous Randolph himself was not better than she, for she had been born with the courage of Bruce, and the wisdom of Solomon.

So it came about, that, while the English gave over wasting arrows for a time, and turned their attention to the building of two great clumsy wooden structures, we would steal down in a body on dark nights to the little postern that opened on the shore, when the waves were dashing against the rocks, and making enough noise to deaden the sound of the picks, and while we women held a lanthorn or two, the men worked with might and main, hewing at the solid rock which stretched out to seaward for a few yards at the foot of the Castle wall. Then, when some huge block was loosened, ropes would be lowered, and with much ado, for our numbers were small, the unwieldy mass would be hoisted up, and placed in position on the top of the Castle, hidden, it is true, behind the battlements, but with the stones in front of it displaced, so that it could be rolled over with ease at a given signal.

We all took a turn at the ropes, and our hands were often raw and frayed with the work. 'Twas my lady who suffered most, for her skin was fine, and up till now she had never known what such labour meant.

At last the day came when the English mounted their great white sows on wheels, and filled them with armed men, and loaded the roofs of them with broad-shouldered, strapping fellows, who carried ladders and irons with which to scale our walls. When all was ready the mighty machines began to move forward, pushed by scores of willing arms, while we watched them in silence.

My lady and I were hidden in old Andrew's tower, for no word that Walter Brand could say could persuade her to go down beside Mistress Marjory, and Mistress Jean, and the serving wenches.

Instead of shooting, our archers stood motionless, stationed in groups behind the great boulders of rock, ready for Walter's signal.

On came the sows, until we could look down and see the men they carried, with upturned faces, and hands busy with the ladders they were raising to place against the walls. They were trundled over the narrow strip of land which connected us with the mainland, and stood still at last, close to our very gates.

"Now, lads," shouted Walter, and before a single ladder could be placed, our great blocks of rock went crashing down on them, hurling the top men in all directions, and driving in the wooden roofs on those who were inside.

Woe's me! Although they were our enemies, our hearts melted at the sight. The timbers of the sows cracked and fell in, and we could see nought but a mass of mangled, bleeding wretches. Had it not been that my lady feared treachery, and that she had sworn not to open the gates except to her husband, I ween she would fain have taken us all out to succour them.

As it was, we could only watch and pity, and keep the bairns in the chambers that looked on the sea, so that their young eyes should not gaze on so ghastly a scene.

And when night fell, and there was no light to guide our archers to shoot, though I trust that, in any case, mercy would have kept them from it, the English stole across the causeway, and pulled away the broken beams, and carried off the dead and wounded, and burned what remained of the sows.

After that day we had no more trouble from any attempts to storm the Castle.

But what force cannot do, hunger may. So my Lord of Salisbury, still sitting in front of our gates with his army, in order to prevent help reaching us from the land, set about starving us into submission. As yet we had had no need to trouble about food, for, as I have said, we had a store of grain, enough to last for some weeks yet, in the dungeon, and, long ere it was done, we looked for help reaching us by the sea, if it could not reach us by land.

It was soon made plain to us, however, that not only my Lord of Salisbury, but his royal master, King Edward, was determined that the "Key of Scotland" should fall into his hand, for one fine March morning a great fleet of ships came sailing round St Abb's Head, and took up their station betwixt us and the Bass Rock, and then we were left, without hope of succour, until our stock of provisions should be eaten up, and starvation forced us to give in.

Ah me! but it was weary work, living through the ever-lengthening days of that cold bleak springtime, waiting for the help which never came, which never could come, so it seemed to us, with that army watching us from the land, and that fleet of ships girding us in on the sea.

And all the time our store of food sank lower and lower, and the wenches' faces grew white, and the men pulled their belts tighter round their middles, and poor little Mistress Jean would turn wearily away from the water gruel which was all we had to give her, and moan and cry for the white bread and the milk to which she was accustomed. Mistress Marjory, on the other hand, being five years old, and wise for her years, never complained, though oft-times she would let the spoon fall into her porringer at supper-time, and, laying her head against my sleeve, would say in a wistful little voice that went to my very heart, "I cannot eat it, Marian; I am not hungry to-night."

As for my lady, she went about in those days in silence, with a stern, set face. It must have seemed to her that when the meal was all gone she must needs give in, for she could not see her children die before her eyes.

But Providence is aye ready to help those who help themselves, and, late one evening, towards the latter end of May, when we had held the castle for five long months, I chanced to be sitting alone in my chamber, when the Countess entered, looking very pale and wan.

"Wrap a plaid round thee, and come to the top of the tower, Marian," she said. "I cannot sleep, and I long for a breath of fresh air. It doth me no good to go up there by day, for I can see nothing but these English soldiers in front, and these English ships behind. But by night it is different. It is dark then, and I forget for a time how closely beset we are, and how few handfuls of meal there are in the girnels.[15] I will tell thee, Marian," and here her voice sank to a whisper, "what as yet only myself and Walter Brand know, that if help doth not come within a week, we must either open our gates, or starve like rats in a hole."

15    Meal-barrels.

"But a week is aye a week," I said soothingly, for I was frightened at the wildness of her look, "and help may come before it passes."

All the same my heart was heavy within me as I threw a wrap round my head, and followed her up the narrow stone stairs, and out on to the flat roof of the tower.

The footing was bad in the darkness, for although the battlements had been built up again since the day that we destroyed the sows, there were stones and pieces of rock lying about in all directions, and not being so young and light of foot as I once had been, I stumbled and fell.

"Do not stir till I get a light," cried my lady; "it is dangerous up here in the dark, and a twisted ankle would not mend matters."

She felt her way over to Andrew's watch-tower, and the old man lighted his lanthorn for her, and she came quickly back again, holding it low in case the enemy should see it, and send a few arrows in our direction. By its light I raised myself, and we went across to the northern turret, which looked straight over to the Bass Rock, and stood there, resting our arms on the wall.

Suddenly a speck of light shone out far ahead in the darkness. It flickered for a second and then disappeared. In a moment or two it appeared again, and then disappeared in the same way. I drew my lady's attention to it.

" 'Tis a light from the Bass," she said in an excited whisper. "Someone is signalling. It can hardly be to the English, for the Rock is held by friends. Is it possible they can have seen our lanthorn? Let us try again. The English loons are likely to be asleep by now; they have had little to disturb their rest for some weeks back, and may well have grown lazy."

Cautiously she raised the lanthorn, and flashed its rays, once, twice, thrice over the waves. It was only for a second, but it was enough. The spark of light appeared three times in answer, and then all was dark again.

"Run and tell Walter," whispered my lady, and her very voice had changed. It was once more full of life and hope. The Bass Rock was but ten miles off, and if there were friends there watching us, and doubtless making plans to help us, was not that enough?

When Walter came we tried our test for the fourth time,

and the answer came back as before.

"We must watch the sea, my lady," he said, when we were safely down in the great hall again. "Help will only come that way, and it will come in the dark. Heaven send that the English sailors have not seen what we have, and keep a double watch in consequence."

After that, we hardly slept. Night after night, we strained our eyes through the darkness in the direction of the Bass, and for five nights our watching was in vain.

But on the sixth, a Sunday, just on the stroke of twelve, the silence which had lasted so long was broken by the sound of shouting, and lights sprang up all round us, first on the ships and then on the land.

With anxious hearts we crowded round the loopholes, for we knew that somewhere, out among the lights, brave men were making a dash for our rescue, and we women, who could do nothing else, lifted up our hearts, and prayed that Heaven and the Holy St Michael would aid their efforts.

Meanwhile, the men manned the walls, ready to shoot if the English ships came within bow-shot, which they were scarce likely to do, as the coast was wild and rocky, and fraught with danger to those who were unacquainted with it.

Presently Walter called for wood to make a fire outside the little postern which opened on the rocks, and we ceased our prayers, and fell to work with a will, with the kitchen-wenches' choppers, on the empty barrels which were piled up in a corner of a cellar. We even drained our last flagon of oil to pour over them, and soon a fire was blazing on the rudely-cut-out landing-stage, and throwing its beams far out over the sea.

And there, dim and shadowy at first, but aye coming nearer and nearer, guided by its light, we saw a boat, not cut in any foreign fashion, but built and rigged near St Margaret's Hope. It was full of men; we could hear them cheering and shouting in our own good Scots tongue, which fell kindly on our ears after the soft mincing English which had been thrown at our heads for so many months.

They were safe now, for, as I have said, the ships through which they had slipped dare not follow them too near the coast, in case they ran upon the rocks, and the Castle sheltered them from any arrows which might be sent from the land. It sheltered us too, and we crowded down to the little landing-stage, and watched with breathless interest the boat which was bringing safety and succour to us.

"Bring down the bairns, Marian," said my lady. "Marjory at least is of an age to remember this."

I hastened to do her bidding, and, calling one of the wenches, we ran up and roused the sleeping lambs, telling them stories of the wonderful boat which was coming over the sea, bringing them nice things to eat once more; for, poor babes, the lack of dainty fare had been the hardest part of all the siege for them.

We had hardly got downstairs again, when the boat ran close up to our roughly constructed landing-stage, which was little more than a ledge of rock, and willing hands seized the ropes which were flung out to them.

Then amidst such cheering as I shall never forget, her crew jumped out. Forty men of them there were, strong, stalwart, strapping fellows, looking very different from our own poor lads, who were pinched and thin from long watching, and meagre fare. Their leader was Sir Alexander Ramsay of Dalhousie, one of the bravest of Scottish knights, and most chivalrous of men, who had risked his life, and the lives of his men, in order to bring us help.

"Now Heaven and all the Saints be thanked, we are in time," he cried, as his eyes rested on my lady, who was standing at the head of the steps which led up to the little postern, with one babe in her arms, and the other clinging to her gown, "for dire tales have reached us of pestilence and starvation which were working their will within these walls."

Then he doffed his helmet, and ran up to where she was standing, and I wot there was not a dry eye in the crowd as he knelt and kissed her hand.

"Here greet I one of the bravest ladies in Christendom," he said, "for, by my troth, as long as the Scots tongue lasts, the story of how thou kept thy lord's castle in his absence will be handed down from father to son."

"Nay, noble sir," she answered, and there was a little catch in her voice as she spoke, "it hath not been so very hard after all. My men have been brave and leal, my walls are thick, and although the wolf hath come very near the door, he hath not as yet entered."

"Nor shall he," said Sir Alexander cheerily, as he picked up Mistress Marjory and kissed her, "for we have brought enough provisions with us to victual your Castle twice over."

And in good sooth they had. It took more than half an hour to unload the boat, and to carry its contents into the great hall. There had been kind hands and thoughtful hearts at the loading of it. There was milk for the bairns, and capons, and eggs. There was meat and ale for the men, and red French wine and white bread for my lady, and bags of grain and meal, and many other things which I scarce remember, but which were right toothsome, I can tell you, after the scanty fare on which we had been living.

And so ended the famous siege of Dunbar Castle, for on the morrow, the English, knowing that now it was hopeless to think of taking it, struck their camp, and by nightfall they were marching southwards, worsted by a woman.

And ere another day had passed, another band of armed men came riding through the woods that lie thickly o'er the valley in which lies the Lamp of Lothian;[16] but this time we knew right well the device which was emblazoned on the banners, and the horses neighed, as horses are wont to do when they scent their own stables, and the riders tossed their caps in the air at the sight of us.

And I trow that if my lady had wished for reward for all the weary months of anxiety which she had passed through, she had it in full measure when at long last she opened the Castle gates, and saw the look on her husband's face, as he took her in his arms, and kissed her, not once, but many times, there, in the courtyard, in the sight of us all.

---

16    The Abbey of Haddington (an old name for it).

# THOMAS THE RHYMER

*"True Thomas lay on Huntly bank;*
*A ferlie he spied with his e'e;*
*And there he saw a ladye bright,*
*Came riding down by the Eildon tree."*

More than six hundred years ago, there lived in the south of Scotland a very wonderful man named Thomas of Ercildoune, or Thomas the Rhymer.

He lived in an old tower which stood on the banks of a little river called the Leader, which runs into the Tweed, and he had the marvellous gift, not only of writing beautiful verses, but of forecasting the future: — that is, he could tell of events long before they happened.

People also gave him the name of True Thomas, for they said that he was not able to tell a lie, no matter how much he wished to do so, and this gift he had received, along with his gift of prophecy, from the Queen of the Fairies, who stole him away when he was young, and kept him in fairyland for seven years and then let him come back to this world for a time, and at last took him away to live with her in fairyland altogether.

I do not say that this is true; I can only say again that Thomas the Rhymer was a very wonderful man; and this is the story which the old country folk in Scotland tell about him.

One St Andrew's Day, as he was lying on a bank by a stream called the Huntly Burn, he heard the tinkling of little bells, just like fairy music, and he turned his head quickly to see where it was coming from.

A short distance away, riding over the moor, was the most beautiful lady he had ever seen. She was mounted on a dapple-gray palfrey, and there was a halo of light shining all around her. Her saddle was made of pure ivory, set with precious stones, and padded with crimson satin. Her saddle girths were of silk, and on each buckle was a beryl stone. Her stirrups were cut out of clear crystal, and they were all set with pearls. Her crupper was made of fine embroidery, and for a bridle she used a gold chain.

She wore a riding-skirt of grass-green silk, and a mantle of green velvet, and from each little tress of hair in her horse's mane hung nine and fifty tiny silver bells. No wonder that, as the spirited animal tossed its dainty head, and fretted against its golden rein, the music of these bells sounded far and near.

She appeared to be riding to the chase, for she led seven greyhounds in a leash, and seven otter hounds ran along the path beside her, while round her neck was slung a hunting-horn, and from her girdle hung a sheaf of arrows.

As she rode along she sang snatches of songs to herself, or blew her horn gaily to call her dogs together.

"By my faith," thought Thomas to himself, "it is not every day that I have the chance of meeting such a beauteous being. Methinks she must be the Virgin Mother herself, for she is too fair to belong to this poor earth of ours. Now will I hasten over the hill, and meet her under the Eildon Tree; perchance she may give me her blessing."

So Thomas hasted, and ran, and came to the Eildon Tree, which grew on the slope of the Eildon Hills, under which, 'tis said, King Arthur and his Knights lie sleeping, and there he waited for the lovely lady.

When she approached he pulled off his bonnet and louted[17] low, so that his face well-nigh touched the ground, for, as I have said, he thought she was the Blessed Virgin, and he hoped to hear some words of benison.

But the lady quickly undeceived him. "Do not do homage to me," she said, "for I am not she whom thou takest me for, and cannot claim such reverence. I am but the Queen of Fairyland, and I ride to the chase with my horn and my hounds."

Then Thomas, fascinated by her loveliness, and loth to lose sight of her, began to make love to her; but she warned him that, if he did so, her beauty would vanish in a moment, and, worse still, she would have the power to throw a spell over him, and to carry him away to her own country. But I wot that her spell had fallen on Thomas already, for it seemed to him that there was nothing on earth to be compared to her favour.

"Here pledge I my troth with thee," he cried recklessly, "and little care I where I am carried, so long as thou art beside me,"

17    Bowed.

and as he said this, he gave her a kiss.

What was his horror, as soon as he had done so, to see an awful change come over the lady. Her beautiful clothes crumbled away, and she was left standing in a long ash-coloured gown. All the brightness round her vanished; her face grew pale and colourless; her eyes turned dim, and sank in her head; and, most terrible of all, one-half of her beautiful black hair went gray before his eyes, so that she looked worn and old.

A cruel smile came on her haggard face as she cried triumphantly, "Ah, Thomas, now thou must go with me, and thou must serve me, come weal, come woe, for seven long years."

Then she signed to him to get up behind her on her gray palfrey, and poor Thomas had no power to refuse. He glanced round in despair, taking a last look at the pleasant country-side he loved so well, and the next moment it vanished from his eyes, for the Eildon Hills opened beneath them, and they sank in gloomy caverns, leaving no trace behind.

For three days Thomas and the lady travelled on, in the dreadful gloom. It was like riding through the darkness of the darkest midnight. He could feel the palfrey moving beneath him; he could hear, close at hand, the roaring of the sea; and, ever as they rode, it seemed to him that they crossed many rivers, for, as the palfrey struggled through them, he could feel the cold rushing water creeping up to his knees, but never a ray of light came to cheer him.

He grew sick and faint with hunger and terror, and at last he could bear it no longer.

"Woe is me," he cried feebly, "for methinks I die for lack of food."

As he spoke these words, the lady turned her horse's head in the darkness, and, little by little, it began to grow lighter, until at last they emerged in open daylight, and found themselves in a beautiful garden.

It was full of fruit trees, and Thomas feasted his eyes on their cool green leaves and luscious burden; for, after the terrible darkness he had passed through, this garden seemed to him like the Garden of Paradise.

There were pear trees in it, covered with pears, and apple trees laden with great juicy apples; there were dates, and damsons, and figs, and grapes. Brightly coloured parrots were flitting about among the branches, and everywhere the thrushes were singing.

The lady drew rein under an apple tree, and, reaching up her hand, she plucked an apple, and handed it to him. "Take this for thine arles,"[18] she said; "it will confer a great gift on thee, for it will give thee a tongue that cannot lie, and from henceforth men shall call thee 'True Thomas.'"

Now, I am sorry to say that Thomas was not very particular about always being truthful, and this did not seem to him to be a very enviable gift. He wondered to himself what he would do if ever he got back to earth, and was always obliged to tell the truth, whether it were convenient or not.

"A bonnie gift, forsooth!" he said scornfully. "My tongue is my own, and I would prefer that no one meddled with it. If I am obliged always to tell the truth, how shall I fare when I once more go back to the wicked world? When I take a cow to market, have I always to point out the horn it hath lost, or the piece of skin that is torn? And when I talk to my betters, and would crave a boon of them, must I always tell them my real thoughts, instead of giving them the flattery which, let me tell you, Madam, goes a long way in obtaining a favour?"

"Now hold thy peace," said the lady sharply, "and think thyself favoured to see food at all. Many miles of our journey lie yet before us, and already thou criest out for hunger. Certs, if thou wilt not eat when thou canst, thou shalt have no more opportunity."

Poor Thomas was so hungry, and the apple looked so tempting, that at last he took it and ate it, and the Grace of Truth settled down on his lips for ever: that is why men called him "True Thomas," when in after years he returned to earth.

Then the lady shook her bridle rein, and the palfrey darted forward so quickly that it appeared to be almost flying. On and on they flew, until they came to the World's End, and a great desert stretched before them. Here the lady bade Thomas dismount and lean his head against her knee. "I have three wonders to show thee, Thomas," she said, "and it is thus that thou canst see them best."

18   Money paid at the engagement of a servant.

Thomas did as he was bid, and when he laid his head against the Fairy Queen's knee, he saw three roads stretching away before him through the sand.

One of them was a rough and narrow road, with thick hedges of thorn on either side, and branches of tangled briar hanging down from them, and lying across the path. Any traveller who travelled by that road would find it beset with many difficulties.

The next road was smooth and broad, and it ran straight and level across the plain. It looked so easy a way that Thomas wondered that anyone ever wanted to go along the narrow path at all.

The third road wound along a hillside, and the banks above it and below it were covered with beautiful brackens, and their delicate fronds rose high on either side, so high, indeed, that they would shelter the wayfarer from the burning heat of the noonday sun.

"That is the best road of all," thought Thomas to himself; "it looks so fresh and cool, I should like to travel along it."

Then the lady's voice sounded in his ears. "Seest thou that narrow path," she asked, "all set about with thorns and briars? That is the Path of Righteousness, and there be but few, oh, so few! who ever ask where it leads to, or who try to travel by it. And seest thou that broad, broad road, that runs so smoothly across the desert? That is the Path of Wickedness, and I trow it is a pleasant way, and easy to travel by. Men think it so, at least, and, poor fools, they do not trouble to ask where it leads to. Some would fain persuade themselves that it leads to Heaven, but Heaven was never reached by an easy road. 'Tis the narrow road through the briars and thorns that leads us thither, and wise are the men who follow it. And seest thou that bonnie, bonnie road, that winds up round the ferny brae? That is the way to Fairyland, and that is the road which lies before us."

Here Thomas was about to speak, and to remonstrate with her for carrying him away, but she interrupted him.

"Hush," she said, "thou must be silent now, Thomas; the time for speech is past. Thou art on the borders of Elfland, and if ever mortal man speak a word in Elfland, he can nevermore go back to his own country."

So Thomas held his peace, and climbed sadly on the palfrey's back, and once more they started on their awful journey. On and on they went. The beautiful road through the ferns was soon left behind, and great mountains had to be crossed, and steep, narrow valleys, until at last, far away in the distance, a splendid castle appeared, standing on the top of a high hill.

It was built of pure white marble, with massive towers, and lovely gardens stretched in front of it.

"That castle is mine," said the lady proudly. "It belongs to me, and to my husband, who is the King of this country. He is a jealous man, and one greatly to be feared, and, if he knew how friendly thou and I have been, he would kill thee in his rage. Remember, therefore, what I told thee about keeping silence. Thou canst talk to me, an thou wilt, if an opportunity offers, but see to it that thou answerest no one else. There are knights and squires in abundance at my husband's court, and doubtless they would fain question thee about the country from whence thou art come, but thou must pay no heed to them, and I shall pretend that thou talkest in an unknown tongue, and that I learned to understand it in thine own country."

While she was speaking, Thomas was amazed to see that a great change had passed over her again. Her face grew bright, and her gray gown vanished, and the green mantle took its place, and once more she became the beauteous being who had charmed his eyes at the Huntly Burn. And he was still more amazed when, on looking down, he found that his own raiment was changed too, and that he was now dressed in a suit of soft, fine cloth, and that on his feet he wore velvet shoon.

The lady lifted the golden horn which hung from a cord round her neck, and blew a loud blast. At the sound of it all the squires, and knights, and great court ladies came hurrying out to meet their Queen, and Thomas slid from the palfrey's back, and walked humbly at her elbow.

As she had foretold, the pages and squires crowded round him, and would fain have learned his name, and the name of the country to which he belonged, but he pretended not to understand what they said, and so they all came into the great hall of the castle.

At the end of this hall there was a dais, and on it were two thrones. The King of Fairyland was sitting on one, and when he saw the Queen, he rose, and stretched out his hand, and led her to the other, and then a rich banquet was served by thirty knights, who offered the dishes on their bended knees. After that all the court ladies went up and did homage to their Royal Mistress, while Thomas stood, and gazed, and wondered at all the strange things which he saw.

At one side of the hall there was a group of minstrels, playing on all manner of strange instruments. There were harps, and fiddles, and gitterns, and psalteries, and lutes and rebecks, and many more that he could not name. And when these minstrels played, the knights and the gay court ladies danced or played games, or made merry jokes amongst themselves; while at the other side of the hall a very different scene went on. There were thirty dead harts lying on the stone floor, and stable varlets carried in dead deer until there were thirty of them stretched beside the harts, and the dogs lay and licked their blood, and the cooks came in with their long knives and cut up the animals, in the sight of all the court.

It was all so weird and horrible that Thomas wondered what manner of folk he had come to dwell among, and if he would ever get back to his own country.

For three days things went on in the same manner, and still he looked and wondered, and still he spoke to no one, not even to the Queen.

At last she spoke to him. "Dress thee, and get thee gone, Thomas," she said, "for thou mayest not linger here any longer. Myself will convey thee on thy journey, and take thee back safe and sound to thine own country again."

Thomas looked at her in amazement. "I have only been here three days," he said, "and methought thou spakest of seven years."

The lady smiled.

"Time passes quickly in this country, Thomas," she replied. "It may not appear so long to thee, but it is seven long years and more, since thou camest into Fairyland. I would fain have kept thee longer; but it may not be, and I will show to thee the reason. Every seven years an evil spirit comes, and chooses someone out of our court, and carries him away to unknown regions, and, as thou art a stranger, and a goodly fellow withal, I fear me his choice would fall on thee; and although I brought thee here, and have kept thee here for seven years, 'twill never be said that I betrayed thee to an evil spirit. Therefore this very night we must be gone."

So once more the gray palfrey was brought, and Thomas and the lady mounted it, and they went back by the road by which they had come, and once more they came to the Eildon Tree.

The sun was shining when they arrived, and the birds singing, and the Huntly Burn tinkling just as it had always done, and it seemed to Thomas more impossible than ever that he had been away from it all for more than seven years.

He felt strangely sorry to say farewell to the beautiful lady, and he asked her to give him some token that would prove to people that he had really been in Fairyland.

"Thou hast already the Gift of Truth," she replied, "and I will add to that the Gift of Prophecy, and of writing wondrous verses; and here is a harp that was fashioned in Fairyland. With its music, set to thine own words, no minstrel on earth shall be to thee a rival. So shall all the world know for certain that thou learnedst the art from no earthly teacher; and some day, perchance, I will return."

Then the lady vanished, and Thomas was left all alone.

After this, he lived at his Castle of Ercildoune for many a long year, and well he deserved the names of Thomas the Rhymer, and True Thomas, which the country people gave him; for the verses which he wrote were the sweetest that they had ever heard, while all the things which he prophesied came most surely to pass.

It is remembered still how he met Cospatrick, Earl of March, one sunny day, and foretold that, ere the next noon passed, a terrible tempest would devastate Scotland. The stout Earl laughed, but his laughter was short, for by next day at noon the tidings came that Alexander III., that much loved King, was lying stiff and stark on the sands of Kinghorn. He also foretold the battles of Flodden and Pinkie, and the dule and woe which would follow the defeat of the Scottish arms; but he also foretold Bannockburn, where

*"The burn of breid*
*Shall run fow reid,"*

and the English be repulsed with great loss. He spoke of the Union of the Crowns of England and Scotland, under a prince who was the son of a French Queen, and who yet had the blood of Bruce in his veins. Which thing came true in 1603, when King James, son of the ill-fated Mary, who had been Queen of France as well as Queen of Scots, began to rule over both countries.

In view of these things, it was no wonder that the fame of Thomas of Ercildoune spread through the length and breadth of Scotland, or that men came from far and near to listen to his wonderful words.

Twice seven years came and went, and Scotland was plunged in war. The English King, Edward I., after defeating John Baliol at Dunbar, had taken possession of the country, and the doughty William Wallace had arisen to try to wrest it from his hand. The tide of war ebbed and flowed, now on this side of the Border, now on that, and it chanced that one day the Scottish army rested not far from the Tower of Ercildoune.

Beacons blazed red on Ruberslaw, tents were pitched at Coldingknowe, and the Tweed, as it rolled down to the sea, carried with it the echoes of the neighing of steeds, and of trumpet calls.

Then True Thomas determined to give a feast to the gallant squires and knights who were camped in the neighbourhood — such a feast as had never been held before in the old Tower of Ercildoune. It was spread in the great hall, and nobles were there in their coats of mail, and high-born ladies in robes of shimmering silk. There was wine in abundance, and wooden cups filled with homebrewed ale.

There were musicians who played sweet music, and wonderful stories of war and adventure went round.

And, best of all, when the feast was over, True Thomas, the host, called for the magic harp which he had received from the hands of the Elfin Queen. When it was brought to him a great silence fell on all the company, and everyone sat listening breathlessly while he sang to them song after song of long ago.

He sang of King Arthur and his Table, and his Knights, and

told how they lay sleeping under the Eildon Hills, waiting to be awakened at the Crack of Doom. He sang of Gawaine, and Merlin, Tristrem and Isolde; and those who listened to the wondrous story felt somehow that they would never hear such minstrelsy again.

Nor did they. For that very night, when all the guests had departed, and the evening mists had settled down over the river, a soldier, in the camp on the hillside, was awakened by a strange pattering of little feet on the dry bent[19] of the moorland.

Looking out of his tent, he saw a strange sight.

There, in the bright August moonlight, a snow-white hart and hind were pacing along side by side. They moved in slow and stately measure, paying little heed to the ever-increasing crowd who gathered round their path.

"Let us send for Thomas of Ercildoune," said someone at last; "mayhap he can tell us what this strange sight bodes."

"Yea, verily, let us send for True Thomas," cried everyone at once, and a little page was hastily despatched to the old tower.

Its master started from his bed when he heard the message, and dressed himself in haste. His face was pale, and his hands shook.

"This sign concerns me," he said to the wondering lad. "It shows me that I have spun my thread of life, and finished my race here."

So saying, he slung his magic harp on his shoulder, and went forth in the moonlight. The men who were waiting for him saw him at a distance, and 'twas noted how often he turned and looked back at his old tower, whose gray stones were touched by the soft autumn moonbeams, as though he were bidding it a long farewell.

He walked along the moor until he met the snow-white hart and hind; then, to everyone's terror and amazement, he turned with them, and all three went down the steep bank, which at that place borders the Leader, and plunged into the river, which was running at high flood.

"He is bewitched! To the rescue! To the rescue, ere it be too late!" cried the crowd with one voice.

19   Withered grass.

But although a knight leaped on his horse in haste, and spurred him at once through the raging torrent, he could see nothing of the Rhymer or his strange companions. They had vanished, leaving neither sign nor trace behind them; and to this day it is believed that the hart and the hind were messengers from the Queen of the Fairies, and that True Thomas went back with them to dwell in her country for ever.

# LORD SOULIS

*"Lord Soulis he sat in Hermitage Castle,*
*And beside him Old Redcap sly; —*
*'Now, tell me, thou sprite, who art meikle of might,*
*The death that I must die.'*

*They roll'd him in a sheet of lead,*
*A sheet of lead for a funeral pall;*
*They plunged him in the cauldron red,*
*And melted him, lead, and bones, and all."*

And so thou hast seen the great cauldron at Skelf-hill, little Annie, standing high up on the hillside, and thou wouldst fain hear its story.

'Tis a weird tale, Sweetheart, and one to make the blood run cold, for 'tis the story of a cruel and a wicked man, and how he came by a violent and a fearsome death. But Grannie will tell it thee, and when thou thinkest of it, thou must always try to remember how true it is what the Good Book says, that "all they that take the sword, shall perish with the sword," which means, I take it, that they who show no mercy need expect none at the hands of others.

'Tis a tale of spirits and of witchcraft, child, things that in our days we do not believe in; but I had it from my grandfather, who had heard it when he was a laddie from the old shepherds out on the hills, and they believed it all and feared to pass that way in the dark.

But to come to the story itself. Long, long ago, in far bygone days, William de Soulis, Lord of Liddesdale, kept high state in his Castle of Hermitage. The royal blood of Scotland flowed in his veins, for he was sixth in descent from Alexander II., and could an ancestress of his have proved her right, he might have sat on the throne of Scotland.

Besides owning Liddesdale, he had lands in Dumfriesshire, and in the Lothians, and he might have been like the "Bold Buccleuch," a succourer of widows, and a defender of the oppressed and the destitute.

But instead of this he worked all manner of wickedness, till his very name was dreaded far and near. He oppressed his vassals; he troubled his neighbours; he was even at enmity with the King himself. And because he feared that his Majesty might come against him with an army, he had fortified his castle with much care. In order to do this thoroughly, he forced his vassals to work like beasts of burden, putting bores[20] on their shoulders, and yoking them to sledges, on which they drew all kinds of building material to the castle.

No wonder, then, that he was hated by rich and poor alike, and no wonder that his heart would quail at times, reckless and hardened though he was, for it is an ill thing not to have a friend in this world. Servants may be hired for money, but 'tis love, and love only, that can buy true friendship. Aye remember that, little Annie, aye remember that.

I say that he had no friends, but I am mistaken. 'Twas said he had one, and mayhap he would have been as well without him. For men would have it that Hermitage Castle was haunted by a familiar spirit.

As a rule he dwelt in a wooden chest, bound with rusty bars of iron; but occasionally, when Lord Soulis was alone, he would come out and talk with him. "Old Redcap," the country folk used to call him, and they said that he was a wee, wee man, with a red pirnie[21] and twisted legs; but whether that be true or no, 'tis not for me to say.

'Twas also said that, one day, when Soulis and his uncanny friend were alone, Soulis asked him what his end would be; if he would die at home in his bed, or out on the hillside in fair fight with his foes? And Redcap made answer that he would throw his spell over him, and that that spell would keep him from all common dangers, from all weapons of war, and from all devices of peace; from arrows, and lances, and knives; from chains, and even from hempen ropes. He would be safe from all these, but there was one thing, and one thing alone, which the charm could not do, and that was to save him if ever men could take him and bind him with ropes of sifted sand.

20 Yokes.
21 Nightcap.

Methinks I can hear Lord Soulis' laugh as Redcap told him this. "Ropes of sand, forsooth!" he would say. "Did ever man hear of ropes of sand?"

But he had forgotten that the Wizard of the North, Sir Michael Scott of Balwearie — the same who studied the wisdom of the East under the Moors at Toledo, in Spain, who could read the stars, and command familiar spirits to come and go at his bidding — had found out the way to forge ropes out of sand, and that, though Michael was dead, his Spae-book yet remained, in which he had written down all his magic.

"Moreover," added Redcap, "if ever danger threatens thee, knock thrice on this old chest, and the lid will rise, and I will speak; but beware lest thou lookest into it. When the lid begins to rise, turn thine eyes away, or the spell will be broken."

Now it chanced soon after this, that one morning, just as the day was breaking, Lord Soulis, as was his wont, sent one of his little pages up to the top of the tower, to look out over the country far and near, to see if there were any travellers who took the road to Hermitage. At first the boy saw nothing, but, as it grew lighter, the figure of a horseman, clad in the royal livery, appeared, riding down the hillside.

"Now what may thine errand be?" cried the page.

"I carry a message to Soulis of Hermitage from the King of Scotland," replied the stranger; "and he bids me tell that cruel Knight, that the report of his ill deeds has come to his Majesty's ears at Holyrood House, and that if ever again such stories reach him, he will send his soldiers to burn the castle, and put its lord to death."

Then the page hasted, and ran, and delivered this message to his master, whose face grew white with rage when he heard it. For he was an awful man, little Annie, an awful man, who in general feared neither God nor the King, and who could not brook to be reproved.

Under the castle there was a deep dungeon, cut out of the solid rock, and the entrance to it was by a hole in the courtyard, which was covered by a great flat stone. The stone rested on beams of oak, and Lord Soulis gave orders that the guards were to keep the King's messenger waiting outside the gate, and pretend to be very kind to him, giving him a tankard of ale, and a hunch of bread, until some of the men inside the castle had cut away those great oak beams.

Then they opened the gate, and told the poor man that Lord Soulis would speak with him if he would ride into the courtyard; and he rode in, and as soon as his horse stepped on the big flat stone that covered the mouth of the dungeon, it gave way beneath its weight, and both man and horse fell down, and were crushed to pieces on the hard stone floor, full thirty feet below.

The King was right wroth when he heard how his messenger had been treated, but before he could set off for Liddesdale to punish Lord Soulis, the punishment came from nearer home.

It chanced that the young Lord of Buccleuch wooed a lovely lady called May o' Gorranberry. 'Twas said that she was the bonniest lass in all Teviotdale, and in all Liddesdale, and the wedding day was fixed. But the wicked Lord Soulis, puffed up with pride at the way in which he had got rid of the King's messenger, and relying, doubtless, on Redcap's charm to protect him from danger, took it into his sinful head that he would like May o' Gorranberry for his wife.

And he sent, and took her, as she was walking on the hillside above her father's house, and brought her to his grim old Castle of Hermitage.

The poor lassie was almost mad with terror, and tore her hair, and cried continually for her lover, until the cruel man threatened that if she did not hold her tongue he would send men to burn down Branksome Tower, and kill all its inmates.

And next morning, because she would not stop weeping, he called his chief man-at-arms, a brave, fearless fellow called Red Ringan, and told him to gather a band of spearmen, and ride over the hills to Teviotdale, and attack the old castle which was the home of the Lords of Buccleuch.

Now it chanced that that very morning, young Buccleuch set out alone to hunt the roe-buck and the dun deer which roamed in the woods that surrounded his castle. He had fine sport, and he went on, and on, and never noticed how far up among the hills he was getting, or how fast the day was passing, until it began to get dark.

Suddenly he looked up, and, to his astonishment, he saw, riding down the glen to meet him, a company of spearmen. He thought they were his own retainers, and walked boldly up to them, and never knew his mistake until he was seized, and bound hand and foot. They were really Lord Soulis' men, with Red Ringan at their head, and Red Ringan had thrown a glamour over his eyes, so that he could not distinguish between friends and foes. Of course Red Ringan was delighted at this piece of good luck, and he set the poor young man on a horse, and sent him over the hills to Hermitage, guarded by a handful of spearmen, while he rode on with the rest of his troop to Branksome, to see what mischief he could work there.

Thou canst think with what triumph my Lord Soulis would greet his prisoner, and with what bitter tears May o' Gorranberry would see him brought in, for she would know about the dungeon, and shudder to think what his fate would be.

'Twas said that the cruel lord mocked at young Buccleuch as he rode under the archway, and cried out to him, as if in jest —

"Thrice welcome, Buccleuch, thrice welcome to my castle. Nathless 'tis as a wedding guest thou comest. Certs, my bonnie May well deserves such a gallant groomsman."

Next morning the sun rose blood red, and just as its rays touched the gray stones of the grim old keep, the page came running to say that Red Ringan was riding down the hillside all alone. Methinks the wicked lord's heart gave a throb of fear, as he hurried out to the gate to meet his henchman.

"Where have ye stabled my gallant steeds?" he cried, "and wherefore do thy comrades tarry, whilst thou ridest home all alone?"

Red Ringan shook his head mournfully. "I bring thee heavy tidings, Master," he said. "The steeds are stabled, sure enough, but 'tis in a stable where they will rest till the Crack of Doom, and their riders lie beside them. Thou knowest Tarras Moss, and how fair and pleasant it lies, and how deep and cruel it is? My men mistook the path in the dark, and rode right into it, and, had it not been for my good brown mare, not one of us had been left to tell the tale. She struggled to firm footing right nobly, and brought me out alive on her back; but when I looked around me, I was all alone, Master, I was all alone."

Lord Soulis made no reply. With heavy steps he sought the low dark room where the great chest stood, with its iron bands, and its three rusty locks.

He shut the door behind him, and then, with clenched fist,

he knocked thrice on the heavy lid. The first time he knocked, and the second time, such a groan came from the chest that his very blood ran cold; but at the third knock the locks opened, and the lid began to rise.

Lord Soulis turned away his head as Redcap had told him to do, and stood listening with all his might. A strange sullen muttering came from the chest, of which he could only distinguish these mysterious words, "Beware of a coming tree," and then the lid shut as slowly as it had opened, and the locks were locked with a jerk, as if by unseen hands.

Meanwhile, over the hills in Teviotdale there had been confusion and dismay when the young Lord of Buccleuch failed to return, and when news came by the country folk that he had been seen, bound hand and foot, being taken to Hermitage by Lord Soulis' men, the anger of the whole clan knew no bounds. For, as it is to-day, little Annie, so it was then. The Scotts of Buccleuch were strong and powerful, and held in honour far and near.

The young lord had one brother, Bold Walter by name. He was a mighty fighter and a right strong man, who carried a bow that no other man could bend, and who loved nothing better than to ride on a foray with all his father's moss-troopers at his back. Methinks Lord Soulis had forgotten Bold Walter when he meddled with his brother and his bride.

It did not take this brave knight long, when he heard the news, to send his riders out to North, and South, and East, and West, to call on his friends and clansmen to ride with him to the fray. And because he had heard of Old Redcap, and knew that Lord Soulis would be protected by his charms, he sent all the way to the Tower of Ercildoune for True Thomas, that wondrous Rhymer, who had been for seven years in Fairyland, and who, on his return to earth, had gone to the Abbey Church of St Mary, at Melrose, and had taken Sir Michael Scott's Spae-book from its dread hiding-place, for its writer had been buried with it in his arms.

So, before the next sun had set, Bold Walter had raised as fair an army as that which the King in Edinburgh had thought to send to Hermitage. The news of this army spread like wildfire over the country, ay, and over the hills to Hermitage, and I ween Lord Soulis' heart sank still lower when he heard of it, and once more he went for counsel to the magic chest. Again he knocked, and again the hollow groan rang out; but as the lid lifted, he forgot in his haste to turn his eyes away, and in a moment the charm was broken. The spirit spoke indeed, but it spoke sullenly and angrily.

"Alas," it said, "thou art undone. Thou hast forgotten my warning, and, instead of turning away thy head, thou hast raised thine eyes to look on me. Therefore thou must lock the door of this chamber, and give the key into my keeping, and for seven long years thou must not return, and I must remain silent."

The wicked may flourish like the green bay tree, little Annie, but vengeance will always overtake them at last; and I trow that Lord Soulis felt that vengeance was close on his heels, as he left that mysterious chamber, and locked the door, and drew the key from the lock, where it had always rested, in his lifetime at least, and threw it over his left shoulder, which is, men say, the right way to give things to wizards and witches, and such-like beings.

The key sank in the ground, and there it remains for aught I know, and 'tis said that even to this day, at the end of every seven years, if anyone cares to listen, they may hear strange and awful sounds coming from that long-locked chamber.[22]

Yet Lord Soulis' heart was not humbled, and he made up his mind, that, come what might, young Buccleuch should die.

---

22 "Somewhere about the autumn of 1806, the Earl of Dalkeith, being encamped near the Hermitage Castle, for the amusement of shooting, directed some workmen to clear away the rubbish from the door of the dungeon in order to ascertain its ancient dimensions and architecture. To the great astonishment of the labourers, a rusty iron key of considerable size was found among the ruins a little way from the dungeon door. The well-known tradition passed from one to another, and it was generally agreed that the malevolent demon who had so long retained possession of the key of the castle dungeon now found himself obliged to resign it to the heir-apparent of the domain." — Note on "Lord Soulis" in *Leyden's Life and Works*.

And in the wickedness and cruelty of his heart he determined that he himself should choose the manner of it.

So he had him brought before him. "What wouldst thou do, young Scott, if thou hadst me as I have thee?" he asked, in his cruel mocking voice.

"I would take thee to the good greenwood," answered Buccleuch haughtily, "and I would hang thee there, and I would make thine own hand wale[23] the tree."

"Good," answered Lord Soulis; "then thou shalt do as thou hast said, and if bonnie May refuse to marry me, then she shall hang on a bush beside thee."

So they led him out to a wood full of tall trees, far up on whose upper branches sat hooded crows, looking down on them in solemn silence.

The first tree that Lord Soulis made his men halt under was a fir.

"Say, wilt thou hang on a fir tree, and let the hooded crows pick thy bones?" he asked roughly.

Young Buccleuch shook his head. "Nay, not so, my Lord of Soulis," he answered in mock humility, "for on windy nights at Branksome, the fir trees rock by the old towers, and the fir cones come pattering to the ground like rain. I heard them when I was a bairn, as I lay awake at night in my cot. Thou surely wouldst not have the heart to hang me on a tree which I have loved all my life."

Then Soulis told his men to pass on, and as they went through the wood their prisoner kept peeping and peering from side to side, and muttering to himself, as if he were looking for something. The men-at-arms could not hear what he was saying, and methinks they would have been much astonished if they had. For he knew the spirit that his brother was of, and he knew that he would not let him hang without an attempt at rescue, and he was saying over and over again to himself, "This death is no' for me, this death is no' for me."

At last they halted again under an aspen tree, whose leaves were quivering mournfully in the wind. Lord Soulis was grow-

23   Choose.

ing impatient.

"Choose, and choose quickly," he cried, "or methinks I must choose for thee."

But again Buccleuch shook his head. "Not on an aspen tree, my lord, not on an aspen tree. I love its gray leaves better than any other, for it was under their shade that May o' Gorranberry and I first plighted our troth."

So on they went, and still the young man peered and looked, first in this direction, then in that, until at last he saw what seemed to be a bank of hazel branches pressing through the trees towards them. Then he gave a great shout, and leaped high in the air. "Methinks I spy a coming tree," he cried, and at the words Lord Soulis' face grew pale, for they recalled to him Redcap's warning, and he feared that his hour had come.

Everyone soon saw what the strange thing was which was coming towards them. It was Bold Walter of Buccleuch and his men, and each of them had stuck a branch of witch's hazel in his basnet, for 'tis said that a twig of hazel protects its wearer from the arts of magic, and they had no mind to be bewitched by the Lord of Hermitage.

So this was the coming tree that Redcap had warned Lord Soulis to beware of, and it had come in right earnest.

But Soulis remembered the charmed life that he bore, and he tried to shake fear from his heart.

"Ay, many may come, but few shall go back," he cried defiantly; "besides, ye come on a bootless errand. There is not a man in broad Scotland who hath the power to wound me."

"By my troth," replied Bold Walter, "but we shall soon prove that," and, drawing his bow, he sent an arrow straight in Lord Soulis' face.

Sure enough it fell harmless to the ground, and there was not even a scratch on the wicked lord's skin, and for a moment Buccleuch was baffled.

But Thomas of Ercildoune stepped forward. "He is bewitched, Sire," he said, "and protected by the charms of Redcap. No steel can break that charm, but mayhap if thy men bore him down with their lances, he might be taken."

In vain the spearmen crowded round, and struck him to the earth. The lances glanced harmlessly off his body, and never left so much as a mark on him.

Then they bound him hand and foot with hempen ropes, but, to their amazement, he burst them as if they had been threads of wool. Then someone brought chains of forged steel, and they bound those round his limbs, thinking that now they surely had him in their power; but he burst them as easily as if they had been made of tow.

At this everyone was daunted, and would have let him go, but Thomas of Ercildoune cried cheerily, "We'll bind him yet, lads, whatever betide."

As he spoke, he drew out from his bosom a little black leather-covered book, and at the sight of it all the spearmen fell back in awe. For it was Sir Michael Scott's "Book of Might," and, as I have said, Sir Michael was a wizard himself, and knew all about warlocks and witches, with their charms and spells, and he could undo everyone of them, and he had written all this knowledge down in his black Spae-book. When he died, the book had been buried deep in his grave in the Abbey at Melrose, and True Thomas had gone there, and recovered it, and he had brought it with him to aid Bold Walter of Buccleuch in rescuing his brother.

He turned over the leaves, and at last he found the place where Sir Michael had told how it was possible to bind a charmed man.

"Ye cannot bind a wizard with ropes," he read, "unless they be ropes of sifted sand."

"Where can we get some sifted sand?" he asked, and every-one looked round in dismay, for there was no sand there, under the trees.

"Come to the Nine-stane Rig," cried a man; "there is a burn[24] runs past the bottom of it, and we will find plenty of sand there."

Thou knowest the Nine-stane Rig, little Annie, the hill that slopes down to Hermitage Water, with the circle of great stones standing on it, which, 'tis said, were placed there by wild and heathen men, hundreds of years ago. Well, they carried Lord Soulis there, and hurried him down to the burn, and they

24   Stream.

shaped ropes out of the sand that lies smooth and clean by the water-side.

But, shape the ropes as they might, they would neither twist nor twine; the dry sand just ran through their fingers, and once again they were baffled. Once more True Thomas turned to the spae-book, and this time he found that the sand would twist more easily if it were mixed with barley chaff, and the men of Teviotdale ran down the valley until they came to a field of growing barley. They pulled the ripe grain and beat it in their hands, and it was not long ere they returned with a napkin full of chaff. They mixed nine handfuls of it with the sand, for it was thus the "Book of Might" directed, and once more they tried to twist the ropes, but once more they failed.

"This is some of the wee man's work," muttered the country folk, who were standing looking on; and they were right. Old Redcap had not deserted his master, although the spell which caused the magic chest to open was broken, and he was at hand, doing his utmost to save him, though unseen by mortal eyes.

Again True Thomas turned over the leaves of Sir Michael's book, in the hope of finding something which would break even the most powerful spell, and at last he came to a page where it told how, if all else failed, the wizard must be boiled in lead.

Ay, thou mayst well shudder, little Annie, and hide thy face in my gown.

'Twas a terrible thing to do, but they did it.

They kindled a fire on the Nine-stane Rig, in the middle of the old Druid stones, and there they placed the great brass cauldron. They heated it red hot, and some of them hasted to Hermitage Castle, and stripped a sheet of lead from the roof, and they wrapped the wicked lord in it, and plunged him in, and stood round in solemn silence till the contents of that awful pot melted — lead, and bones, and all — and nought remained but a seething sea of molten metal.

So came the sinful man by his end, and to this day the cauldron remains, as thou knowest, child. It was brought over to the Skelf-hill, and there it stands, a fearful warning to evil-doers, while, on the spot where it was boiled, within the circle of stones on the Nine-stane Rig, the ground lies bare and fallow, for the very grass refuses to grow where such a terrible deed was done.

# THE BROWNIE OF BLEDNOCK

*"There came a strange wight to our town en',*
*An' the fient a body did him ken;*
*He twirled na' lang, but he glided ben,*
*Wi' a weary, dreary hum.*

*His face did glow like the glow o' the West,*
*When the drumly cloud had it half o'ercast;*
*Or the struggling moon when she's sair distrest.*
*O, Sirs! it was Aiken-Drum."*

Did you ever hear how a Brownie came to our village of Blednock, and was frightened away again by a silly young wife, who thought she was cleverer than anyone else, but who did us the worst turn that she ever did anybody in her life, when she made the queer, funny, useful little man disappear?

Well, it was one November evening, in the gloaming, just when the milking was done, and before the bairns were put to bed, and everyone was standing on their doorsteps, having a crack about the bad harvest, and the turnips, and what chances there were of good prices for the stirks[25] at the Martinmas Fair, when the queerest humming noise started down by the river.

It came nearer and nearer, and everyone stopped their clavers[26] and began to look down the road. And, 'deed, it was no wonder that they stared, for there, coming up the middle of the highway, was the strangest, most frightsome-looking creature that human eyes had ever seen.

He looked like a little wee, wee man, and yet he looked almost like a beast, for he was covered with hair from head to foot, and he wore no clothing except a little kilt of green rashes which hung round his waist. His hair was matted, and his head

---

25    Bullocks.
26    Idle talk.

hung forward on his breast, and he had a long blue beard, which almost touched the ground.

His legs were twisted, and knocked together as he walked, and his arms were so long that his hands trailed in the mud.

He seemed to be humming something over and over again, and, as he came near us we could just make out the words, "Hae ye wark for Aiken-Drum?"

Eh, but I can tell you the folk were scared. If it had been the Evil One himself who had come to our quiet little village, I doubt if he would have caused more stir.[27] The bairns screamed, and hid their faces in their mothers' gown-tails; while the lassies, idle huzzies that they were, threw down the pails of milk, which should have been in the milkhouse long ago, if they had not been so busy gossiping; and the very dogs crept in behind their masters, whining, and hiding their tails between their legs. The grown men, who should have known better, and who were not frightened to look the wee man in the face, laughed and hooted at him.

"Did ye ever see such eyes?" cried one.

"His mouth is so big, he could swallow the moon," said another.

"Hech, sirs, but did ye ever see such a creature?" cried a third.

And still the poor little man went slowly up the street, crying wistfully, "Hae ye wark for Aiken-Drum? Any wark for Aiken-Drum?"

Some of us tried to speak to him, but our tongues seemed to be tied, and the words died away on our lips, and we could only stand and watch him with frightened glances, as if we were bewitched.

Old Grannie Duncan, the oldest, and the kindest woman in the village, was the first to come to her senses. "He may be a ghost, or a bogle, or a wraith," she said; "or he may only be a harmless Brownie. It is beyond me to say; but this I know, that if he be an evil spirit, he will not dare to look on the Holy Book." And with that she ran into her cottage, and brought out the great leather-bound Bible which aye lay on her little table by

27   Excitement.

the window.

She stood on the road, and held it out, right in front of the creature, but he took no more heed of it than if it had been an old song-book, and went slowly on, with his weary cry for work.

"He's just a Brownie," cried Grannie Duncan in triumph, "a simple, kindly Brownie. I've heard tell of such folk before, and many a long day's work will they do for the people who treat them well."

Gathering courage from her words, we all crowded round the wee man, and now that we were close to him, we saw that his hairy face was kind and gentle, and his tiny eyes had a merry twinkle in them.

"Save us, and help us, creature!" said an old man reprovingly, "but can ye no speak, and tell us what ye want, and where ye come from?"

For answer the Brownie looked all round him, and gave such a groan, that we scattered and ran in all directions, and it was full five minutes before we could pluck up our courage and go close to him again.

But Grannie Duncan stood her ground, like a brave old woman that she was, and it was to her that the creature spoke.

"I cannot tell thee from whence I come," he said. "'Tis a nameless land, and 'tis very different from this land of thine. For there we all learn to serve, while here everyone wishes to be served. And when there is no work for us to do at home, then we sometimes set out to visit thy land, to see if there is any work which we may do there. I must seem strange to human eyes, that I know; but if thou wilt, I will stay in this place awhile. I need not that any should wait on me, for I seek neither wages, nor clothes, nor bedding. All I ask for is the corner of a barn to sleep in, and a cogful of brose set down on the floor at bedtime; and if no one meddles with me, I will be ready to help anyone who needs me. I'll gather your sheep betimes on the hill; I'll take in your harvest by moonlight. I'll sing the bairns to sleep in their cradles, and, though I doubt you'll not believe it, you'll find that the babes will love me. I'll kirn your kirns[28] for you,

28   A churn.

goodwives, and I'll bake your bread on a busy day; while, as for the men folk, they may find me useful when there is corn to thrash, or untamed colts in the stables, or when the waters are out in flood."

No one quite knew what to say in answer to the creature's strange request. It was an unheard-of thing for anyone to come and offer their services for nothing, and the men began to whisper among themselves, and to say that it was not canny, and 'twere better to have nothing to do with him.

But up spoke old Grannie Duncan again. "'Tis but a Brownie, I tell you," she repeated, "a poor, harmless Brownie, and many a story have I heard in my young days about the work that a Brownie can do, if he be well treated and let alone. Have we not been complaining all summer about bad times, and scant wages, and a lack of workmen to work the work? And now, when a workman comes ready to your hand, ye will have none of him, just because he is not bonnie to look on."

Still the men hesitated, and the silly young wenches screwed their faces, and pulled their mouths. "But, Grannie," cried they, "that is all very well, but if we keep such a creature in our village, no one will come near it, and then what shall we do for sweethearts?"

"Shame on ye," cried Grannie impatiently, "and on all you men for encouraging the silly things in their whimsies. It's time that ye were thinking o' other things than bonnie faces and sweethearts. 'Handsome is that handsome does,' is a good old saying; and what about the corn that stands rotting in the fields, an' it past Hallowe'en already? I've heard that a Brownie can stack a whole ten-acre field in a single night."

That settled the matter. The miller offered the creature the corner of his barn to sleep in, and Grannie promised to boil the cogful of brose, and send her grandchild, wee Jeannie, down with it every evening, and then we all said good-night, and went into our houses, looking over our shoulders as we did so, for fear that the strange little man was following us.

But if we were afraid of him that night, we had a very different song to sing before a week was over. Whatever he was, or wherever he came from, he was the most wonderful worker that men had ever known. And the strange thing was that he did most of it at night. He had the corn safe into the stackyards, and the stacks thatched, in the clap of a hand, as the old folk say.

The village became the talk of the countryside, and folk came from all parts to see if they could catch a glimpse of our queer, hairy little visitor; but they were always unsuccessful, for he was never to be seen when one looked for him. One might go into the miller's barn twenty times a day, and twenty times a day find nothing but a heap of straw; and although the cog of brose was aye empty in the morning, no one knew when he came home, or when he supped it.

But wherever there was work to be done, whether it was a sickly bairn to be sung to, or a house to be tidied up; a kirn that would not kirn, or a batch of bread that would not rise; a flock of sheep to be gathered together on a stormy night, or a bundle to be carried home by some weary labourer; Aiken-Drum, as we learned to call him, always got to know of it, and appeared in the nick of time. It looked as if we had all got wishing-caps, for we had just to wish, and the work was done.

Many a time, some poor mother, who had been up with a crying babe all night, would sit down with it in her lap, in front of the fire, in the morning, and fall fast asleep, and when she awoke, she would find that Aiken-Drum had paid her a visit, for the floor would be washed, and the dishes too, and the fire made up, and the kettle put on to boil; but the little man would have slipped away, as if he were frightened of being thanked.

The bairns were the only ones who ever saw him idle, and oh, how they loved him! In the gloaming, or when the school was out, one could see them away down in some corner by the stream-side, crowding round the little dark brown figure, with its kilt of rushes, and one would hear the sound of wondrous low sweet singing, for he knew all the songs that the little ones loved.

So by and by the name of Aiken-Drum came to be a household word amongst us, and although we so seldom saw him near at hand, we loved him like one of our ain folk.

And he might have been here still, had it not been for a silly, senseless young wife who thought she knew better than everyone else, and who took some idle notion into her empty head that it was not right to make the little man work, and give him no wage.

She dinned[29] this into our heads, morning, noon, and night, and she would not believe us when we told her that Aiken-Drum worked for love, and love only.

Poor thing, she could not understand anyone doing that, so she made up her mind that she, at least, would do what was right, and set us all an example.

"She did not mean any harm," she said afterwards, when the miller took her to task for it; but although she might not mean to do any harm, she did plenty, as senseless folk are apt to do when they cannot bear to take other people's advice, for she took a pair of her husband's old, mouldy, worn-out breeches, and laid them down one night beside the cogful of brose.

By my faith, if the village folk had not remembered so well what Aiken-Drum had said about wanting no wages, they would have found something better to give him than a pair of worn-out breeks.

Be that as it may, the long and the short of it was, that the dear wee man's feelings were hurt because we would not take his services for nothing, and he vanished in the night, as Brownies are apt to do, so Grannie Duncan says, if anyone tries to pay them, and we have never seen him from that day to this, although the bairns declare that they sometimes hear him singing down by the mill, as they pass it in the gloaming, on their way home from school.

29   Impressed this upon us.

# SIR PATRICK SPENS

*"The king sits in Dunfermline town,*
*Drinking the blude-red wine;*
*'O whare will I get a skeely skipper,*
*To sail this new ship o' mine?'*

*   *   *   *

*Half owre, half owre to Aberdour,*
*'Tis fifty fathoms deep,*
*And there lies gude Sir Patrick Spens,*
*Wi' the Scots lords at his feet."*

Now hearken to me, all ye who love old stories, and I will tell you how one of the bravest and most gallant of Scottish seamen came by his death.

'Tis the story of an event which brought mourning and dule to many a fair lady's heart, in the far-off days of long ago.

Now all the world knows that his Majesty, King Alexander the Third, who afterwards came by his death on the rocks at Kinghorn, had one only daughter, named Margaret, after her ancestress, the wife of Malcolm Canmore, whose life was so holy, and her example so blessed, that, to this day, men call her Saint Margaret of Scotland.

King Alexander had had much trouble in his life, for he had already buried his wife, and his youngest son David, and 'twas no wonder that, as he sat in the great hall of his Palace at Dunfermline, close to the Abbey Church, where he loved best to hold his Court, that his heart was sore at the thought of parting with his motherless daughter.

She had lately been betrothed to Eric, the young King of Norway, and it was now full time that she went to her new home. So a stately ship had been prepared to convey her across the sea; the amount of her dowry had been settled; her attendants chosen; and it only remained to appoint a captain to the charge of the vessel.

But here King Alexander was at a loss. It was now past midsummer, and in autumn the Northern Sea was wont to be wild and stormy, and on the skilful steering of the Royal bark many precious lives depended.

He thought first of one man skilled in the art of seamanship, and then he thought of another, and at last he turned in his perplexity to his nobles who were sitting around him.

"Canst tell me," he said, fingering a glass of red French wine as he spoke, "of a man well skilled in the knowledge of winds and tides, yet of gentle birth withal, who can be trusted to pilot this goodly ship of mine, with her precious burden, safely over the sea to Norway?"

The nobles looked at one another in silence for a moment, and then one of them, an old gray-haired baron, rose from his seat by Alexander's side.

"Scotland lacks not seamen, both gentle and simple, my Liege," he said, "who could be trusted with this precious charge. But there is one man of my acquaintance, who, above all others, is worthy of such a trust. I speak of young Sir Patrick Spens, who lives not far from here. Not so many years have passed over his head, but from a boy he has loved the sea, and already he knows more about it, and its moods, than white-haired men who have sailed on it all their lives. 'Tis his bride, he says, an' I trow he speaks the truth, for, although he is as fair a gallant as ever the eye of lady rested on, and although many tender hearts, both within the Court, and without, beat a quicker measure when his name is spoken, he is as yet free of love fancies, and aye bides true to this changeful mistress of his. Truly he may well count it an honour to have the keeping of so fair a flower entrusted to him."

"Now bring me paper and pen," cried the King, "and I will write to him this instant with mine own hand."

Slowly and laboriously King Alexander penned the lines, for in these days kings were readier with the sword than with the pen; then, folding the letter and sealing it with the great signet ring which he wore on the third finger of his right hand, he gave it to the old baron, and commanded him to seek Sir Patrick Spens without loss of time.

Now Sir Patrick dwelt near the sea, and when the baron arrived he found him pacing up and down on the hard white sand by the sea-shore, watching the waves, and studying the course of the tides. He was quite a young man, and 'twas little wonder if the story which the old baron had told was true, and if all the ladies' hearts in Fife ached for love of him, for I trow never did goodlier youth walk the earth, and men said of him that he was as gentle and courteous as he was handsome.

At first when he began to read the King's letter, his face flushed with pride, for who would not have felt proud to be chosen before all others in Scotland, to be the captain of the King's Royal bark? But the smile passed away almost as soon as it appeared, and a look of great sadness took its place. In silence he gazed out over the sea. Did something warn him at that moment that this would prove his last voyage; — that never again would he set foot in his beloved land?

It may be so; who can tell? Certain it is — the old baron recalled it to his mind in the sad days that were to come — that, when the young sailor handed back the King's letter to him, his eyes were full of tears.

" 'Tis certainly a great honour," he said, "and I thank his Majesty for granting it to me, but methinks it was no one who loved my life, or the lives of those who sail with me, who suggested our setting out for Norway at this time of year."

Then, anxious lest the baron thought that he said this out of fear, or cowardice, he changed his tone, and hurried him up to his house to partake of some refreshment after his ride, while he gave orders to his seamen to get everything ready.

"Make haste, my men," he shouted in a cheerful, lusty voice, "for a great honour hath fallen to our lot. His Majesty hath deigned to entrust to us his much loved daughter, the Princess Margaret, that we may convey her, in the stately ship which he hath prepared, to her husband's court in Norway. Wherefore, let every man look to himself, and let him meet me at Aberdour, where the ship lies, on Sunday by nightfall, for we sail next day with the tide."

So on the Monday morning early, ere it struck eight of the clock, a great procession wound down from the King's Palace at Dunfermline to the little landing-stage at Aberdour, where the stately ship was lying, with her white sails set, like a gigantic swan.

Between the King and his son, the Prince of Scotland, rode the Princess Margaret, her eyes red with weeping, for in those days it was no light thing to set out for another land, and she felt that the parting might be for ever. And so, in good sooth, it proved to be, in this world at least, for before many years had passed all three were in their graves; but that belongs not to my tale.

Next rode the high and mighty persons who were to accompany the Princess to her husband's land, and be witnesses of the fulfilment of the marriage contract. These were their Graces the Earl and Countess of Menteith, his Reverence the Abbot of Balmerino, the good Lord Bernard of Monte-Alto, and many others, including a crowd of young nobles, five and fifty in all, who had been asked to swell the Princess's retinue, and who were only too glad to have a chance of getting a glimpse of other lands.

Next came a long train of sumpter mules, with the Princess's baggage, and that of her attendants. And last of all, guarded well by men-at-arms, came the huge iron-bound chests which contained her dowry: seven thousand merks in good white money; and there were other seven thousand merks laid out for her in land in Scotland.

Sir Patrick Spens was waiting to receive the Princess on board the ship. Right courteously, I ween, he handed her to her cabin, and saw that my Lady of Menteith, in whose special care she was, was well lodged also, as befitted her rank and station. But I trow that his lip curled with scorn when he saw that the five and fifty young nobles had provided themselves with five and fifty feather beds to sleep on.

He himself was a hardy man, as a sailor ought to be, and he loved not to see men so careful of their comfort.

At last the baggage, and the dowry, and even the feather beds were stowed away; and the last farewells having been said, the great ship weighed anchor, and sailed slowly out of the Firth of Forth.

Ah me, how many eyes there were, which watched it sail away, with husband, or brother, or sweetheart on board, which would wait in vain for many a long day for its return!

Sir Patrick made a good voyage. The sea was calm, the wind was in his favour, and by the evening of the third day he brought his ship with her precious burden safe to the shores of Norway.

"Now the Saints be praised," he said to himself as he cast anchor, "for the Princess is safe, let happen what may on our return voyage."

In great state, and with much magnificence, Margaret of Scotland was wedded to Eric of Norway, and great feasting and merry-making marked the event. For a whole month the rejoicing went on. The Norwegian nobles vied with each other who could pay most attention to the Scottish strangers. From morning to night their halls rang with music, and gaiety, and dancing. No wonder that the young nobles; — nay, no wonder that even Sir Patrick Spens himself, careful seaman though he was, forgot to think of the homeward journey, or to remember how soon the storms of winter would be upon them.

In good sooth they might have remained where they were till the spring, and then this tale need never have been told, had not a thoughtless taunt touched their Scottish pride to the quick.

The people of Norway are a frugal race, and to the older nobles all this feasting and junketing seemed like wild, needless extravagance.

"Our young men have gone mad," they said to each other; "if this goes on, the country will be ruined. 'Tis those strangers who have done it. It would be a good day for Norway if they would bethink themselves, and sail for home."

That very night there was a great banquet, an' I warrant that there was dire confusion in the hall when a fierce old noble of Royal blood, an uncle of the King, spoke aloud to Sir Patrick Spens in the hearing of all the company.

"Now little good will the young Queen's dowry do either to our King or to our country," he said, "if it has all to be eaten up, feasting a crowd of idle youngsters who ought to be at home attending to their own business."

Sir Patrick turned red, and then he turned white. What the old man said was very untrue; and he knew it. For, besides the young Queen's dowry, a large sum of money had been taken over in the ship, to pay for the expenses of her attendants, and of the nobles in her train.

"'Tis false. Ye lie," he said bluntly; "for I wot I brought as much white money with me as would more than pay for all that hath been spent on our behalf. If these be the ways of Norway, then beshrew me, but I like them not."

With these words he turned and left the hall followed by all the Scottish nobles. Without speaking a word to any of them, he strode down to the harbour, where his ship was lying, and ordered the sailors to begin to make ready at once, for he would sail for home in the morning.

The night was cold and dreary; there was plainly a storm brewing. It was safe and snug in the harbour, and the sailors were loth to face the dangers of the voyage. But their captain looked so pale and stern, that everyone feared to speak.

"Master," said an old man at last — he was the oldest man on board, and had seen nigh seventy years — "I have never refused to do thy bidding, and I will not begin to-night. We will go, if go we must; but, if it be so, then may God's mercy rest on us. For late yestreen I saw the old moon in the sky, and she was nursing the new moon in her arms. It needs not me to tell thee, for thou art as weather-wise as I am, what that sign bodes."

"Say ye so?" said Sir Patrick, startled in spite of his anger; "then, by my troth, we may prepare for a storm. But tide what may, come snow or sleet, come cold or wet, we head for Scotland in the morning."

So the stately ship set her sails once more, and for a time all went well. But when they had sailed for nigh three days, and were thinking that they must be near Scotland, the sky grew black and the wind arose, and all signs pointed to a coming storm.

Sir Patrick took the helm himself, and did his best to steer the ship through the tempest which soon broke over them, and which grew worse and worse every moment. The sailors worked with a will at the ropes, and even the foolish young nobles, awed by the danger which threatened them, offered their assistance. But they were of little use, and certs, one would have laughed to have seen them, had the peril not been so great, with their fine satin cloaks wrapped round them, and carrying their feathered hats under their arms, trying to step daintily across the deck, between the rushes of the water, in order that they might not wet their tiny, cork-heeled, pointed-toed shoes.

Alack, alack, neither feathered hats, nor pointed shoon, availed to save them! Darker and darker grew the sea, and every moment the huge waves threatened to engulf the goodly vessel.

Sir Patrick Spens had sailed on many a stormy sea, but never in his life had he faced a tempest like this. He knew that he and all his gallant company were doomed men unless the land were near. That was their only hope, to find some harbour and run into it for shelter.

Soon the huge waves were breaking over the deck, and the bulwarks began to give way. Truly their case was desperate, and even the gay young nobles grew grave, and many hearts were turned towards the homes which they would never see again.

"Send me a man to take the helm," shouted Sir Patrick hoarsely, "while I climb to the top of the mast, and try if I can see land."

Instantly the old sailor who had warned him of the coming storm, the night before, was at his side.

"I will guide the ship, captain," he said, "if thou art bent on going aloft; but I fear me thou wilt see no land. Sailors who are out on their last voyage need not look for port."

Now Sir Patrick was a brave man, and he meant to fight for life; so he climbed up to the mast head, and clung on there, despite the driving spray and roaring wind, which were like to drive him from his foothold. In vain he peered through the darkness, looking to the right hand and to the left; there was no land to be seen, nothing but the great green waves, crested with foam, which came springing up like angry wolves, eager to swallow the gallant ship and her luckless crew.

Suddenly his cheek grew pale, and his eyes dark with fear. "We are dead men now," he muttered; for, not many feet below him, seated on the crest of a massive wave, he saw the form of a beautiful woman, with a cruel face and long fair hair, which floated like a veil on the top of the water. 'Twas a mermaid, and he knew what the sight portended.

She held up a silver bowl to him, with a little mocking laugh on her lips. "Sail on, sail on, my guid Scots lords," she cried, and her sweet, false voice rose clear and shrill above the tumult of the waves, "for I warrant ye'll soon touch dry land."

"We may touch the land, but 'twill be the land that lies fathoms deep below the sea," replied Sir Patrick grimly, and then the weird creature laughed again, and floated away in the darkness.

When she had passed Sir Patrick glanced down at the deck, and the sight that met him there only deepened his gloom.

Worn with the beating of the waves, a bolt had sprung in the good ship's side, and a plank had given way, and the cruel green water was pouring in through the hole.

Verily, they were facing death itself now; yet the strong man's heart did not quail.

He had quailed at the sight of the mermaid's mocking eyes, but he looked on the face of death calmly, as befitted a brave and a good man. Perhaps the thought came to him, as it came to another famous seaman long years afterwards, that heaven is as near by sea as by land, and in the thought there was great comfort.

There was but one more thing to be done; after that they were helpless.

"Now, my good Scots lords," he cried, and I trow a look of amusement played round his lips even at that solemn hour, "now is the time for those featherbeds of thine. There are five and fifty of them; odds take it, if they be not enough to stop up one little hole."

At the words the poor young nobles set to work right manfully, forgetting in their fear, that their white hands were bruised and bleeding, and their dainty clothes all wet with seawater.

Alack! alack! ere half the work was done, the good ship shivered from bow to stern, and went slowly down under the waves; and Sir Patrick Spens and his whole company met death, as, in their turn, all men must meet him, and passed to where he had no more power over them.

So there, under the waters of the gray Northern Sea he rested, lying in state, as it were, with the Scottish lords and his own faithful sailors round him; while there was dule and woe throughout the length and breadth of Scotland, and fair women wept as they looked in vain for the husbands, and the brothers, and the lovers who would return to them no more.

And, while the long centuries come and go, he is resting there still, with the Scots lords and his faithful sailors by him, waiting for a Day, whose coming may be long, but whose coming will be sure, when the sea shall give up its dead.

# YOUNG BEKIE

*"Young Bekie was as brave a knight*
*As ever sailed the sea;*
*And he's done him to the Court of France*
*To serve for meat and fee.*

*He hadna been in the Court of France*
*A twelvemonth, nor sae lang,*
*Till he fell in love with the King's daughter,*
*And was thrown in prison strang."*

It was the Court of France: the gayest, and the brightest, and the merriest court in the whole world. For there the sun seemed always to be shining, and the nobles, and the fair Court ladies did not know what care meant.

In all the palace there was only one maiden who wore a sad and troubled look, and that was Burd Isbel, the King's only daughter.

A year before she had been the lightest-hearted maiden in France. Her face had been like sunshine, and her voice like rippling music; but now all was changed. She crept about in silence, with pale cheeks, and clouded eyes, and the King, her father, was in deep distress.

He summoned all the great doctors, and offered them all manner of rewards if only they would give him back, once more, his light-hearted little daughter. But they shook their heads gravely; for although doctors can do many things, they have not yet found out the way to make heavy hearts light again.

All the same these doctors knew what ailed the Princess, but they dare not say so. That would have been to mention a subject which nearly threw the King into a fit whenever he thought of it.

For just a year before, a brave young Scottish Knight had come over to France to take service at the King's Court. His name was Young Bekie, and he was so strong and so noble that at first the King had loved him like a son. But before long the young man had fallen in love with Burd Isbel, and of course Burd Isbel had fallen in love with him, and he had gone straight to the King, and asked him if he might marry her; — and then the fat was in the fire.

For although the stranger seemed to be brave, and noble, and good, and far superior to any Frenchman, he was not of royal birth, and the King declared that it was a piece of gross impertinence on his part ever to think of marrying a king's daughter.

It was in vain that the older nobles, who had known Burd Isbel since she was a child, begged for pity for the young man, and pointed out his good qualities; the King would not listen to them, but stamped, and stormed, and raged with anger. He gave orders that the poor young Knight should be shut up in prison at once, and threatened to take his life; and he told his daughter sharply that she was to think no more about him.

But Burd Isbel could not do that, and she used to creep to the back of the prison door, when no one was near, and listen wistfully, in the hope that she might hear her lover's voice. For a long time she was unsuccessful, but one day she heard him bemoaning his hard fate — to be kept a prisoner in a foreign land, with no chance of sending a message to Scotland of the straits that he was in.

"Oh," he murmured piteously to himself, "if only I could send word home to Scotland to my father, he would not leave me long in this vile prison. He is rich, and he would spare nothing for my ransom. He would send a trusty servant with a bag of good red gold, and another of bonnie white silver, to soften the cruel heart of the King of France."

Then she heard him laugh bitterly to himself.

"There is little chance that I will escape," he muttered, "for who is likely to carry a message to Scotland for me? No, no, my bones will rot here; that is clear enough. And yet how willingly I would be a slave, if I could escape. If only some great lady needed a servant, I would gladly run at her horse's bridle if she could gain me my liberty. If only a widow needed a man to help her, I would promise to be a son to her, if she could obtain my freedom. Nay, if only some poor maiden would promise to wed me, and crave my pardon at the King's hand, I would in return carry her to Scotland, and dower her with all my wealth; and that is not little, for am I not master of the forests, and the lands, and the Castle of Linnhe?"

Many a maiden would have been angry had she heard her lover speak these words; but Burd Isbel loved him too much to be offended at anything which he said, so she crept away to her chamber with a determined look on her girlish face.

"'Tis not for thy lands or thy Castle," she whispered, "but for pure love of thee. Love hath made maidens brave ere now, and it will make them brave again."

That night, when all the palace was quiet, Burd Isbel wrapped herself in a long gray cloak, and crept noiselessly from her room. She might have been taken for a dark shadow, had it not been for her long plait of lint-white hair and her little bare feet, which peeped out and in beneath the folds of her cloak, as she stole down the great polished staircase.

Silently she crept across the hall, and peeped into the guard-room.

All the guards were asleep, and, on the wall above their heads hung the keys of the palace, and beside them a great iron key. That was the key of the prison. She stole across the floor on tip-toe, making no more noise than a mouse, and, stretching up her hand, she took down the heavy key, and hid it under her cloak. Then she sped quickly out of the guard-room, and through a turret door, into a dark courtyard where the prison was. She fitted the key in the lock. It took all her strength to turn it, but she managed it at last, and, shutting the door behind her, she went into the little cell where Young Bekie was imprisoned.

A candle flickered in its socket on the wall, and by its light she saw him lying asleep on the cold stone floor. She could not help giving a little scream when she saw him, for there were three mice and two great rats sitting on the straw at his head, and they had nibbled away nearly all his long yellow hair, which she had admired so much when first he came to Court. His beard had grown long and rough too, for he had had no razors to shave with, and altogether he looked so strange that she hardly knew him.

At the sound of her voice he woke and started up, and the mice and the rats scampered away to their holes. He knew her at once, and in a moment he forgot his dreams of slaves, and widows, and poor maidens. He sprang across the floor, and knelt at her feet, and kissed her little white hands.

"Ah," he said, "now would I stay here for ever, if I might always have thee for a companion."

But Burd Isbel was a sensible maiden, and she knew that if her lover meant to escape, he must make haste, and not waste time in making pretty speeches. She knew also that if he went out of prison looking like a beggar or a vagabond, he would soon be taken captive again, so she hurried back to the palace, and went hither and thither noiselessly with her little bare feet, and presently she returned with her hands full of parcels.

She had brought a comb to comb the hair which the rats had left on his head, and a razor for him to shave himself with, and she had brought five hundred pounds of good red money, so that he might travel like a real Knight.

Then, while he was making his toilet, she went into her father's stable, and led out a splendid horse, strong of limb, and fleet of foot, and on it she put a saddle and a bridle which had been made for the King's own charger.

Finally, she went to the kennels, and, stooping down, she called softly, "Hector, Hector."

A magnificent black hound answered her call and came and crouched at her feet, fawning on them and licking them. After him came three companions, all the same size, and all of them big enough to kill a man.

These dogs belonged to Burd Isbel, and they were her special pets. A tear rolled down her face as she stooped and kissed their heads.

"I am giving you to a new master, darlings," she said. "See and guard him well."

Then she led them to where the horse was standing, saddled and bridled; and there, beside him, stood Young Bekie. Now that his beard was trimmed, and his hair arranged, he looked as gallant, and brave, and noble as ever.

When Burd Isbel told him that the money, and the hounds, and the horse with its harness, were all his, he caught her in his arms, and swore that there had never been such a brave and generous maiden born before, and that he would serve her in life and death.

Then, as time was pressing, and the dawn was beginning to break, they had to say farewell; but before they did so, they vowed a solemn vow that they would be married to each other within three years. After this Burd Isbel opened the great gate, and her lover rode away, with money in his pocket, and hounds by his side, like the well-born Knight that he was; and nobody who met him ever imagined that he was an escaped prisoner, set free by the courage of the King's daughter.

Alas, alas, for the faithfulness of men! Young Bekie was brave, and gentle, and courteous, but his will was not very strong, and he liked to be comfortable. And it came about that, after he had been back in Scotland for a year, the Scotch King had a daughter for whom he wanted to find a husband, and he made up his mind that Young Bekie would be the very man for her.

So he proposed that he should marry her, and was quite surprised and angry when the young man declined.

"It is an insult to my daughter," he said, and he determined to force Bekie to do as he wanted, by using threats. So he told the Knight, that, if he agreed to marry his daughter, he would grow richer and richer, but, if he refused, he would lose all his lands, and the Castle of Linnhe.

Poor Young Bekie! I am afraid he was not a hero, for he chose to marry the Princess and keep his lands, and he tried to put the thought of Burd Isbel and what she had done for him, and the solemn vow that he had made to her, out of his head.

Meanwhile Burd Isbel lived on at her father's court, and because her heart was full of faith and love, it grew light and merry again, and she began to dance and to sing as gaily as ever.

But early one morning she woke up with a start, and there, at the foot of her bed, stood the queerest little manikin that she had ever seen. He was only about a foot high, and he was dressed all in russet brown, and his face was just like a wrinkled apple.

"Who art thou?" she cried, starting up, "and what dost thou want?"

"My name is Billy Blin," said the funny old man. "I am a Brownie, and I come from Scotland. My family all live there, and we are all very kind-hearted, and we like to help people. But it is no time to be talking of my affairs, for I have come to help thee. I have just been wondering how thou couldst lie there and sleep so peacefully when this is Young Bekie's wedding day. He is to be married at noon."

"Oh, what shall I do? what shall I do?" cried poor Burd Isbel in deep distress. "It is a long way from France to Scotland, and I can never be there in time."

Billie Blin waved his little hand. "I will manage it for thee," he said, "if thou wilt only do what I tell thee. Go into thy mother's chamber as fast as thou canst, and get two of thy mother's maids-of-honour. And, remember, thou must be careful to see that they are both called Mary. Then thou must dress thyself in thy most beautiful dress. Thou hast a scarlet dress, I know, which becomes thee well, for I have seen thee wear it. Nay, be not surprised; we Brownies can see people when they do not see us. Put that dress on, and let thy Maries be dressed all in green. And in thy father's treasury there are three jewelled belts, each of them worth an earl's ransom. These thou must get, and clasp them round thy waists, and steal down to the sea-shore, and there, on the water, thou wilt see a beautiful Dutch boat. It will come to the shore for thee, and thou must step in, and greet the crew with a Mystic Greeting. Then thy part is done. I will do the rest."

The Brownie vanished, and Burd Isbel made haste to do exactly what he had told her to do.

She ran to her mother's room, and called to two maids called Mary to come and help her to dress. Then she put on her lovely scarlet robe, and bade them attire themselves in green, and she took the jewelled girdles out of the treasury, and gave one to each of them to put on; and when they were dressed they all went down to the sea-shore.

There, on the sea, as the Brownie had promised, was a beautiful Dutch boat, with its sails spread. It came dancing over the water to them, and when Burd Isbel stepped on board, and greeted the sailors with a Mystic Greeting, they turned its prow towards Scotland, and Billy Blin appeared himself, and took the helm.

Away, away, sailed the ship, until it reached the Firth of Tay, and there, high up among the hills, stood the Castle of Linnhe.

When Burd Isbel and her maidens went to the gate they heard beautiful music coming from within, and their hearts sank. They rang the bell, and the old porter appeared.

"What news, what news, old man?" cried Burd Isbel. "We have heard rumours of a wedding here, and would fain know if they be true or no?"

"Certs, Madam, they are true," he answered; "for this very day, at noon, the Master of this place, Young Bekie, will be married to the King of Scotland's daughter."

Then Burd Isbel felt in her jewelled pouch, and drew out three merks. "Take these, old man," she said, "and bid thy master speak to me at once."

The porter did as he was bid, and went upstairs to the great hall, where all the wedding guests were assembled. He bent low before the King, and before the Queen, and then he knelt before his young lord.

"I have served thee these thirty and three years, Sire," he said, "but never have I seen ladies come to the gate so richly attired as the three who wait without at this moment. There is one of them clad in scarlet, such scarlet as I have never seen, and two are clad in green, and they have girdles round their waists which might well pay an earl's ransom."

When the Scottish Princess heard these words, she tossed her head haughtily. She was tall and buxom, and she was dressed entirely in cloth of gold.

"Lack-a-day," she said, "what a to-do about three strangers! This old fool may think them finely dressed, but I warrant some of us here are every whit as fine as they."

But Young Bekie sprang to his feet. He knew who it was, and the thought of his ingratitude brought the tears to his eyes.

"I'll wager my life 'tis Burd Isbel," he cried, "who has come over the sea to seek me."

Then he ran downstairs, and sure enough it was Burd Isbel.

He clasped her in his arms, and kissed her, and now that he had her beside him, it seemed to him as if he had never loved anyone else.

But the wedding guests came trooping out, and when they heard the story they shook their heads.

"A likely tale," they cried. "Who is to believe it? If she be really the King of France's daughter, how came she here alone, save for those two maidens?"

But some of them looked at the jewelled girdles, and held their peace.

Then Burd Isbel spoke out clearly and simply. "I rescued my love out of prison," she said, "and gave him horse and hounds. And if the hounds know me not, then am I proved false." So saying she raised her voice. "Hector, Hector," she cried, and lo! the great black hound came bounding out of its kennel, followed by its companions, and lay down fawning at her feet, and licked them.

Then the wedding guests knew that she had told the truth, and they turned their eyes on Young Bekie, to see what he would do. He, on his part, was determined that he would marry Burd Isbel, let happen what might.

"Take home your daughter again," he cried impatiently to the King, "and my blessing go with her; for she sought me ere I sought her. This is my own true love; I can wed no other."

"Nay," answered the King, in angry astonishment, "but this thing cannot be. Whoever heard of a maiden being sent home unwed, when the very wedding guests were assembled? I tell thee it cannot be."

In despair Young Bekie turned to the lady herself. "Good lack, Madam," he cried, "is there no one else whom thou canst marry? There is many a better and manlier man than I, who goes seeking a wife. There, for instance, stands my cousin John. He is taller and stronger than I, a better fighter, and a right good man. Couldst thou not accept him for a husband? If thou couldst, I would pay him down five hundred pounds of good red gold on his wedding day."

A murmur of displeasure ran through the crowd of wedding guests at this bold proposal, and the King grasped his sword in a rage. But, to everyone's amazement, the Princess seemed neither displeased nor daunted. She blushed rosy red, and smiled softly.

"Keep thy money to thyself, Bekie," she answered. "Thy cousin John and I have no need of it. Neither doth he require a bribe to make him willing to take me for his wife. To speak truth, we loved each other long ere I set eyes on thee, and 'twas but the King, my father, who would have none of him. Perchance by now he hath changed his mind."

So there were two weddings in the Castle of Linnhe instead of one. Young Bekie married Burd Isbel, and his cousin John married the King's daughter, and they "lived happy, happy, ever after."

# THE EARL OF MAR'S DAUGHTER

*"It was intil a pleasant time,*
*Upon a simmer's day,*
*The noble Earl of Mar's daughter*
*Went forth to sport and play."*

Long, long ago, in a country far away over the sea, there lived a Queen who had an only son. She was very rich, and very great, and the only thing that troubled her was that her son did not want to get married in the very least.

In vain his mother gave grand receptions and court balls, to which she asked all the young countesses and baronesses, in the hope that the Prince would take a fancy to one of them. He would talk to them, and dance with them, and be very polite, but, when his mother hinted that it was time that he looked for a wife, he only shrugged his shoulders and said that there was not a pretty girl amongst them.

And perhaps there was some truth in his answer, for the maidens of that country were all fat, and little, and squat, and everyone of them waddled like a duck when she walked.

"If thou canst not find a wife to thy liking at home," the Queen would say, "go to other countries and see the maidens there; surely somewhere thou wouldst find one whom thou couldst love."

But Prince Florentine, for that was his name, only shook his head and laughed.

"And marry a shrew," he would say mockingly; "for when the maidens heard my name, and knew for what purpose I had come, they would straightway smile their sweetest, and look their loveliest, and I would have no chance of knowing what manner of maidens they really were."

Now the Queen had a very wonderful gift. She could change a man's shape, so that he would appear to be a hare, or a cat, or a bird; and at last she proposed to the Prince that she should turn him into a dove, and then he could fly away to foreign countries, and go up and down until he saw some maiden whom he thought he could really love, and then he could go back to his real shape, and get to know her in the usual way.

This proposal pleased Prince Florentine very much. "He would take good care not to fall in love with anyone," he told himself; but, as he hated the stiffness and ceremony of court life, it seemed to him that it would be good fun to be free to go about as he liked and to see a great many different countries.

So he agreed to his mother's wishes; and one day she waved a little golden wand over his head, and gave him a very nasty draught to drink, made from black beetles' wings, and wormwood, and snails' ears, and hedgehogs' spikes, and before he knew where he was, he was changed into a beautiful gray dove, with a white ring round its neck.

At first when he saw himself in this changed guise he was frightened; but his mother quickly tied a tiny charm round his neck, and hid it under his soft gray feathers, and taught him how to press it against his heart until a fragrant odour came from it, and as soon as he did this, he became once more a handsome young man.

Then he was very pleased, and kissed her, and said farewell, promising to return some day with a beautiful young bride; and after that he spread his wings, and flew away in search of adventure.

For a year and a day he wandered about, now visiting this country, now that, and he was so amused and interested in all the strange and wonderful things that he saw, that he never once wanted to turn himself into a man, and he completely forgot that his mother expected that he was looking out for a wife.

At last, one lovely summer's day, he found himself flying over broad Scotland, and, as the sun was very hot, he looked round for somewhere to shelter from its rays. Just below him was a stately castle, surrounded by magnificent trees.

"This is just what I want," he said to himself; "I will rest here until the sun goes down."

So he folded his wings, and sank gently down into the very heart of a wide-spreading oak tree, near which, as good fortune would have it, there was a field of ripening grain, which provided him with a hearty supper. Here, for many days, the Prince took up his abode, partly because he was getting rather tired of flying about continually, and partly because he began to feel interested in a lovely young girl who came out of the castle every day at noon, and amused herself with playing at ball under the spreading branches of the great tree. Generally she was quite alone, but once or twice an old lady, evidently her governess, came with her, and sat on a root, which formed a comfortable seat, and worked at some fine embroidery, while her pupil amused herself with her ball.

Prince Florentine soon found out that the maiden's name was Grizel, and that she was the only child of the Earl of Mar, a nobleman of great riches and renown. She was very beautiful, so beautiful, indeed, that the Prince sat and feasted his eyes upon her all the time that she was at play, and then, when she had gone home, he could not sleep, but, sat with wide-open eyes, staring into the warm twilight, and wondering how he could get to know her. He could not quite make up his mind whether he should use his mother's charm, and take his natural shape, and walk boldly up to the castle and crave her father's permission to woo her, or fly away home, and send an ambassador with a train of nobles, and all the pomp that belonged to his rank, to ask for her hand.

The question was settled for him one day, however, and everything happened quite differently from what he expected.

On a very hot afternoon, Lady Grizel came out, accompanied by her governess, and, as usual, the old lady sat down to her embroidery, and the girl began to toss her ball. But the sun was so very hot that by and by the governess laid down her needle and fell fast asleep, while her pupil grew tired of running backwards and forwards, and, sitting down, began to toss her ball right up among the branches. All at once it caught in a leafy bough, and when she was gazing up, trying to see where it was, she caught sight of a beautiful gray dove, sitting watching her. Now, as I have said, Lady Grizel was an only child, and she had had few playmates, and all her life she had been passionately fond of animals, and when she saw the bird, she stood up and called gently, "Oh Coo-me-doo, come down to me, come down." Then she whistled so softly and sweetly, and stretched out her white hands above her head so entreatingly, that Prince Florentine left his branch, and flew down and alighted gently on her shoulder.

The delight of the maiden knew no bounds. She kissed and fondled her new pet, which perched quite familiarly on her arm, and promised him a latticed silver cage, with bars of solid gold.

The bird allowed the girl to carry him home, and soon the beautiful cage was made, and hung up on the wall of her chamber, just inside the window, and Coo-me-doo, as the dove was named, placed inside.

He seemed perfectly happy, and grew so tame that soon he went with his mistress wherever she went, and all the people who lived near the castle grew quite accustomed to seeing the Earl's daughter driving or riding with her tame dove on her shoulder.

When she went out to play at ball, Coo-me-doo would go with her, and perch up in his old place, and watch her with his bright dark eyes. One day when she was tossing the ball among the branches it rolled away, and for a long time she could not find it, and at last a voice behind her said, "Here it is," and, turning round, she saw to her astonishment a handsome young man dressed all in dove-gray satin, who handed her the ball with a stately bow.

Lady Grizel was frightened, for no strangers were allowed inside her father's park, and she could not think where he had come from; but just as she was about to call out for help, the young man smiled and said, "Lady, dost thou not know thine own Coo-me-doo?"

Then she glanced up into the branches, but the bird was gone, and as she hesitated (for the stranger spoke so kindly and courteously she did not feel very much alarmed), he took her hand in his.

" 'Tis true, my own love," he said; "but if thou canst not recognise thy favourite when his gray plumage is changed into gray samite, mayhap thou wilt know him when the gray samite is once more changed into softest feathers; and, pressing a tiny gold locket which he wore, to his heart, he vanished, and in his stead was her own gray dove, hovering down to his resting-place on her shoulder.

"Oh, I cannot understand it, I cannot understand it," she cried, putting up her hand to stroke her pet; but the feathers seemed to slip from between her fingers, and once more the gallant stranger stood before her.

"Sit thee down and rest, Sweetheart," he said, leading her to the root where her governess was wont to sit, while he stretched himself on the turf at her feet, "and I will explain the mystery to thee."

Then he told her all. How his mother was a great Queen away in a far country, and how he was her only son. Lady Grizel's fears were all gone now, and she laughed merrily as he described the girls who lived in his own country, and told her how little and fat they were, and how they waddled when they walked; but when he told her how his mother had used her magic and turned him into a dove, in order that he might bring home a wife, her face grew grave and pale.

"My father hath sworn a great oath," she said, "that I shall never wed with anyone who lives out of Scotland; so I fear we must part, and thou must go elsewhere in search of a bride."

But Prince Florentine shook his head.

"Nay," he said, "but rather than part from thee, I will live all my life as a dove in a cage, if I may only be near thee, and talk to thee when we are alone."

"But what if my father should want me to wed with some Scottish lord?" asked the maiden anxiously; "couldst thou bear to sit in thy cage and sing my wedding song?"

"That could I not," answered Prince Florentine, drawing her closer to him; "and in order to prevent such a terrible thing happening, Sweetheart, we must find ways and means to be married at once, and then, come what may, no one can take thee from me. This very evening I must go and speak to thy father."

Now the Earl of Mar was a violent man, and his fear lay on all the country-side — even his only child was afraid of him — and when her lover made this suggestion she clung to him and begged him with tears in her eyes not to do this. She told him what a fiery temper the Earl had, and how she feared that when he heard his story he would simply order him to be hanged on the nearest tree, or thrown into the dungeon to starve to death. So for a long time they sat and talked, now thinking of one plan, now of another, but none of them seemed of any use, and it seemed as though Prince Florentine must either remain in the shape of her pet dove, or go away altogether.

All at once Lady Grizel clapped her hands. "I have it, I have it," she cried; "why cannot we be married secretly? Old Father John out at the chapel on the moor could marry us; he is so old and so blind, he would never recognise me if I went bare-headed and bare-footed like a gipsy girl; and thou must go dressed as a woodman, with muddy shoes, and an axe over thine arm. Then we can dwell together as we are doing now, and no one will suspect that the Earl of Mar's daughter is married to her tame pet dove, which sits on her shoulder, and goes with her wherever she goes. And if the worst comes to the worst, and some gallant Scotch wooer appears, why, then we must confess what we have done, and bear the consequences together."

A few days later, in the early morning, when old Father John, the priest who served the little chapel which stood on the heather-covered moor, was preparing to say Mass, he saw a gipsy girl, bare-headed and bare-footed, steal into the chapel, followed by a stalwart young woodman, clad all in sober gray, with a bright wood-axe gleaming on his shoulder.

In a few words they told him the purpose for which they had come, and after he had said Mass the kindly old priest married them, and gave them his blessing, never doubting but that they were a couple of simple country lovers who would go home to some tiny cottage in the woods near by. Little did he think that only half a mile away a page boy, wearing the livery of the Earl of Mar, was patiently waiting with a white palfrey until his young mistress should return, accompanied by her gray dove, from visiting an old nurse, "who," she told her governess, "was teaching her how to spin."

And little did her father, or her governess, or any of the servants at the castle, think that Lady Grizel was leading a double life, and that the gray dove which was always with her, and which she seemed to love more than any other of her pets, was a gray dove only when anyone else was by, but turned into a gallant young Prince, who ate, and laughed, and talked with her the moment they were alone.

Strange to say, their secret was never found out for seven long years, even although every year a little son was born to them, and carried away under the gray dove's wing to the country far over the sea. At these times Lady Grizel used to cry and be very sad, for she dare not keep her babies beside her, but had to kiss them, and let them go, to be brought up by their Grandmother whom she had never seen.

Every time Prince Florentine carried home a new baby, he brought back tidings to his wife how tall, and strong, and brave her other sons were growing, and tender messages from the Queen, his mother, telling her how she hoped that one day she would be able to come home with her husband, and then they would be all together.

But year after year went by, and still the fierce old Earl lived on, and there seemed little hope that poor Lady Grizel would ever be able to go and live in her husband's land, and she grew pale and thin. And year after year her father grew more and more angry with her, because he wanted her to marry one of the many wooers who came to crave her hand; but she would not.

"I love to dwell alone with my sweet Coo-me-doo," she used to say, and the old Earl would stamp his foot, and go out of her chamber muttering angry words in his vexation.

At last, one day, a very great and powerful nobleman arrived with his train to ask the Earl's daughter to marry him. He was very rich, and owned four beautiful castles, and the Earl said, "Now, surely, my daughter will consent."

But she only gave her old answer, "I love best to live alone with my sweet Coo-me-doo."

Then her father slammed the door in a rage, and went into the great hall, where all his men-at-arms were, and swore a mighty oath, that on the morrow, before he broke his fast, he would wring the neck of the wretched bird, which seemed to have bewitched his daughter.

Now just above his head, in the gallery, hung Coo-me-doo's cage with the golden bars, and he happened to be sitting in it, and when he heard this threat he flew away in haste to his wife's room and told her.

"I must fly home and crave help of my mother," he said; "mayhap she may be able to aid us, for I shall certainly be no help to thee here, if my neck be wrung to-morrow. Do thou fall in with thy father's wishes, and promise to marry this nobleman; only see to it that the wedding doth not take place until three clear days be past."

Then Lady Grizel opened the window, and he flew away, leaving her to act her part as best she might.

Now it chanced that next evening, in the far distant land over the sea, the Queen was walking up and down in front of her palace, watching her grandsons playing at tennis, and thinking sadly of her only son and his beautiful wife whom she had never seen. She was so deep in thought, that she never noticed that a gray dove had come sailing over the trees, and perched itself on a turret of the palace, until it fluttered down, and her son, Prince Florentine, stood beside her.

She threw herself into his arms joyfully, and kissed him again and again; then she would have called for a feast to be set, and for her minstrels to play, as she always did on the rare occasions when he came home, but he held up his hand to stop her.

"I need neither feasting nor music, Mother," he said, "but I need thy help sorely. If thy magic cannot help me, then my wife and I are undone, and in two days she will be forced to marry a man whom she hates," and he told the whole story.

"And what wouldst thou that I should do?" asked the Queen in great distress.

"Give me a score of men-at-arms to fly over the sea with me," answered the Prince, "and my sons to help me in the fray."

But the Queen shook her head sadly.

" 'Tis beyond my power," she said; "but mayhap Astora, the old dame who lives by the sea-shore, might help me, for in good sooth thy need is great. She hath more skill in magic than I have."

So she hurried away to a little hut near the sea-shore where the wise old woman lived, while her son waited anxiously for her return.

At last she appeared again, and her face was radiant.

"Dame Astora hath given me a charm," she said, "which will turn four-and-twenty of my stout men-at-arms into storks, and thy seven sons into white swans, and thou thyself into a gay gos-hawk, the proudest of all birds."

Now the Earl of Mar, full of joy at the disappearance of the gray dove, which seemed to have bewitched his daughter, had bade all the nobles throughout the length and breadth of fair Scotland to come and witness her wedding with the lover whom he had chosen for her, and there was feasting, and dancing, and great revelry at the castle. There had not been such doings since the marriage of the Earl's great-grandfather a hundred years before. There were huge tables, covered with rich food, standing constantly in the hall, and even the common people went in and out as they pleased, while outside on the green there was music, and dancing, and games.

Suddenly, when the revelry was at its height, a flock of strange birds appeared on the horizon, and everyone stopped to look at them. On they came, flying all together in regular order, first a gay gos-hawk, then behind him seven snow-white swans, and behind the swans four-and-twenty large gray storks. When they drew near, they settled down among the trees which surrounded the castle green, and sat there, each on his own branch, like sentinels, watching the sport.

At first some of the people were frightened, and wondered what this strange sight might mean, but the Earl of Mar only laughed.

"They come to do honour to my daughter," he said; "'tis well that there is not a gray dove among them, else had he found an arrow in his heart, and that right speedily," and he ordered the musicians to strike up a measure.

The Lady Grizel was amongst the throng, dressed in her bridal gown, but no one noticed how anxiously she glanced at the great birds which sat so still on the branches.

Then a strange thing happened. No sooner had the musicians begun to play, and the dancers begun to dance, than the twenty-four gray storks flew down, and each of them seized a nobleman, and tore him from his partner, and whirled him round and round as fast as he could, holding him so tightly with his great gray wings that he could neither draw his sword nor struggle. Then the seven white swans flew down and seized the bridegroom, and tied him fast to a great oak tree. Then they flew to where the gay gos-hawk was hovering over Lady Grizel, and they pressed their bodies so closely to his that they formed a soft feathery couch, on which the lady sat down, and in a moment the birds soared into the air, bearing their precious burden on their backs, while the storks, letting the nobles go, circled round them to form an escort; and so the strange army of birds flew slowly out of sight, leaving the wedding guests staring at one another in astonishment, while the Earl of Mar swore so terribly that no one dare go near him.

*And although the story of this strange wedding is told in Scotland to this day, no one has ever been able to guess where the birds came from, or to what land they carried the beautiful Lady Grizel.*

# HYNDE HORN

*"'Oh, it's Hynde Horn fair, and it's Hynde Horn free;*
*Oh, where were you born, and in what countrie?'*
*'In a far distant countrie I was born;*
*But of home and friends I am quite forlorn.'"*

Once upon a time there was a King of Scotland, called King
Aylmer, who had one little daughter, whose name was Jean.
She was his only daughter, and, as her mother was dead, he
adored her. He gave her whatever she liked to ask for, and her
nursery was so full of toys and games of all kinds, that it was a
wonder that any little girl, even although she was a Princess,
could possibly find time to play with them all.

She had a beautiful white palfrey to ride on, and two pie-
bald ponies to draw her little carriage when she wanted to
drive; but she had no one of her own age to play with, and often
she felt very lonely, and she was always asking her father to
bring her someone to play with.

"By my troth," he would reply, "but that were no easy matter, for thou art a royal Princess, and it befits not that such as
thou shouldst play with children of less noble blood."

Then little Princess Jean would go back to her splendid
nurseries with the tears rolling down her cheeks, wishing with
all her heart that she had been born just an ordinary little girl.

King Aylmer had gone away on a hunting expedition one
day, and Princess Jean was playing alone as usual, in her nursery, when she heard the sound of her father's horn outside the
castle walls, and the old porter hurried across the courtyard to
open the gate. A moment later the King's voice rang through
the hall, calling loudly for old Elspeth, the nurse.

The old dame hurried down the broad staircase, followed by
the little Princess, who was surprised that her father had returned so early from his hunting, and what was her astonishment to see him standing, with all his nobles round him,
holding a fair-haired boy in his arms.

The boy's face was very white, and his eyes were shut, and
the little Princess thought that he was dead, and ran up to a
gray-haired baron, whose name was Athelbras, and hid her face

against his rough hunting coat.

But old Elspeth ran forward and took the boy's hand in hers, and laid her ear against his heart, and then she asked that he might be carried up into her own chamber, and that the housekeeper might be sent after them with plenty of blankets, and hot water, and red wine.

When all this had been done, King Aylmer noticed his little daughter, and when he saw how pale her cheeks were, he patted her head and said, "Cheer up, child, the young cock-sparrow is not dead; 'tis but a swoon caused by the cold and wet, and methinks when old Elspeth hath put a little life into him, thou wilt mayhap have found a playfellow."

Then he called for his horse and rode away to hunt again, and Princess Jean was once more left alone. But this time she did not feel lonely.

Her father's wonderful words, "Thou wilt mayhap have found a playfellow," rang in her ears, and she was so busy thinking about them, sitting by herself in the dark by the nursery fire, that she started when old Elspeth opened the door of her room and called out, "Come, Princess, the young gentleman hath had a sweet sleep, and would fain talk with thee."

The little Princess went into the room on tip-toe, and there, lying on the great oak settle by the fire, was the boy whom she had seen in her father's arms. He seemed about four years older than she was, and he was very handsome, with long yellow hair, which hung in curls round his shoulders, and merry blue eyes, and rosy cheeks.

He smiled at her as she stood shyly in the doorway, and held out his hand. "I am thy humble servant, Princess," he said. "If it had not been for thy father's kindness, and for this old dame's skill, I would have been dead ere now."

Princess Jean did not know what to say; she had often wished for someone who was young enough to play with her, but now that she had found a real playmate, she felt as if someone had tied her tongue.

"What is thy name, and where dost thou come from?" she asked at last.

The boy laughed, and pointed to a little stool which stood beside the settle. "Sit down there," he said, "and I will tell thee. I have often wished to have a little sister of my own, and now I will pretend that thou art my little sister."

Princess Jean did as she was bid, and went and sat down on the stool, and the stranger began his tale.

"My name is Hynde Horn," he said, "and I am a King's son."

"And I am a King's daughter," said the little Princess, and then they both laughed.

Then the boy's face grew grave again.

"They called my father King Allof," he said, "and my mother's name was Queen Godyet, and they reigned over a beautiful country far away in the East. I was their only son, and we were all as happy as the day was long, until a wicked king, called Mury, came with his soldiers, and fought against my father, and killed him, and took his kingdom. My mother and I tried to escape, but the fright killed my mother — she died in a hut in the forest where we had hidden ourselves, and some soldiers found me weeping beside her body, and took me prisoner, and carried me to the wicked King.

"He was too cruel to kill me outright — he wanted me to die a harder death — so he bade his men tie my hands and my feet, and carry me down to the sea-shore, and put me in a boat, and push it out into the sea; and there they left me to die of hunger and thirst.

"At first the sun beat down on my face, and burned my skin, but by and by it grew dark, and a great storm arose, and the boat drifted on and on, and I grew so hungry, and then so thirsty — oh! I thought I would die of thirst — and at last I became unconscious, for I remember nothing more until I woke up to find yonder kind old dame bending over me."

"The boat was washed up on our shore, just as his Highness the King rode past," explained old Elspeth, who was stirring some posset over the fire, and listening to the story.

"And what did you say your name was?" demanded the little Princess, who had listened with eager attention to the story.

"Hynde Horn," repeated the boy, whose eyes were wet with tears at the thought of all that he had gone through.

"Prince Hynde Horn," corrected Princess Jean, who liked always to have her title given to her, and expected that other people liked the same.

"Well, I suppose I ought to be King Horn now, were it not for that wicked King who hath taken my Kingdom, as well as my father's life; but the people in my own land always called me Hynde Horn, and I like the old name best."

"But what doth it mean?" persisted the little Princess.

The boy blushed and looked down modestly. "It is an old word which in our language means 'kind' or 'courteous,' but I am afraid that they flattered me, for I did not always deserve it."

The little Princess clapped her hands. "We will call thee by it," she said, "until thou provest thyself unworthy of it."

After this a new life opened up for the little girl.

King Aylmer, finding that the young Prince who had been so unexpectedly thrown on his protection was both modest and manly, determined to befriend him, and to give him a home at his Court until he was old enough to go and try to recover his kingdom, and avenge his parents' death, so he gave orders that a suite of rooms in the castle should be given to him, and arranged that Baron Athelbras, his steward, should train him in all knightly accomplishments, such as hawking and tilting at the ring. He soon found out too that Hynde Horn had a glorious voice, and sang like a bird, so he gave orders that old Thamile, the minstrel, should teach him to play the harp; and soon he could play it so well, that the whole Court would sit round him in the long winter evenings, and listen to his music.

He was so sweet-tempered, and lovable, that everyone liked him, and would say to one another that the people in his own land had done well to name him Hynde Horn.

To the little Princess he was the most delightful companion, for he was never too busy or too tired to play with her. He taught her to ride as she had never ridden before, not merely to jog along the road on her fat palfrey, but to gallop alongside of him under the trees in the forest, and they used to be out all day, hunting and hawking, for he trained two dear little white falcons and gave them to her, and taught her to carry them on her wrist; and she grew so fat and rosy that everyone said it was a joyful day when Hynde Horn was washed up on the sea-shore in the boat.

But alas! people do not remain children for ever, and, as years went on, Hynde Horn grew into as goodly a young man as anyone need wish to see, and of course he fell in love with Princess Jean, and of course she fell in love with him. Everyone was quite delighted, and said, "What is to hinder them from being married at once, and then when Princess Jean comes to be Queen, we will be quite content to have Hynde Horn for our King?"

But wise King Aylmer would not agree to this. He knew that it is not good for any man to have no difficulties to overcome, and to get everything that he wants without any trouble.

"Nay," he said, "but the lad hath to win his spurs first, and to show us of what stuff he is made. Besides, his father's Kingdom lies desolate, ruled over by an alien. He shall be betrothed to my daughter, and we will have a great feast to celebrate the event, and then I will give him a ship, manned by thirty sailors, and he shall go away to his own land in search of adventure, and when he hath done great deeds of daring, and avenged his father's death, he shall come again, and my daughter will be waiting for him."

So there was a splendid feast held at the castle, and all the great lords and barons came to it, and Princess Jean and Hynde Horn were betrothed amidst great rejoicing, for everyone was glad to think that their Princess would wed someone whom they knew, and not a stranger.

But the hearts of the two lovers were heavy, and when the feast was over, and all the guests had gone away, they went out on a little balcony in front of the castle, which overlooked the sea. It was a lovely evening, the moon was full, and by its light they could see the white sails of the ship lying ready in the little bay, waiting to carry Hynde Horn far away to other lands. The roses were nodding their heads over the balcony railings and the honeysuckle was falling in clusters from the castle walls, but it might have been December for all that poor Princess Jean cared, and the tears rolled fast down her face as she thought of the parting.

"Alack, alack, Hynde Horn," she said, "could I but go with thee! How shall I live all these years, with no one to talk to, or to ride with?"

Then he tried to comfort her with promises of how brave he would be, and how soon he would conquer his father's enemies and come back to her; but they both knew in their hearts that this was the last time that they would be together for long years to come.

At last Hynde Horn drew a long case from his pocket, out of which he took a beautifully wrought silver wand, with three little silver laverocks[30] sitting on the end of it. "This," he said, "dear love, is for thee; the sceptre is a token that thou rulest in my heart, as well as over broad Scotland, and the three singing laverocks are to remind thee of me, for thou hast oft-times told me that my poor singing reminds thee of a lark."

Then Princess Jean drew from her finger a gold ring, set with three priceless diamonds. It was so small it would only go on the little finger of her lover's left hand. "This is a token of my love," she said gravely, "therefore guard it well. When the diamonds are bright and shining, thou shalt know that my love for thee will be burning clear and true; but if ever they lose their lustre and grow pale and dim, then know thou that some evil hath befallen me. Either I am dead, or else someone tempts me to be untrue."

Next morning the fair white ship spread her sails, and carried Hynde Horn far away over the sea. Princess Jean stood on the little balcony until the tallest mast had disappeared below the horizon, and then she threw herself on her bed, and wept as though her heart would break.

After this, for many a long day, there was nothing heard of Hynde Horn, not even a message came from him, and people began to say that he must be dead, and that it was high time that their Princess forgot him, and listened to the suit of one of the many noble princes who came to pay court to her from over the sea. She would not listen to them, however, and year after year went by.

Now it happened, that, when seven years had passed, a poor beggar went up one day to the castle in the hope that one of the servants would see him, and give him some of the broken bread and meat that was always left from the hall table. The porter knew him by sight and let him pass into the courtyard, but although he loitered about for a whole hour, no one appeared to have time to speak to him. It seemed as if something unusual were going on, for there were horses standing about in

30    Larks.

the courtyard, held by grooms in strange liveries, and servants were hurrying along, as if they were so busy they hardly knew what to do first. The old beggar man spoke to one or two of them as they passed, but they did not pay any attention to him, so at last he thought it was no use waiting any longer, and was about to turn away, when a little scullery-maid came out of the kitchen, and began to wash some pots under a running tap. He went up to her, and asked if she could spare him any broken victuals.

She looked at him crossly. "A pretty day to come for broken victuals," she cried, "when we all have so much to do that we would need twenty fingers on every hand, and four pairs of hands at the very least. Knowst thou not that an embassage has come from over the sea, seeking the hand of our Princess Jean for the young Prince of Eastnesse, he that is so rich that he could dine off diamonds every day, an' it suited him, and they are all in the great hall now, talking it over with King Aylmer? Only 'tis said that the Princess doth not favour the thought; she is all for an old lover called Hynde Horn, whom everyone else holds to be dead this many a year. Be it as it may, I have no time to talk to the like of thee, for we have a banquet to cook for fifty guests, not counting the King and all his nobles. The like of it hath not been seen since the day when Princess Jean and that Hynde Horn plighted their troth these seven years ago. But hark'ee, old man, it might be well worth thy while to come back to-morrow; there will be plenty of picking then." And, flapping her dish-clout in the wind, she ran into the kitchen again.

The old beggar went away, intending to take her advice and return on the morrow; but as he was walking along the sands to a little cottage where he sometimes got a night's lodging, he met a gallant Knight on horseback, who was very finely dressed, and wore a lovely scarlet cloak.

The beggar thought that he must be one of the King's guests, who had come out for a gallop on the smooth yellow sands, and he stood aside and pulled off his cap; but the Knight drew rein, and spoke to him.

"God shield thee, old man," he said, "and what may the news be in this country? I used to live here, but I have been in far-off lands these seven years, and I know not how things go on."

"Sire," answered the beggar, "things have gone on much as usual for these few years back, but it seems as if changes were in the air. I was but this moment at the castle, and 'twas told me that the young Prince Eitel, heir to the great Kingdom of Eastnesse, hath sent to crave the hand of our Princess; and although the young lady favours not his suit (she being true to an old love, one Hynde Horn, who is thought to be dead), the King her father is like to urge her to it, for the King of Eastnesse is a valuable ally, and fabulously rich."

Then a strange light came into the stranger's eyes, and, to the beggar's astonishment, he sprang from his horse, and held out the rein to him. "Wilt do me a favour, friend?" he said. "Wilt give me thy beggar's wallet, and staff, and cloak, if I give thee my horse, and this cloak of crimson sarsenet? I have a mind to turn beggar."

The beggar scratched his head, and looked at him in surprise. "He hath been in the East, methinks," he muttered, "and the sun hath touched his brain, but anyhow 'tis a fair exchange; that crimson cloak will sell for ten merks any day, and for the horse I can get twenty pounds," and presently he cantered off, well pleased with the bargain, while the other, — the beggar's wallet in his hand, his hat drawn down over his eyes, and leaning on his staff, — began to ascend the steep hill leading to the castle.

When he reached the great gate, he knocked boldly on the iron knocker, and the knock was so imperious that the porter hastened to open it at once. He expected to see some lordly knight waiting there, and when he saw no one but a weary-looking beggar man, he uttered an angry exclamation, and was about to shut the great gate in his face, but the beggar's voice was wondrously sweet and low, and he could not help listening to it.

"Good porter, for the sake of St Peter and St Paul, and for the sake of Him who died on the Holy Rood, give a cup of wine, and a little piece of bread, to a poor wayfarer."

As the porter hesitated between pity and impatience, the pleading voice went on, "And one more boon would I crave, kind man. Carry a message from me to the fair bride who is to be betrothed this day, and ask her if she will herself hand the bite and the sup to one who hath come from far?"

"Ask the Bride! ask the Princess Jean to come and feed thee with her own hands!" cried the man in astonishment. "Nay, thou art mad. Away with thee; we want no madmen here," and he would have thrust the beggar aside; but the stranger laid his hand on his shoulder, and said calmly, as if he were giving an order to a servant, "Go, tell her it is for the sake of Hynde Horn." And the old porter turned and went without a word.

Meanwhile all the guests in the castle were gathered at the banquet in the great banqueting hall. On a raised dais at the end of the room sat King Aylmer and the great Ambassador who had come from Prince Eitel of Eastnesse, and between them sat Princess Jean, dressed in a lovely white satin dress, with a little circlet of gold on her head. The King and the Ambassador were in high spirits, for they had persuaded the Princess to marry Prince Eitel in a month and a day from that time; but poor Princess Jean looked pale and sad.

As all the lords and nobles who were feasting in the hall below stood up and filled their glasses, and drank to the health of Prince Eitel of Eastnesse and his fair bride, she had much ado to keep the tears from falling, as she thought of the old days when Hynde Horn and she went out hunting and hawking together.

Just at that moment the door opened, and the porter entered, and, without looking to the right hand or to the left, marched straight up the hall and along the dais, until he came to where Princess Jean sat; then he stooped down and whispered something to her.

In a moment the Princess' pale face was like a damask rose, and, taking a glass full of ruby-red wine in one hand, and a farl of cake in the other, she rose, and walked straight out of the hall.

"By my faith," said King Aylmer, who was startled by the look on his daughter's face, "something hath fallen out, I ween, which may change the whole course of events," and he rose and followed her, accompanied by the Ambassador and all the great nobles.

At the head of the staircase they stopped and watched the Princess as she went down the stairs and across the courtyard, her long white robe trailing behind her, with the cup of ruby-red wine in one hand, and the farl of cake in the other.

When she came to the gateway, there was no one there but a poor old beggar man, and all the foreign noblemen looked at each other and shook their heads, and said, "Certs, but it misdoubts us if this bride will please our young Prince, if she is wont to disturb a court banquet because she must needs serve beggars with her own hands."

But Princess Jean heard none of this. With trembling hands she held out the food to the beggar. He raised the wine to his lips, and pledged the fair bride before he drank it, and when he handed the glass back to her, lo! in the bottom of it lay the gold ring which she had given to her lover Hynde Horn, seven long years before.

"Oh," she cried breathlessly, snatching it out of the glass, "tell me quickly, I pray thee, where thou didst find this? Was't on the sea, or in a far-off land, and was the hand that it was taken from alive or dead?"

"Nay, noble lady," answered the beggar, and at the sound of his voice Princess Jean grew pale again, "I did not get it on the sea, or in a far-off land, but in this country, and from the hand of a fair lady. It was a pledge of love, noble Princess, which I had given to me seven long years ago, and the diamonds were to be tokens of the brightness and constancy of that love. For seven long years they have gleamed and sparkled clearly, but now they are dim, and losing their brightness, so I fear me that my lady's love is waning and growing cold."

Then Princess Jean knew all, and she tore the circlet of gold from her head and knelt on the cold stones at his feet, and cried, "Hynde Horn, my own Hynde Horn, my love is not cold, neither is it dim; but thou wert so long in coming, and they said it was my duty to marry someone else. But now, even if thou art a beggar, I will be a beggar's wife, and follow thee from place to place, and we can harp and sing for our bread."

Hynde Horn laughed a laugh that was pleasant to hear, and he threw off the beggar's cloak, and, behold, he was dressed as gaily as any gallant in the throng.

"There is no need of that, Sweetheart," he said. "I did it but to try thee. I have not been idle these seven years; I have killed the wicked King, and come into my own again, and I have fought and conquered the Saracens in the East, and I have gold enough and to spare."

Then he drew her arm within his, and they crossed the courtyard together and began to ascend the stairs. Suddenly old Athelbras, the steward, raised his cap and shouted, "It is Hynde Horn, our own Hynde Horn," and then there was such a tumult of shouting and cheering that everyone was nearly deafened. Even the Ambassador from Eastnesse and all his train joined in it, although they knew that now Princess Jean would never marry their Prince; but they could not help shouting, for everyone looked so happy.

And the next day there was another great banquet prepared, and riders were sent all over the country to tell the people everywhere to rejoice, for their Princess was being married, not to any stranger, but to her old lover, Hynde Horn, who had come back in time after all.

# THE GAY GOS-HAWK

*"'Oh weel is me, my gay gos-hawk,*
*If your feathering be sheen!'*
*'Oh waly, waly, my master dear,*
*But ye look pale and lean!'"*

It was the beautiful month of June, and among the bevy of fair maidens who acted as maids-of-honour to Queen Margaret at Windsor, there was none so fair as the Lady Katherine, the youngest of them all.

As she joined in a game of bowls in one of the long alleys under the elm trees, or rode out, hawk on wrist, in the great park near the castle, her merry face, with its rosy cheeks and sparkling blue eyes, was a pleasure to see. She had gay words for everyone, even for the sharp-tongued, grave-faced old Baroness who acted as governess to the Queen's maids, and kept a sharp lookout lest any of the young ladies under her charge should steal too shy glances at the pages and gentlemen-at-arms who waited on the King.

The old lady loved her in return, and pretended to be blind when she noticed, what every maid-of-honour had noticed for a fortnight, that there was one Knight in particular who was always at hand to pick up Lady Katherine's balls for her, or to hold her palfrey's rein if she wanted to alight, when she was riding in the forest.

This gallant Knight was not one of the King's gentlemen, but the son of a Scottish earl, who had been sent to Windsor with a message from the King of Scotland.

Lord William, for that was his name, was so tall, and strong, and brave, and manly, it was no wonder that little Lady Katherine fell in love with him, and preferred him to all the young English lords who were longing to lay their hearts at her feet.

So things went merrily on, in the pleasant June weather, until one sunny afternoon, when Lady Katherine was riding slowly through the park, under the shady beech trees, with Lord William, as usual, by her side. He was telling her how much he loved her, a story which he had told her very often before, and describing the old ivy-covered gray castle, far away in the North, where he would take her to live some day, when a little page, clad all in Lincoln green, ran across the park and bowed as he stopped at the palfrey's side. "Pardon, my lady," he said breathlessly, "but the Baroness Anne sent me to carry tidings to thee that thy Duchess mother hath arrived, and would speak with thee at once."

Then the bright red roses faded from the poor little lady's cheeks, for she knew well that the Duchess, who was not her real mother, but only her step-mother, wished her no good. Sorrowfully she rode up to the castle, Lord William at her side, and it seemed to both of them as if the little birds had stopped singing, and the sun had suddenly grown dim.

And it was indeed terrible tidings that the little maiden heard when she reached the room where her stern-faced step-mother awaited her. An old Marquis, a friend of her father's, who was quite old enough to be her grandfather, had announced his wish to marry her, and, as she had five sisters at home, all waiting to get a chance to become maids-of-honour, and see a little of the world, her step-mother thought it was too good an opportunity to let slip, and she had come to fetch her home.

In vain poor Lady Katherine threw herself at the Duchess's feet, and besought her to let her marry the gallant Scottish knight. Her ladyship only curled her lip and laughed. "Marry a beggarly Scot!" she said. "Not as long as I have any power in thy father's house. No, no, wench, thou knowest not what is for thy good. Where is thy waiting-maid? Let her pack up thy things at once; thou hast tarried here long enough, I trow."

So Lady Katherine was carted off, bag and baggage, to the great turreted mansion on the borders of Wales, where her five sisters and her grandfatherly old lover were waiting for her, without ever having a chance of bidding Lord William farewell.

As for that noble youth, he mounted his horse, and called his men-at-arms together, and straightway rode away to Scotland, and never halted till he reached the old gray castle, three days' ride over the Border. When he arrived there he shut himself up in the great square tower where his own apartments were, and frightened his family by growing so pale and thin that they declared he must have caught some fever in England,

and had come home to die. In vain the Earl, his father, tried to persuade him to ride out with him to the chase; he cared for nothing but to be left alone to sit in the dim light of his own room, and dream of his lost love.

Now Lord William was fond of all living things, horses, and dogs, and birds; but one pet he had, which he loved above all the others, and that was a gay gos-hawk which he had found caught in a snare, one day, and had set free, and tamed, and which always sat on a perch by his window.

One evening, when he was sitting dreaming sadly of the days at Windsor, stroking his favourite's plumage meanwhile, he was startled to hear the bird begin to speak. "What mischance hath befallen thee, my master?" it said, "that thou lookest so pale and unhappy. Hast been defeated in a tourney by some Southron loon, or dost still mourn for that fair maiden, the lovely Lady Katherine? Can I not help thee?"

Then a strange light shone in Lord William's eye, and he looked at the bird thoughtfully as it nestled closer to his heart.

"Thou shalt help me, my gay gos-hawk," he whispered, "for, for this reason, methinks, thou hast received the gift of speech. Thy wings are strong, and thou canst go where I cannot, and bring no harm to my love. Thou shalt carry a letter to my dear one, and bring back an answer," and in delight at the thought, the young man rose and walked up and down the room, the gos-hawk preening its wings on his shoulder, and crooning softly to itself.

"But how shall I know thy love?" it said at last.

"Ah, that is easy," answered Lord William. "Thou must fly up and down merrie England, especially where any great mansion is, and thou canst not mistake her. She is the fairest flower of all the fair flowers that that fair land contains. Her skin is white as milk, and the roses on her cheeks are red as blood. And, outside her chamber, by a little postern, there grows a nodding birch tree, the leaves of which dance in the slightest breeze, and thou must perch thereon, and sing thy sweetest, when she goes with her sisters and maids to hear Mass in the little chapel."

That night, when all the country folk were asleep, a gay gos-hawk flew out from a window in the square tower, and sped swiftly through the quiet air, on and on, above lonely houses, and sleeping towns, and when the sun rose it was still flying, hovering now and then over some great castle, or lordly manor house, but never resting long, never satisfied. Day and night it travelled, up and down the country, till at last it came one evening to a great mansion on the borders of Wales, in one side of which was a tiny postern, with a high latticed window near it, and by the door grew a birch tree, whose branches nodded up and down against the panes.

"Ah," said the gos-hawk to itself, "I will rest here." And it perched on a branch, and put its head under its wing, and slept till morning, for it was very tired. As soon as the sun rose, however, it was awake, with its bright eyes ready to see whatever was to be seen.

Nor had it long to wait.

Presently the bell at the tiny chapel down by the lake began to ring, and immediately the postern opened, and a bevy of fair maidens came laughing out, books in hand, on their way to the morning Mass. They were all beautiful, but the gay gos-hawk had no difficulty in telling which was his master's love, for the Lady Katherine was the fairest of them all, and, as soon as he saw her, he began to sing as though his little throat would burst, and all the maidens stood still for a moment and listened to his song.

When they returned from the little chapel he was still singing, and when Lady Katherine went up into her chamber the song sounded more beautiful than ever. It was a strange song too, quite unlike the song of any other bird, for first there came a long soft note, and then a clear distinct one, and then some other notes which were always the same, "Your love cannot come here; your love cannot come here." So they sounded over and over again, in Lady Katherine's ears, until the roses on her cheeks disappeared, and she was white and trembling.

"To the dining-hall, maidens; tarry not for me," she said suddenly. "I would fain be alone to enjoy this lovely song." And, as the fresh morning air had made them all hungry, they obeyed her without a moment's thought.

As soon as she was alone she ran to the window and opened it, and there, just outside, sat a gay gos-hawk, with the most beautiful plumage that she had ever seen.

"Oh," she cried faintly, "I cannot understand it; but something in my heart tells me that you have seen my own dear love."

Then the gay gos-hawk put his head on one side, and whistled a merry tune; then he looked straight into her eyes and sang a low sweet one; then he pecked and pecked at one of his wings until the tender-hearted little lady took hold of him gently to see if he were hurt, and who can describe her delight and astonishment when she found a tiny letter from Lord William tied in a little roll under his wing.

The letter was very sad, and the tears came into her eyes as she read it. It told her how he had already sent her three letters which had never reached her, and how he felt as if he must soon die, he was so sick with longing for her.

When she had read it she sat for a long time thinking, with her face buried in her hands, while the gay gos-hawk preened his feathers, and crooned to himself on the window sill. At last she sprang to her feet, her eyes flashing and her mouth set determinedly. Taking a beautiful ring from her hand, she tied it with trembling fingers under the bird's wing where the letter had been.

"Tell him that with the ring I send him my heart," she whispered passionately, and the gay gos-hawk just gave one little nod with his head, and then sat quite still to hear the rest of her message. "Tell him to set his bakers and his brewers to work," she went on firmly, "to bake rich bridal cake, and brew the wedding ale, and while they are yet fresh I will meet him at the Kirk o' St Mary, the Kirk he hath so often told me of."

At these words the gay gos-hawk opened his eyes a shade wider. "Beshrew me, lady," he said to himself, "but thou talkest as if thou hadst wings"; but he knew his duty was to act and not to talk, so with one merry whistle he spread his wings, and flew away to the North.

That night, when all the people in the great house were asleep, the little postern opened very gently, and a gray-cloaked figure crept softly out. It went slowly in the shadow of the trees until it came to the little chapel by the lake; then it ran softly and lightly through the long grass until it reached a tiny little cottage under a spreading oak tree. It tapped three times on the window, and presently a quavering old voice asked who was there.

"'Tis I, Dame Ursula; 'tis thy nursling Katherine. Open to me, I pray thee; I am in sore need of thy help."

A moment later the door was opened by a little old woman, with a white cap, and a rosy face like a wrinkled apple.

"And what need drives my little lady to me at this time of night?" she asked.

Then the maiden told her story, and made her request.

The old woman listened, shaking her head, and laughing to herself meanwhile. "I can do it, I can do it," she cried, "and 'twere worth a year's wages to see thy proud stepdame's face when thy brothers return to tell the tale." Then she drew Lady Katherine into her tiny room, and set her down on a three-legged stool by the smouldering fire, while she pottered about, and made up a draught, taking a few drops of liquid from one bottle, and a few drops from another; for this curious old woman seemed to keep quite a number of bottles, as well as various bunches of herbs, on a high shelf at one end of her kitchen.

At last she was finished, and, turning to the maiden, she handed her a little phial containing a deep red-coloured mixture.

"Swallow it all at once," she chuckled, "when thou requirest the spell to work. 'Twill last three days, and then thou wilt wake up as fresh as a lark."

Next morning the Duke and his seven sons were going a-hunting, and the courtyard rang with merry laughter as one after another came out to mount the horses which the pages held ready for them. The ladies were on the terrace waiting to wave them good-bye, when, just as the Duke was about to mount his horse, his eldest daughter, whom he loved dearly, ran into the courtyard and knelt at his feet.

"A boon, a boon, dear father," she cried, and she looked so lovely with her golden hair waving in the wind, and her bright eyes looking up into his, that he felt that he could not refuse her anything.

"Ask what thou wilt, my daughter," he said kindly, laying his hand on her head, "and I will grant it thee. Except permission to marry that Scottish squire," he added, laughing.

"That will I never ask, Sire," she said submissively; "but though thou forbiddest me to think of him, my heart yearns for Scotland, the country that he told me of, and if 'tis thy will that I marry and live in England, I would fain be buried in the North. And as I have always had due reverence for Holy Church, I pray thee that when that day comes, as come it must some day, that thou wilt cause a Mass to be sung at the first Scotch kirk we come to, and that the bells may toll for me at the second kirk, and that at the third, at the Kirk o' St Mary, thou wilt deal out gold, and cause my body to rest there."

Then the Duke raised her to her feet.

"Talk not so, my little Katherine," he said kindly. "My Lord Marquis is a goodly man, albeit not too young, and thou wilt be a happy wife and mother yet; but if 'twill ease thy heart, child, I will remember thy fancy." Then the kind old man rode away, and Katherine went back to her sisters.

"What wert thou asking, girl?" asked her jealous stepmother with a frown as she passed.

"That I may be buried in Scotland when my time comes to die," said Katherine, bowing low, with downcast eyes, for in those days maidens had to order themselves lowly to their elders, even although they were Duke's daughters.

"And did he grant thy strange request?" went on the Duchess, looking suspiciously at the girl's burning cheeks.

"Yes, an' it please thee, Madam," answered her step-daughter meekly, and then with another low curtsey she hurried off to her own room, not waiting to hear the lady's angry words: "I wish, proud maiden, that I had had the giving of the answer, for, by my troth, I would have turned a deaf ear to thy request. Buried in Scotland, forsooth! Thou hast a lover in Scotland, and it is he thou art hankering after, and not a grave."

Two hours afterwards, when the Duke and his sons came back from hunting, they found the castle in an uproar. All the servants were running about, wringing their hands, and crying; and indeed it was little wonder, for had not Lady Katherine's waiting-woman, when she went into her young lady's room at noon, found her lying cold and white on her couch, and no one had been able to rouse her? When the poor old Duke heard this, he rushed up to her chamber, followed by all his seven sons; and when he saw her lying there, so white, and still, he covered his face with his hands, and cried out that his little Katherine, his dearly loved daughter, was dead.

But the cruel step-mother shook her head and said nothing.

Somehow she did not believe that Lady Katherine was really dead, and she determined to do a very cruel thing to find out the truth. When everyone had left the room she ordered her waiting-maid, a woman who was as wicked as herself, to melt some lead, and bring it to her in an iron spoon, and when it was brought she dropped a drop on the young girl's breast; but she neither started nor screamed, so the cruel Duchess had at last to pretend to be satisfied that she was really dead, and she gave orders that she should be buried at once in the little chapel by the lake.

But the old Duke remembered his promise, and vowed that it should be performed.

So Lady Katherine's seven brothers went into the great park, and cut down a giant oak tree, and out of the trunk of it they hewed a bier, and they overlaid it with silver; while her sisters sat in the turret room and sewed a beautiful gown of white satin, which they put on Lady Katherine, and laid her on the silver bier; and then eight of her father's men-at-arms took it on their shoulders, and her seven brothers followed behind, and so the procession set out for Scotland.

And it all fell out as the old Duke had promised. At the first Scotch kirk which the procession came to, the priests sang a solemn Mass, and at the second, they caused the bells to toll mournfully, and at the third kirk, the Kirk o' St Mary, they thought to lay the maiden to rest.

But, as they came slowly up to it, what was their astonishment to find that it was surrounded by a row of spearmen, whose captain, a tall, handsome young man, stepped up to them as they were about to enter the kirk, and requested them to lay down the bier. At first Lady Katherine's seven brothers objected to this being done. "What business of the stranger's was it?" they asked, and they haughtily ordered the men-at-arms to proceed. But the young soldier gave a sign to his men, and in an instant they had crossed their spears across the doorway, and the rest surrounded the men who carried the bier, and compelled them to do as they were bid.

Then the young captain stepped forward to where Lady Katherine was lying in her satin gown, and knelt down and took hold of her hand.

Immediately the rosy colour began to come back to her

cheeks, and she opened her eyes; and when they fell on Lord William — for it was he who had come to meet her at the Kirk o' St Mary, as she had bidden him — she smiled faintly and said, "I pray thee, my lord, give me one morsel of bread and a mouthful of thy good red wine, for I have fasted for three days, ever since the draught which my old nurse Ursula gave me, began to do its work."

When she had drunk the wine her strength came back, and she sprang up lightly, and a murmur of delight went round among Lord William's spearmen when they saw how lovely she was in the white satin gown which her sisters had made, and which would do beautifully for her wedding.

But her seven brothers were very angry at the trick which had been played on them, and if they had dared, they would have carried her back to England by force; but they dare not, because of all the spearmen who stood round.

"Thou wilt rue this yet, proud girl," said her eldest brother; "thou mightest have been a Marchioness in England, with land, and castles, and gold enough and to spare, instead of coming to this beggarly land, and breaking thy father's, and thy mother's heart."

Then the little lady put her hand in that of her lover, and answered quietly, "Nay, but I had no mind to wed with one who was already in his dotage; little good the lands, and castles, and gold would have done me, had I been obliged to spend my time in nursing an old man; and, as for my father, I know he will secretly rejoice when he hears, that, after all, I shall wed my own true love, who, I would have him know, is an Earl's son, although he may not be so rich as is my lord the Marquis; and, as for my cruel step-mother, 'tis no matter what she thinks."

Her brother stamped his foot in useless anger. "Then," said he, pointing to the silver bier lying forgotten on the grass, "I swear that that bier on which thou camest hither shall be the only wedding portion that thy husband will ever see of thine; mayhap poverty will bring thee to thy senses."

But his sister only laughed as she pressed closer to her bridegroom and said bravely, "Happiness is more than gold, brother, and the contented heart better than the restless one which is ever seeking riches."

So the seven brothers went back to England in a rage, while

Lord William married his brave little bride in the old Kirk o' St Mary; and then they rode home to the gray ivy-covered castle, where the gay gos-hawk was waiting on the square tower to sing his very sweetest song to greet them.

## THE END

www.ingramcontent.com/pod-product-compliance
Lightning Source LLC
Chambersburg PA
CBHW032010240626
47153CB00003B/1197